Rise of the Anarchy March

A
NOVEL
BY

RUSS LIPPITT

F.T.W. Rise of the Anarchy March
Copyright © 2020 by Russ Lippitt

For information, address Ravenhawk Books, a division of the
6DOF-Ravenhawk™ Company: The6DOFCompany@gmail.com
Facebook.com/6DOFRavenhawk | Twitter.com/Ravenhawk™ Book

First edition, first printing 2020
Manufactured in the United States of America

Library of Congress Cataloging-in-Publication Data
Lippitt, Russ;   —
F.T.W. ... / Lippitt, Russ - 1st ed. p.c.m.

A Ravenhawk™ Book

ISBN 978-1-893660-30-4

1.Title

2020 LCCN

Original book design, interior design by Spider
Cover design, original artwork by Fly

The world as we know it

Foreword

I would like to thank all the politicians around the world for all of your dedication and hard work, and most of all, your honesty. Without you, none of this would have been possible. I cannot even imagine a world without government. I mean, where would we be? Who would guide us through the scary opposition we call life? Thank you for sharing your supreme intellect and showing us how the world should run, one turn at a time. Your leadership surpasses all expectations, and with that, I know we are truly blessed. Just one thing, next time you take me for a walk, try not to jerk the leash too hard, I am a human being after all.

PROLOGUE

A shiny, mint-condition fire truck wailed, shaking up the quiet night. A team of firefighters sat ready, waiting to arrive at a fire engulfing the distant horizon.

"What's on today's watch, sir?" Fitzgerald asked, eager for some action. "Section C, rookie," the captain replied.

"Section C, sir? That can't be right. Isn't that in homestead territory?"

"Boy, you catch on quick. Where did you say you're from?" Wilson studied Fitzgerald with mock superiority.

"From the West Coast, country of California. Graduated top of my class. Where are you from?"

Wilson put on a fire-retardant mask, ignoring the question.

"Sunny ol' California. Not so sunny anymore since the Fifth of November, huh? I heard the Povs out there are trying to cross the border. Over my dead body," Walker stated as he spat thick and brown.

The captain turned around, "Hey, leave him alone!"

"Just breaking in the new kid, captain. Shit, we all been through it."

He fixated on Fitzgerald, "We are not going into Section C's fire, just protecting Section A in case the fire jumps."

Fitzgerald sat silent, gauging the captain's orders.

The road became increasingly damaged; the fire truck rocked steadily over jagged concrete that suddenly eased and turned into a dirt path continuing as far as the line of sight allowed. An invisible barrier was drawn between the sections, obvious only by the run-down buildings and the broken society leaning precariously toward the pristine domiciles, with their white picket fences and all. The crew reached Section A and pulled to a stop at the border. The blazing fire was burning down a block. It bounced from house to house like a sick and twisted dance, consuming the old wooden shanties built in the late eighties.

"Engage the I.F.S. and I want two men on the hose for secondary douse," commanded the captain. Two large speakers rose from the tail end of the truck and began to emit a low-level frequency. Two of the four firefighters jumped out of the truck. Wilson began to pull out the fire hose and attach it to a fire hydrant when he noticed Fitzgerald staring off into the distance. He was watching the fire rage in the forlorn community while the destitute frantically helped each other put out fires.

"Hey rookie, you wanna help me with this or you gonna stand there looking stupid all day?!"

Fitzgerald ran back to Wilson and helped him hook up the fire hose. The firefighters stood holding it steady, ready to pounce on the first house in Section A.

An older woman, gripping on to her six-year-old boy whose pallid flesh was sullied and broken open into soot-covered burn marks, staggered up to the firefighters. "Help us! Help us!" she cried, holding out her young boy. "My baby is still in the house."

"Do you have a G.R. card?" the staunch captain asked.

"Help me please! My baby!"

"Ma'am, do you have a G.R. card?"

"No! There's no money! Save my baby!"

The captain returned his focus to the first house in Section A, lowering the pitch level on the speaker.

"We are still human beings! You bastard! For the love of God!"

"Sir, can't we just—"

"Stand down, rookie! You know the law."

Her house began to crumble; the flames licked out the windows as the firefighters ignored the shattering edifice and continued to spotlight the first house in Section A.

A large man ran across the street and charged past the firefighters, trying to grab some fire-retardant gear.

"Stop that Pov!" roared the captain.

Wilson pulled out a gun and fired up into the night air. "Get away from that or I promise my next shot will be a lot closer."

The man turned around and looked at his house immersed

in a hellish fire. He grabbed the gear, and without further consideration, Wilson shot the pitiful man in the back.

"You're monsters! All a yous!" The woman put down the little boy on the curb. "Doyle, I want you to stay here. Mommy will be right back." She ran into her house, desperate to save her baby.

"This is not right. Back home we help everyone in need."

"Times have changed. We do our jobs and obey the laws here." Wilson spotted an orange flame arcing from a house in Section A, aimed the hose, and doused it.

The woman ran out of her blazing house clutching an infant engulfed in flames. She collapsed to the ground.

"No!" Fitzgerald let go of the hose and ran to the woman. He tried to smother the fire raging all over her body. When the smoke cleared, Fitzgerald was left holding a charred baby, frozen in its innocence. Tears streaked clean down his soiled face.

The captain nodded at Wilson; he took aim and shot Fitzgerald in the head. Fitzgerald collapsed on the ground, the charred remnants stuck to his fire-retardant gloves.

"I knew that boy wasn't gonna last." Walker spat more chew.

"Hey captain, so much for the California kid." Wilson spotted another arc threatening the house in Section A and put it out. "Captain? Hey captain?"

"Focus on your job," the captain said, grinding his teeth.

"Sorry, cap."

The dazed little boy crawled past Fitzgerald to his baby brother and mother's side. He peered back at the uniformed firefighters, those who were once his heroes became villainous and unworthy.

A man dressed in black looked down from the top of a brush-covered hill through binoculars. His emotionless, camouflage-painted face blended into his surroundings as he admired the fire that illuminated the raging chaos and burning houses in Section C. He unlatched a handheld transceiver from the side of his hip. "Operation Fire-Top has begun, over."

"Good work, Private Stripes. Keep this up, and you might be up for a promotion. Report back to base. Over."

The man took one more look around through his binoculars and saw a swarm of people running out of their burning houses. His hawkish eyes stopped on a little boy sitting next to a blackened figure, holding what was left of its hand. "Not in my Section."

Testament I

COMING OF RAGE

"Government is not reason; it is not eloquent; it is force. Like fire, it is a dangerous servant and a fearful master."

— George Washington (1732–1799)

world like ours was unsustainable. Immersed with selfish hate, darker than the deepest abyss, creating an endless void that could only be filled with power and greed overflowing to that brink of nothingness, one had to ask: What in human nature causes someone to strive to be better than the person standing next to them? Or is it taught? To some, this world is a beautiful place, occupied with colorful and monumental characters that help shape the existence that we breathe. To others, it is a cesspool of human waste and depraved dreams, and they welcome death kicking down their doors. It is all in the eye of the beholder. However, what if you lived in a world without reason, without care or compromise? A world where you're told to obey, or else, suffer the consequences. How would you determine what is right or what is wrong? How would you, as a human being, fit in? In dire times people will be tested; some will bring their best and others will bring their worst. To that I say, fuck this world, fuck that dream world, and fuck the machine world with a big middle finger raised ever so proudly. Sleep tight and safe tonight because it could be your last. When you wake up in the morning, you just might have to fight for what you believe in and for what you once had. It might be too late before you can recognize the truth, and reality will be nothing but a fading memory. Welcome to my world.

It seems like an eternity ago that I saw my mom burned alive, fifteen years to be exact. I relive that nightmare every time I close my eyes. The burning stench of her flesh, her eyes bugging with horror, will haunt me till the day I die. Where has the world gone? After the Fifth of November, the so-called government decided it was in its best interest to divide up the United States of America into sovereign countries. Some countries thrived and some wasted on their borders. That was when the first war broke out between the countries, and the rich and the poor. The government is now known as the Prominent Municipality; a theory that had been pondered in the minds of the wealthy during the last century was actualized and cultivated in an overwhelmingly loyal environment. They protect only those who can afford the price. Police, fire, hospital, education, sanitation, the list goes on. All governmental departments offer their services to the highest bidder. The East Coast sections became the most promising of all the land, leaving other countries barren. The people who rejected the brutality formed a revolution called the Anarchy March. Though we're divided into sections and spread out across this former country that once stood for freedom and justice, the Anarchy March gains support. We live in the underbelly of a recalcitrant society and are the unspoken allies to freedom and equality. The Prominent Municipality recognized our group as a threat and has since formed small militias that roam the sections looking to take us out. And so begins the rise of the Anarchy March.

The sun rose over the hills, breaching the last standing letters of the Hollywood sign, which cast a shadow upon the landscape. The light shone on the face of a young man lying on the side of the curb. Taking a deep breath of the smoggy, yellowed air, he awoke coughing and spat out blood on the side of the ruined road. All that surrounded him was deserted terrain, jagged and mangled in confusion.

"Hey, Doyle! We gotta move." Jack tugged on Doyle's threadbare shirt.

"Why? What's going on?" Doyle stood up and held his head. His dyed celadon-colored mohawk was now stained red with blood.

"P.M.'s coming. We gotta move, now."

"Where's Darla?"

"I'm right here, Horsey. Come on, we're almost to my mom's house." Darla grabbed Doyle's hand and pulled him across the road, out of sight.

"Wait up! This backpack is heavy!" Jack put on his headphones and slid in his favorite cassette tape, tuning out the world and turning up the punk rock. He hefted the large backpack, heavier than Darla's and Doyle's, higher on his shoulder. He scratched at the black scabs on his shaved head, then ran across the road.

"You need help carrying that?" Doyle reached his hand out.

"I got it. I got it, I said!" Jack held the backpack a little closer to his body. As they pushed forward, the town became still save for the tanks and trucks of the Prominent Municipality approaching. Windows and doors slammed shut and were bolted, urging disinterest and compliance.

"Over here, quick!" Darla pushed Doyle and Jack toward a building that should have been condemned, unfit for even sewer dwellers.

A woman, weathered and downtrodden with gray matted hair that seemed to stand out at points on its own accord, waved at them.

"This is your mom's place? I thought she lived on the lower east side?" Doyle looked up at the decrepit structure with the spray-painted message on the wall reading: *The Singularity is near*. He smiled at the woman, who was oblivious that her hole-ridden nightgown exposed a wilted breast.

"Yeah, the last place was a real dump." Darla pulled Doyle's boney wrist, and a round pin with a logo came off his jacket. It landed with a slight ping on a rotted stump.

The three hurried inside, slamming the door shut behind them. They ran through what used to be a beautiful townhouse, but it had since fallen into disorder. Cracked walls, distorted floorboards, and a persistent leak molded and warped the space. They took cover in a smaller room that could have once been a dining room.

"How have you been, honey? Are you hungry? You look cold. Here's a blanket." Darla's mom wrapped her daughter in a moth-infested, damp blanket. She lit up a lantern.

"I'm fine, Mom. Thanks for taking us in."

"Yeah thanks, Mom!" Jack joked.

"So, they finally discovered the library?"

"We ran out the backdoor as they burnt the place to the ground. The last of the fucking Proudhon books, gone."

Doyle looked around at the disarray. A few strangers were huddled up in a corner, holding on to each other as if they were sewn together.

"Mom, I would like you to meet Doyle, my fiancé." Darla pulled Doyle's hand in, matching them up with crudely formed chain-link rings, a symbolic gesture.

"Oh honey, I didn't know you were getting eloped. We should celebrate!" She stood, but Darla pulled her back down.

"Mom, keep your voice down."

"Nonsense, we have to tell your dad."

"Dad's been dead for over ten years. Fuck, Mom!"

Doyle dug in his pocket and found nothing but an old piece of chewed-up gum from his childhood. He squeezed Darla's arm. "Babe, do we have any ration capsules left? I'm starving and fading fast."

"Oh, Horsey, I know. You passed out and hit your head, huh? Did you kill some brain cells?" Darla teased, curling her lip and revealing her jagged chipped teeth. She lifted up her shirt, exposing her emaciated ribs.

Doyle caressed her waist.

"Stop it, that tickles."

Doyle smiled and dug in between her ribs to a sunken crevice, shrapnel remnants of an old trip-mine wound, and found a small red-and-blue capsule. "You're the best." Doyle popped the capsule in his mouth and swallowed, feeling immediate relief.

"I know, but that's our last one. Next month we will have to find a trade."

Darla's mother opened up Doyle's hand and forced a smashed pendant into his palm, saying, "I want you to have this, my son. It is not much, but it's my gift to you."

Doyle examined the pendant. It contained a small tattered picture of his mother-in-law in her youth; better times; she resembled Darla when she smiled. Doyle looked up at her — she had the same smile but now with somber wrinkles around her mouth and a black hole where her white teeth used to be.

A rumbling through the house shook the crumbling remains as the Prominent Municipality's tanks and trucks, filled with armed military personnel, pulled up to the town.

The streets were empty, not even the slightest breeze could be heard. The lead tank stopped, and two well-dressed officials climbed out.

General Stripes, wearing a peaked cap with an olive green pressed uniform covered in layers of multicolored medals, examined the dismal surroundings. He adjusted his epaulets. "Lieutenant Bachmann, what on God's green earth do you call this filthy Pov section?" The general looked around in disgust.

Lieutenant Bachmann opened his hand, a holographic display appeared, showing the section's layout. "It's an unmarked section, sir. Hollywood land," he asserted.

"Holy Saint Mary and Joseph! They say this place used to have streets of gold and rivers of wine. Tinsel Town they used to call it." The general spotted a round pin on the ground, sticking out from under a rotten log. He kicked over the log, sending the cockroaches and black winged insects scampering.

"Sir?" Lieutenant Bachmann looked at the general stooping down and adjusted his thick, oval Windsor glasses.

"You have to know your enemy." The general picked up the pin and caressed it, he noticed unfamiliar black stripes. He handed it to Lieutenant Bachmann and pulled out a handkerchief to wipe his hands. "What is this? Code?"

Bachmann swiped the pin across his hand, and the holographic read-out revealed, "It's a band pin, a punk band to be more precise. They were called 'Black Flag,' popular in the movement of the early eighties. Interesting, it says here that, not only were they—"

"Shut up! I don't wanna hear about that Pov propaganda. All I need to know is where there's a punk, there is the Anarchy March." The general looked at a shattered edifice. "Break it in!"

The military trucks formed and surrounded the house. The general walked back to the tank and stood on top. He pulled out a Throat Thrower, a small triangular device and put it up to his Adam's apple. His voice became amplified by 90 decibels piercing through the walls of the house.

"This is the Prominent Municipality. Under code 356456-9586712-11134-H, we are entering your house under suspicion that you might be harboring a threat to national security."

"Oh shit, they're coming in!" Jack ran into the kitchen and hid in a little cabinet under the sink.

"Just stay cool everyone. They don't know who we are." Doyle stood up, strengthened by a full stomach.

"Clear!" An explosion ripped; the door flew against a back wall. The military SWAT team bolted in. "Hands up, Povs! Nobody move!"

"Oh, we have guests. Honey, bring out the good China." Darla's mom moved toward the kitchen.

Darla, staggered by the aggressive team pointing their guns at her mother, yelled, "No! Stop! She's not okay!" She jumped in front of the men, but her tiny stature failed to shield the ailing woman.

The armed men threw Darla to the ground. Doyle leaped forward and got a gun in his face for his trouble as the general walked in.

"Why are Povs moving in here when I heard my men specifically, in detail say, do not move?"

Darla got back to her feet and inched closer to her mother. "I'm sorry, my mom is sick. She needs medical attention."

"Fa-la-la-la, la la, la, la..." Darla's mom sang as she shuffled into the kitchen looking for her best China. She opened up a cabinet revealing Jack, shivering, who, despite attempting to cover himself with metal pans, was exposed to all the military personnel. She closed the cabinet and continued to look for the proper dinnerware.

"Hey, get out from under there!" Lieutenant Bachmann yelled.

Jack climbed out and lined up with everyone else.

The general pulled out his Robusto cigar and stuffed it in his mouth, as he walked to Doyle.

"Hey kid, you have a light?"

"I got a light, General Stripes, sir!" yelled a soldier standing by the door.

Doyle's, Darla's, and Jack's eyes met. The infamous name now had a face to hate.

"I'm asking this kid for a light, and the next time you use my rank outside of Section A, I'll have you and your family thrown over the wall."

"Yeah, I got a light." Doyle reached into his pocket and pulled out some matches, offering them to the general.

Doyle hesitated, unsure what to expect from the authority figure, then struck the match.

The general observed the pale burn scars stretched across Doyle's right cheek and jawbone, hairless compared to an otherwise scruffy visage. "Have we met before? I never forget a face."

"I don't think so." Doyle pulled out a hand-rolled cigarette and lit it.

"Did I say you can smoke?" The general blew a puff of smoke in Doyle's face.

Doyle dropped the cigarette from his mouth.

The general strolled over to Darla. "So, you say your mother's sick. As in a mental illness?"

"No, no, no, she's just exhausted and tired, I mean." Darla moved toward the kitchen, grabbing her mom and covering her with a blanket. "She hasn't had much to eat, you see."

"Oh, okay, of course not. Well thank God, because you know the law on the mentally ill? Right?"

"Honey, is this Jesus coming to take us to Disneyland? I hope so." Darla's mom peered out from under her cover.

The general lifted the blanket off of her head. Smoke streamed out of the general's nostrils.

"Are you Jesus?" Darla's mom looked at the general.

"Not quite, but I am God." He ripped the woman from Darla's arms and put her in a chokehold.

"No, don't hurt her. She poses no threat to you!"

"She doesn't, but she's harboring potential threats, members of the Anarchy March."

"There is no Anarchy March here, just us simple people trying to survive." Jack said, scratching his shoulder attempting to cover a telltale patch.

"Was I talking to you?"

"He's right. We are simple people with simple lives. Please show some pity for us." Doyle affirmed.

The general drew his handgun and placed it against the mother's temple. "Oh spare me the misfortunes and woes of the Povs. Now we can do this the hard way or the Prominent Municipality's way. Just tell me where the camp is for this section."

Darla, Doyle, and Jack stood in solidarity.

"So be it." The general began to squeeze the trigger.

"No wait!" Darla screamed.

"You have something you want to say?"

"Yes, you forgot to say please."

The entire SWAT team's attention was on the general to see his reaction to the young girl's condescension.

A tear rolled down her mother's face. She smiled at her daughter.

The general laughed, he pulled the trigger, and the woman's head exploded open. Blood, skull fragments, brain matter splattered Darla's face, yet she remained still, hiding her agony.

A pall of evil consumed the general, "Is there anything else you—"

An explosion shook the dilapidated house.

A military officer ran into the house. "Sir, we are under attack, it's the A.M."

The general dropped the lifeless body and marched out the doorway. As he passed the military guard by the door, he ordered, "Kill them all."

"Sir, yes, sir! I will neutralize these Povs, sir!"

His staff followed him.

One of the guards posed a question, "So, who wants to die first, huh?"

To his surprise, Jack, Darla, and Doyle were gone.

The guard turned his attention on two people quivering in the corner, praying. "Hey, Povs! Where did they go?"

"Hail Mary, full of grace. The lord is with thee. Blessed art thou amongst women, and blessed is the fruit of thy womb, Jesus."

The guard walked up to them with his gun drawn and finger on the trigger.

"Holy Mary, mother of God, pray for us sinners, now and at the hour of our death."

"God doesn't listen to the prayers of the filthy Povs." The guard opened fire on them, pelting their bodies. "Amen."

Just then, a small canister hit the guard in the chest and landed next to his feet. "What is this? Stupid Povs. Is that all you got! Throwing canned goods at me!" The guard picked up the canister. Green gas leaked from it and then burst, filling the room with smoke.

He screamed as his clothes began to melt away. Pieces of his scalp and hair melted and dripped onto the ground. The burning gas stuck to his skin, consuming it. Soon, only goo remained. The guard fell to a fetal position succumbing to the unbearable pain. The gas seeped through his flesh, his bones, leaving behind a pile of mush.

Doyle, Darla, and Jack walked out of the house. They were dressed in radioactive suits and gas masks. Explosions erupted, covering the area with gray smoke and dust, and as the air cleared, Doyle saw the general walking beside a tank toward the battle in the distance.

"Let's get out of here." Doyle ran off the main street with Darla and Jack close behind.

The general pulled out the Throat Thrower again, but this time he put it in front of his eyes. He zoomed in on a location much further than the naked eye could see. As he walked along the side of the tank that trekked forward, he shouted out target commands.

Return fire and explosions ripped through the air, but the general was oblivious to the danger and continued to press ahead.

"Sir, you were right. It seems like this section has an Anarchy March, though their numbers are low."

"I can see that, Bachmann. Seven o'clock, fire!"

The tank fired on his command. The heavy weaponry destroyed a hidden bunker. Bodies flew out and a severed arm landed next to the general, an Anarchy March armband smoldered.

"Sir, maybe you should take cover!" Lieutenant Bachmann said, peaking his head out from inside the tank.

"Nonsense, this is where the action is. Three o'clock, fire!"

The tank rotated its massive gun. The general ducked under the swaying cannon as it unloaded a barrage of heavy fire upon the target.

"Take some notes, Bachmann. Inside that tank you can't see squat. Out here I can see all the—" a bullet pierced his Medal of Honor and lodged itself in his right arm. The impact knocked his cap to the ground revealing his balding head. He looked down at the wound and raised his head in disgust: "Goddamn Pov shot me." He snatched his cap from the ground, shook off the dirt, and restored it, "Eleven o'clock, FIRE!"

The tank's gun rotated and shot. The exploding projectile ripped through the crumbling edifice, and the return fire ceased.

Lieutenant Bachmann looked at a holographic image on his palm; the remaining Anarchy March members were running for their lives. "Sir, they are on the retreat."

"Good, then this area is clear. Only a few more and Section Y will be under the rule of the Prominent Municipality."

"Should we follow the fleeing rebels? See if they lead us to the next camp?"

The steely-eyed general stopped dead in his tracks, "Now where is the fun in that? Twelve o'clock high, fire!"

Doyle, Darla, and Jack made their way to an old highway, long forgotten by time. Cars laid still and abandoned after the rationing of natural crude oil. Heavy smog and debris allowed for only a twenty-yard visibility radius.

"Fuck yeah! Did you see that shot of gas I gave that guard? I told you my throwing arm was better than yours, Doyle." Jack took off his gas mask and pulled out another can, feigning a throw. "My old man was right."

"Hey, be careful with that stuff! It could explode in your hand." Doyle ripped the canister from his grasp and put it back in Jack's backpack.

"Doesn't work that way, man."

"Your father was a genius, and let's make sure his death was not in vain."

Darla stopped and fell to her knees. Sobbing, she took off her gas mask and breathed deep.

"Are you alright, baby?" Doyle took off his gas mask.

"She was crazy, but she did not deserve *that*." She wiped her tears away as soon as they formed.

"I know. Don't worry though, her death, just like everyone else's, is for the greater cause."

"We can't even give her a proper burial. We have to go back."

"You know we can't do that. Here." Doyle handed her the pendant that her mother gave him. "We have five minutes. I'll leave you alone." Doyle hugged her tight then stood up and walked back to join Jack.

Darla stared at the photo in the pendant, smiling. She reminisced when she took the snapshot on an old 35mm. "I love you, Mom. I will never forget." A tear dropped on the pendant and seeped through the broken glass. Darla dug at the hardened soil with her knife and laid the jewellery inside a shallow hole, pushing the dry dirt over it. She took a moment then pulled out a little notebook and scribbled her mother's name within, accompanying the countless names she had recorded in the book of unmarked graves and locations of the dearly departed.

Doyle approached Jack, sitting on a large rock with his back turned. "Jack, how far are we to the underground tunnels? Jack!" Doyle smacked the headphones off his head.

"What?!"

"The underground tunnels, how far?"

"Fuck, I don't know ... let me check my handy-dandy map." Jack opened up a tattered paper with a hand-drawn map. "If we continue on the old 101, we can reach the tunnels in two days. Or we can go to Section S, eat a nice meal, have a clean bath, and maybe get a ride."

"I don't want to go to Savage Town!" Darla bellowed as she approached them.

"We can rest up there and still make it to the tunnels in two days. Besides, you know the 101 is riddled with chaser mines."

"We don't have any electronics that would set off the mines. The only reason you want to go to Savage Town is so you can get laid and bet on the fights."

"And see a good show. When was the last time we went to a good punk show? Please. We have been traveling for a while now. Let's take a break. We might also be able to get a vehicle from Benny and skip the tunnels entirely. Pretty please." Jack dropped down to his knees and begged Darla. "I'm low on batteries too. Are you gonna deprive me of traveling music?"

Darla looked back at her mother's shallow grave. "I can definitely use a bath and a break from all this killing."

Doyle hushed them and ran behind a car that had been torched and devoured by flames. Darla and Jack followed him.

"What's up?" Jack peeked over ravaged metal but saw only the desolate region.

Doyle grabbed Jack and pulled him back down. "I heard a moan. This place was bombed by the P.M. a ways back. Could still be some Nukies running around."

"Ew, I hate those beasts. Let's get out of here." Darla began sneaking off the freeway.

"Yeah, I don't want to mess with those freaks, let's get out of here." Doyle followed her.

"Man, I'll fuck them up." Jack pulled out his canister as he heard a gurgling moan. "Hey, wait up guys!" Jack ran after them heading for the highway's exit.

Testament II

SAVAGE TOWN

An abortion of the human spirit is how some characterized it. I remember first coming into Section S, a former Anarchy March stronghold turned sour and now resides by the nickname Savage Town. Vagabonds and merchants originally built it around an old Indian casino as a halfway point from hell. The seven deadly sins were a stroll in the park compared to this abhorrent city. The worst of the worst gathered here to trade: drugs, gambling, prostitution, murder, bestiality, you name it. It all went down here. It was a place where the illicit flocked like hungry dogs as if commanded by their self-appointed king, Benny Hall. Hall came from a generation of preachers and had been friends with the Anarchy March for as long as I'd known him. I don't know why, and no one really asked, but the P.M. left this place alone. When there was no law, the curious went missing. Benny was a man of the cloth, and I never trusted him.

Doyle, Darla, and Jack reached the corroded metal gate of Savage Town. The noise from beyond sounded as if wild animals had been starved into a frenzied hunger, scratching and clawing to escape their menagerie.

An armed guardsman shot a single bullet, kicking up the dirt in front of Doyle. He then raised his weapon, stopping Doyle from entering the town.

Doyle removed his jacket and exposed his arm, revealing a black band with a red A and M enclosed in a circle. The attentive man signaled down to another guardsman, and the rusted gate creaked open. Doyle put his jacket back on, and the trio walked through.

"Hey, dip-shit! Maybe you should ask questions first before

shooting, you could have shot one of us!" Darla yelled up at the guardsman.

The guardsman stuck his half-missing tongue out and made a chopping gesture with his hand across his neck.

"Forget it, babe, let's just do what we gotta do and get out of here."

Jack flipped the guardsman off. He smiled, revealing the last of his decayed teeth as he went back to his post.

Doyle's tattered shoes were not equipped to handle walking through the town of mud and garbage; every footstep sunk into the muck, and the sludge sloshed between his toes. Pop-up tents and derelict structures, where families lived in penury and disease, replaced houses. A utopian haven for the flies that buzzed around, eating and vomiting on the dead. Darla swatted at the black waves, opening a path to clear the air. She held her nostrils closed with her other hand and stepped over a rotting animal protruding from the soil.

Savage Town was infamous for its salacious circus acts. The inhumane displays of torture brought pleasure to the wicked willing to pay, and Darla knew that all too well. One of the first acts they passed consisted of a soiled and skeletal old man trading pain for food. He was bleeding from small cuts all over his body. A crudely spray-painted sign read: *Bulls-eyes mark the spot*. He had laid out sharp objects on a table: darts, knives, hammers, and basic household items to throw at him at will. A trade was made, and a crowd gathered around to watch the show.

"Let's check this out." Doyle fought his way through the crowd to get a better view.

"Alright you young whippersnapper. The trade is four throws for four food capsules. Did everyone hear that?"

A grumble of acknowledgment from the onlookers, and the old, beaten man shook the trader's hand in agreement. He walked over to his standing picnic table and nonchalantly leaned against it.

"You ready, old man?" The trader picked up his first weapon, a hammer, slamming the hefty steel into his palm to check its durability.

"Get it over with!" The old man closed his eyes and his mouth salivated at the visions of food that would ease his ensuing pain.

The trader grinned and threw the hammer, hitting the old man in the chest. The crowd cheered as he buckled and groaned in pain.

"Hey, I'm not too bad at this," the trader boasted as he grabbed for his next weapon, a meat-cleaver.

The old man held his trembling hand up to his chest and rubbed the brightening red bruise. He stood up determined, ready to finish this deal. He spat out blood and taunted the trader, "Is that it, is that all you got, sonny? Try, try not using your hand you whip your dipper with."

The crowd laughed at the trader's expense. "Fucking crazy, old man. I'll teach you." The trader cocked back and threw the meat cleaver in anger. The dirty metal handle broke off and the cleaver whizzed past the old man's ear, penetrating the wooden picnic table.

"Smart old man," Doyle marveled.

The crowd responded with angry jeers. They wanted blood, and the trader was disappointing them.

"Alright, old man, this one's gonna hurt," he said while picking up a large butcher knife and testing the blade's sharpness with the tips of his fingers.

The old man closed his eyes again, hoping the next throw would not kill him before he was able to enjoy a final meal. The trader focused in and chucked the knife straight into the old man's bicep, as if he had practiced this feat over and over again. The old man's legs gave out, but the knife, lodged into the wooden frame behind him, had pinned him. He screamed in pain as the crowd cheered for blood.

Darla turned her head in horror, grabbing on to Doyle. "Alright I had enough, can we go?" she urged.

"Wait, I need to see what happens."

Darla walked away as the old man reached with his other arm and wrapped his hand around the knife's handle. He twisted it around to loosen it from the frame and pulled it out. "Is ... is that all, gasser?" the old man yelled, throwing the knife on the ground as he slumped forward.

"Tough son of a bitch. Tell you what, I'll make the last one easy." The trader picked up a single, small dart.

The old man was shaking from the excruciating pain as he closed his tearing eyes for the final throw. Thoughts of food capsules kept his mind off the agony. He knew the weeks without a meal would pay off after this last toss. No more radiated rats or the vile aftertaste of cockroach legs sticking between his teeth. Soon he would be eating like a king.

The trader took aim and feigned his throw. The crowd reacted with an, "Aww!"

As the old man opened his eyes to see what was happening, the trader threw the dart into his right eye. He fell to the ground and passed out.

"Cry your eye out, why don't you, sucker!" The trader bolted through the crowd to escape his debt.

Doyle, incensed by the trader's disregard for the old man, stuck his leg out and tripped the scammer. The crowd surrounded the trader and began to stomp him as if they were putting out a fire that could spread. Doyle grabbed Jack as he continued to watch the trader get kicked in the head until his body stopped moving.

Doyle and Jack found Darla, her arms folded. She was standing in the muck by the door of a shanty. A withered old woman with a crooked spine opened up the door and said, "Excuse me, honey." Her broom swept out the rats from inside, and she shut the door.

"So, did you guys get your kicks back there?"

"Vigilante justice still presides in Savage Town. Sorry, I needed to know. We can tread safely now."

Darla scoffed, "Safe and Savage Town do not belong in the same sentence, not even in the same Section."

"Come on, babe. You should know by now, when you don't have anything, your word becomes priceless."

Through the crowd a well-dressed pimp strolled up to Doyle and put his arm around him. He smelled of grease and musk, and his smile exposed a wide golden grin. "You look like a man who wants to see a woman fucked in every orifice."

Darla pushed the pimp away and grabbed him by his velvet cerulean encased testicles. "You look like a man about to lose his nuts!" She pushed the circus pimp to the ground, releasing her steel grip.

"Thanks, babe."

"This fucking town disgusts me, I swear if it did not have ... Jack? Get over here!"

Jack was talking to another circus pimp. Jack came running, a befuddled look dominated his face. "What? I was trading for some batteries and checking what time the fights start."

"Whatever, let's not split up, alright?" She demanded, "Alright?!"

"Yeah, yeah, sure, sure. I'm on top of it," he nodded, as he scanned the perimeter. He spied the arena and jogged toward it.

"Damn it, Jack!"

"He'll be fine, let him go and have his fun."

"I know. I just don't want him to get into any trouble. I'm tired of bailing him out."

Doyle embraced Darla and kissed her softly. "How about me and you go to the top of the hill, like old times."

"As much as I hate this town, it's eerily infectious. Only if I get to use the whip," she cooed.

"Hell no, I still have scars from the last time!"

"You said you'd try anything once."

"I was thinking more like a three-way." Doyle pointed out a tousled hooker walking by them. She heard Doyle's comment, and swayed toward them on unsteady legs. She tried to focus on Doyle and Darla through crusty, blackened eyes.

Darla whacked him in the arm, "Yeah, right. In your wildest dreams."

The hooker shrugged her shoulders and strolled away.

Doyle looked into Darla's eyes, "My dreams only have you in it."

"Oh, nice one. It gets better every time I hear it. I fucking love you."

"I fucking love you, more."

They embraced in the middle of the grime, lost in their own ravenous bliss and love for one another. Doyle pulled away, "First, let's go and see Benny. Business before pleasure." Despite his ignited passion, he knew they had more pressing matters to attend to. He grasped her hand and led her up to the shiny house on a hill.

Jack hurried to the arena, dodging and swaying between all the seedy characters looking for their next kick. He bumped shoulders with someone who had a giant green Mohawk, "Hey! Watch it buddy!"

"Jack?"

He looked closer at the person with the Mohawk and the torn sequin dress, but could not focus his memory.

"Holy dog shit! Jack the Ripper. It's me, Shawn. Shawn Smash."

"Smash, huh? Not ringing a bell."

"You dared me to drink all that rubbing alcohol the night before the Diablo Canyon incursion."[1]

"Oh yeah, how's it going? How's the arm?" Jack reached out to give a handshake but instead was given his frayed wallet back.

"Still not there." Shawn twisted their body and revealed a stump where an arm used to be.

Jack put his wallet back in his pocket and laughed at Shawn's pick-pocketing dexterity despite only having one arm.

"So, what are you doing in Savage Town besides picking pockets? Are you on a mission for the Anarchy March?"

"No, I'm kinda laying low for a while. A few months back, my

---

[1] Diablo Canyon, at the border of Section Y, imploded after the Fifth of November. This was the first of many nuclear power plants to shut down improperly, exposing the people to extreme levels of radiation. The first wave of Nukies swarmed over the nearby towns, destroying all in their path. The Anarchy March put up a counter front and held back the Nukies for a brief time before getting overwhelmed and eventually retreating, suffering casualties in the thousands.

town in Section U was burned to the ground and the P.M. ran everyone else out. My family had to relocate to this fucking mess here." Shawn waved their one arm as if they were pulling back an invisible curtain, revealing Savage Town. A desperate family knee-deep in muck cried out together as the mud seemed to swallow them.

"Nothing? What have you been doing for the cause?" Jack inquired.

"Nothing at all, comrade. I can't bear arms. Ha-ha!" Shawn laughed but then grew grave. "I'm just living day by day, trying to make ends meet."

"Fuck, that sucks. Hey, you got any batteries?"

"Double A? I'll trade ya, what tapes you got?"

"Let me see here." Jack rifled through his collection in his backpack, "I gots some Bad Brains, Dead Kennedys, um ... some Conflict, Crass, MDC."

"A pack of Double As for your MDC, deal?"

"Fuck yeah." They made the exchange with a secret handshake. "Good to see you, Jack. What are you doing here?"

"You know Doyle, right? Leader of Anarchy March in Section Y? We're making a quick pit stop before we go to — see, yeah, never mind, it's kinda top secret."

"What? No secrets between comrades; it's the oath, friend."

"You said you were out of commission, and besides, this place has ears and eyes everywhere."

"You looking for some help? I'm lusting for some action."

"We might be." Jack heard a roar coming from the arena. "Who's fighting tonight?"

"Oh, it's a good time to be in Savage Town, my man. Tonight, Kongo is defending his title, and Reagan's Children is playing at The Church."

"What the fuck are we standing around here for?"

"Come on, I know somebody, and we can get the best seats in town." Shawn wrapped their arm around Jack, and the two ran to the arena.

As they entered the old ice hockey arena, the smell of blood, sweat, and oil hit Jack in the face, sticking to his pores. The rink was walled off in an octagon shape with barbed wire, fencing in any escape. The concrete floors were stained with tire marks and blood. The first dueling fight had been going on for a while. One wrecked car smashed up against the wall, laying on its side engulfed in flames. An old muscle car with a flamethrower attached to its hood was chasing a bloodied man around the rink. Jack and Shawn climbed to the front of the seats where two vagabonds were slumped over, passed out.

Shawn threw the drunken men out into the crowd and wiped the seats clean, "What did I say, best seats in the house."

"This is great! Who's running the arena now?"

"Benny Hall won it in a poker game. I heard he won it with a pair of aces and eights. Lucky bitch."

The bloodied man dodged the car as it slammed into the wall. The sound of metal against concrete ricocheted through the arena, while the crowd's uproar of cheers echoed through the town. The driver lay unconscious as the man jumped on the hood of the car and pulled off the flamethrower, pointing it into the driver-side window. He pulled the trigger and set the driver on fire. The angry crowd threw their trash into the rink as the man raised his hand in victory. He stumbled up to the entrance gate, and as he was let out, a man wearing a tailored double-breasted wool and silk three-piece suit, gripping an alligator suitcase, greeted him.

"Well done, here's your winnings," he said, handing him twelve food capsules, "Do you want to go double or nothing?" A gleam sparkled from his eye along with a fiendish smile.

"Fuck off, Benny!"

"Touchy. Your loss," Benny said with crooked jawline. His underbite was infamous in Section S, broken in three pieces as a child by an uncle and posed as a constant reminder of his family's sovereignty.

Benny walked out to the middle of the rink with a bullhorn in hand. The crowd quieted down, anticipating the main event. "A lot of people have come and died in Savage Town, fought for riches, fucked a whore, killed for capsules, whatever your little heart desires. Savage Town is not a place for imperialist dreams, to start over, have a family ... oh no, no, no, no. This is our place! Do what you want to do and except no substitute."

The frenzied crowd roared, banging chains and pots. Benny quieted the crowd like a conductor of a feral orchestra. "There are those who say, we are uncivilized, not proper if you will. HA! I laugh in their faces because we are truly free. So laugh with me, will you? Laugh at oppression, laugh at him." A P.M. soldier was forcibly shoved into the rink and stripped of his bloodstained blindfold and makeshift earmuffs. His hands were untied and mouth ungagged. All of his senses were exposed at once to the horrors that awaited him. Fear crippled his every being as he shuddered, spinning in a three-sixty degree at the ravenous taunts from the animalistic spectators. Benny turned up the knob to full blast on the bullhorn to get everyone's attention. "Now, introducing a man who takes away our freedom, our homes, and our very existence. Please help me in giving a very cold and unwelcoming jeer to the arena. He is currently an active soldier-of-fortune from the P.M. ... Well, I really don't know what his name is. Let's call him, Dead Meat! Place your final bets and now ... it's show time!"

A grubby man missing a leg hobbled up to Benny and whispered something into his ear. He mouthed, "Darla?" and then waved the man away. "Now, I have the pleasure to welcome to the arena, our one and only defending world champion, hailing from Section D and a member of our beloved Anarchy March. Please help me welcome, Kongo!"

The crowd stood up and howled at the towering man, with full body tattoos and piercings. His flat nose looked to be broken a few times over, and his deep-set eyes were as dark as night. He rode out into the rink on a spiked motorcycle, revving the engine.

"Fuck yeah! Kill 'em all, Kongo!" Shawn screamed. "Here, have some of this."

Jack looked at Shawn's hand that held a fluorescent powder.

"You didn't tell me you were carrying."

"You didn't ask, and this is the good shit. It's not cut with glass," Shawn replied with a laugh.

Jack buried his nose in the powder and snorted it.

"I've been saving this for a special occasion, and this is about as special as it's gonna get. F.T.W., baby!"

"Fuck the world," Jack said shoveling the powder into his nose.

Benny signaled at someone manning the door and then left. The gate locks clanged together behind him, and he jumped onto a handcrafted elevator that ascended to his V.I.P. box seat.

A few blunt weapons were thrown into the rink. The P.M. soldier picked up a two-by-four and jumped into attack position.

Kongo unwound the chain that decorated his chest and began to twirl it in the air. He pulled back the throttle, peeling out toward the soldier. The P.M. soldier swung his board and hit Kongo, splitting the piece of wood in half. Kongo did a sharp turn, and twirled the chain across the soldier's mouth, slamming him head-first into the concrete.

Kongo kicked down the bike's stand and jumped off. The soldier spat out his teeth. Blood dripped from a large gash on his head. He wobbled to his feet. Kongo wrapped his chain around both his hands and pulled it apart. He clanged his fists together, sparks flew. The frightened soldier took off running, trying to scale the walls. He managed to climb over, but the revenge-hungry crowd threw him back into the pit.

Kongo stalked the soldier, who had broken out into a fearful sweat. The soldier jumped and took a swinging punch at Kongo's face. Unfazed, Kongo picked up the soldier and threw him back in the middle of the rink like a doll. He stood over him and delivered vicious punches to his bloodied face. A horn sounded and Kongo backed off. All the while his face remained expressionless.

The beaten soldier lay unconscious with his foot twisted backward and his clothes ripped. A crew of people ran into the rink and pulled at the soldier, trying to revive him with smelling salts and a shot of adrenaline. He awoke and was carried to his corner and plopped onto a stool.

Over the loudspeaker, Benny introduced round two. "One down

and two more to go!" Benny sipped from an etched wine glass as he observed the chaos below. "Now let's see if Dead Meat can survive the slice and dice!"

Buckets of oil and water were dumped onto the concrete floor. Baskets were handed out to the crowd, filled with a variety of small, sharp items. From needles to razor blades, the crowd took handfuls and threw them into the rink, covering the floor. Kongo was fitted with steel biker boots and was given a large sledgehammer. He stood up from his stool after his corner men watered him down.

"Kongo! Kongo! Kongo!" The crowd chanted en masse.

A metal pole was thrown into the middle of the rink. The soldier stumbled off of his stool and traversed the concrete floor toward his only weapon. Kongo strolled over to meet the soldier halfway. As the soldier limped across the combat zone, he stepped on a broken glass bottle. It pierced his foot, and he screamed in agony. He reached for the pole, but just as he grabbed it, a sledgehammer pounded his chest. The soldier flew back, sliding across the floor. Needles were embedded all over him as he slammed against the wall. His blood splattered against the side of the rink, leaving a gruesome portrait of post-modern art. Jack rose out of his seat with a voracious roar, exciting the crowd as they too erupted for their bloodlust: punish the wicked and unjust with no mercy! The soldier leaned up against the wall, his intestines spilling out. He sucked in deep, dying breaths as Kongo approached.

Jack grabbed Shawn by the shoulder. "Let's get out of here."

"What? The best part is coming up. Kongo is gonna smash his head in."

"I don't like the finishing. I just like the fighting. It's no fun knowing the end, you know? Anyway, let's get to The Church, the night's still young."

"You're a weird dude. Fuck it!" Shawn threw the last handful of sharp items into the rink.

As they left, fighting through the crowd toward the exit, a loud shattering of bones echoed through the arena.

Doyle and Darla reached a large, dark house on the top of a hill. The Gothic-style home mirrored a chapel with flying buttresses and thinly pointed spires. It was the only structure in Section S that was built with a primeval quality; fit for a king or queen. Doyle struck a knocker attached to the huge wooden doors and waited.

"I hope he remembers us." Darla looked up at the towering house.

"Hell, I hope he doesn't kill us."

"I'd protect you, Horsey."

"I know you would, babe, you would kill him with your constant nagging," Doyle joked.

"You love my nagging."

Doyle grabbed Darla close and said, "No, I love your sweet spot!"

"Mmm, let's get this over with so we can go to our special place."

Doyle kissed her on the neck ever so gently as the double-door swung open and a young, pretty boy greeted them. "Yes, how can I help you?" he said with a haughty tone.

"We're here to see Benny, the Anarchy March needs his help."

"Sorry, the master is out at the fights at the moment," the servant boy stated as he rolled his eyes back, swinging the door shut.

Doyle caught the door before it closed and forced it open. "Well, can you call him? It's kind of an emergency."

The pretty boy rolled his eyes again and huffed, "Like I have time for this … come in, I guess."

Doyle and Darla walked into the enormous house. The servant boy led them into an Art Deco-style room, passing two armed men who stood like statues. They sat down on a plush, pitchy-velvet couch. The floor was made of glass but was covered by a red cloth from the underside. The servant boy closed the door, leaving them alone. Old paintings from earlier centuries lined the walls like wallpaper, almost depreciating them. They stretched upward to the high ceiling and circled the wrought iron chandelier.

Doyle stood up and pointed out infamous and lost paintings throughout the centuries. Munch's *The Scream*, Dalí's *The Face of War*, ending in da Vinci's *Mona Lisa*. "Where the fuck does Benny get this shit from? I don't like it."

"I thought you liked art?"

"No, it's not that, I don't like him having it. These pieces just don't pop up out of nowhere. I know there's back-stabbing behind each and every one of these pieces."

"You're just jealous, Horsey. He has been an ally of the Anarchy March for a long time, I'm sure they give him kick-backs for all his help."

"Jealous? Jealous of what? All I know is his family mysteriously dies, and all of a sudden, he acquires vast amounts of riches." Doyle picked up an antique vase and examined it, looking for something that would tie Benny to devious endeavors.

Darla nestled into the couch, putting her feet up on an ebony and glass Art Deco table.

"Plus, I don't like him because you used to work for him."

"Why do you have to bring that up again?" Darla said. "I don't know what to tell you. Why can't you just leave the past in the past?"

The doors swung open and Benny entered wearing a heavily brocaded robe. Benny had one of those faces that always looked like he smelled something pungently sweet, a touch of bitter mixed with an air of pride. Doyle wanted to punch him in that smug face. Darla grabbed Doyle's hand, feeling his discomfort.

"Well, well, well, look who's come back to Savage Town. My beloved Darla and Dangle. Do you like my exhibition room?"

"It's Doyle!"

"Touchy. Doyle it is." Benny summoned his servant boy over and whispered in his ear followed by a gentle kiss. "Sorry I took so long, I had to change my clothes. My new arena gets bloodier and bloodier. So, what brings such a succulent couple back to Savage Town? Looking for work, darling Darla?"

"No, the Anarchy March takes care of me now."

"Bones and scraps, you know you had a better trade here," he said with an insouciant flip of his wrist.

"Hey fuck-face, she doesn't do that shit anymore, now are you going to help us or not?"

"Now, now. That's no way to ask for help."

The servant boy returned with three large crystal glasses containing a deep garnet-colored wine.

"Drink up. It's the finest wine in this Section."

They reluctantly took the wine glasses. Doyle smelled the wine suspiciously, while Darla drank.

"Now, what can I do for the Anarchy March today?"

"We need a car or a tank, something that can transport us safely to Section X," Doyle asserted.

"Interesting. Why? If you don't mind my asking." Benny sipped from his wine glass.

"A new bio–" Doyle nudged Darla, interrupting her sentence. "It really doesn't concern you," Doyle stated.

"So, let me get this straight, you come barging in here, unannounced, and expect me to bend over," Benny winked at his servant boy, "and let you take one of my special vehicles, for unknown reasons?"

"Um, yeah, that's how it is. The less you know the better," Doyle blurted out.

Benny sat quiet for a few moments, staring at the color of his wine. "Ha! I like you, Dangle. You have balls." Benny exclaimed as he uncrossed his legs and stood up. He walked to the *Mona Lisa*. Reaching out, he pressed a concealed button on the side of its frame. "Maybe Darla can seal the deal. ... I think I don't need to remind you two what will happen if I don't receive my property back in one piece."

"You know I'm good for it, don't make me beg," Darla said as she gulped down her wine.

A sadistic smile tore across Benny's face and his eyes locked with Darla's.

"Fuck this! Come on, babe. This person is not interested in helping the cause."

Doyle stepped in between them and grabbed Darla's arm.

"Did I ever show you my latest masterpiece?" Benny turned a knob on the wall that was next to the button. The red cloth floated apart from under the glass floor and disappeared. "I call it, Purgatory." It revealed a haunting set of Hell viewed through the glass. Decapitated heads were speared on poles that lined the ground. Burnt bodies were satirically positioned, and the look of horror was cast on the faces of the wicked. Acrylic painted flames roared up the sides of the walls. And in the middle sat a small, gold cage with what appeared to be a man reaching up at the gawking Darla for help.

"What do you think? Do you think I caught an eternal Hell moment?" Benny sipped from his glass. Suddenly he bit down, cracking it.

Darla stomped out of the room.

"It's ... it's something. We'll be in touch." Doyle trailed after Darla; they were escorted out of the house.

Benny looked down at the caged man and sneered, turning the knob back. The caged man stared up at Benny as the red cloth sealed shut, leaving him in his own private Hell.

The heavy front doors slammed behind them. "What a sick bastard. I hate Savage Town."

"If he can help us, it's worth it. Now forget about it, let's go to our special spot." Doyle took Darla's hand and led her on an unbeaten path to a forgotten overlook.

"Fuck yeah, oh yeah, fuck, oh yes, yes! Rock 'n' roll!" Jack rolled off the prostitute, "Oh yeah, honey, you just got Jacked."

The prostitute rolled her eyes and lit up a cigarette.

"Hey, you done over there or what?" Jack looked into the adjacent room, separated by a thin sheet, and saw Shawn slamming against the backside of another prostitute.

Jack took the cigarette from the apathetic woman's mouth and took a big drag. "Well, it's been real, honey." Jack jumped out of the makeshift bed that sat on cinder blocks and pulled up his pants. He ran through the hanging sheet and put out his cigarette on Shawn's ass. "Let's get to the show!"

"What the fuck! Can I finish at least?"

"No time. Ye-ow!" Jack howled and ran out of the large, hole-ridden tent.

"I'm sorry, Johnny. Can I get a rain check? Say hi to your mom for me." Shawn pulled up their underwear and stumbled out of the tent, running after Jack. "Why are you in such a rush all the fucking time?" Shawn secured the safety pin holding their dress together.

"Do you have any more happy on you?"

"You're a fiend." Shawn pulled out the baggie and handed it to Jack.

He stuck his nose in the bag and took a deep breath. His eyes glossed over red as he got lost inside of Shawn's shimmering beads.

"Dude, are you okay?"

"Whad'ya know, any who?" Jack rambled off.

"Man, you need to calm down on that shit. It's fucking with your mind."

"You're right, it's a mind fuck!" Jack took off running, and Shawn chased after him.

They arrived at an abandoned, graffiti-marked church. Jack broke in the front door and was greeted by a blistering sound of raw punk rock blaring through two distorted speakers. A young punk band banged on their instruments with ferocity that could wake the Gods. The adolescent kids looked no older than twelve, but no one could have guessed by the way they played their instruments. They slammed through the chords like a riot, but the crowd harassed them, spitting and throwing broken bottles.

"Isn't it bedtime, kiddies?" a punk rocker in the pit yelled.

"No, your fucking mom hasn't called me for bed yet," taunted the rebellious musician.

"Yeah, that dirty fucking whore swallowed last time I was over." The guitarist spat at the crowd and sneered with delight. "Fuck you, you little snot-nosed punks!"

Debris continued to fly up on stage, while the crowd and the band continued to taunt one another.

"Fuck you and your mom!"

The punk rocker stormed the stage with his fists clenched but was smashed in the side of the head with a guitar.

"Batter's up!" The guitarist mocked and then checked his instrument for any damages.

"Alright! Are you ready for some real punk rock, real punk rock! This song goes out to the Anarchy March! One, two, three, FOUR!" the lead singer bellowed as he grabbed the microphone and kicked over the mic stand.

The band slammed into a blistering frenzy of untamed music. The crowd started a large, violent pit releasing their aggression and frustration from the years of oppression. The music spoke when reason didn't.

Jack ran into the pit and slipped on the piss-saturated ground. "God, I'm home!" He sprang to his feet and rushed into the pit to slam dance.

Bibles were tossed around the room, once used as an instrument to coerce, but now with a new-found purpose. One Bible struck the lead singer in the head. Blood flowed down from his forehead. A fistfight broke out in back of the room, while a punk couple fucked in the corner. Scenes of debauchery like this were no stranger to Savage Town, and Jack was in sin heaven. The music and drugs consumed his being. Shawn jumped in the pit as fists and feet flew. Jack slammed into a large skinhead, who punched him to the ground. He lay on the floor getting trampled. In a beaten daze he stared up at the broken stained-glass windows and then at a spray-painted Jesus statue erected over the stage.

He stood up in a rage and yelled at the statue, "You fucker! I hate you and your fucking religion! Look what you create! Look at me! Who do ya think you are?" Jack fell to his knees. "Answer me!"

The statue twisted its head and out of its mouth, "Go to Hell!" it began to bleed from its eyes.

Crazed Jack stood up. Pulling out one of his canisters, he threw it at the Jesus figure. The green gas exploded, engulfing the statue. Jack snapped out of his daze and realized his stupidity. He turned and tried to run but was tripped by a fallen punker. Five canisters flew out of his backpack across the floor and under the pews. A punker, half passed out, slumped over the bench and saw the canisters roll to a stop under his feet.

"Free beer!" The punker yelled as he dove under the pews for the canisters. He opened one, only to have it explode in his face and set off the others in chain reaction. The gas engulfed the crowd and the band. It ate at their skin and began to dissolve it while they continued to play. The adrenaline-pumped crowd continued to slam dance as their skin dripped off their bodies, momentarily oblivious to the pain.

Then they began to scream, "Get it off of me! It burns!" The crowd broke into a panic.

Jack pulled his radioactive suit out of his backpack and began searching for Shawn. The gas billowed out the doors and windows, leaving the scene of pandemonium inside.

Doyle and Darla reached the top of the hill and laid on a frayed blanket down at the edge of the scenic lookout. The sun began to set as they stared out, looking over smoggy Savage Town with its eerie congested glow. Fire raged out of control on the west side and shots could be heard echoing through the valley.

"Ah, finally just the two of us. Alone." Darla batted her long lashes.

"You mean besides the couple fucking in the bushes over there." Doyle pointed to the rustling bushes where they could hear moaning. "I guess our special place is no longer a secret."

"Let's just make the best of it." Darla found comfort in Doyle's arms.

"I remember when we first came here, you had that sexy red dress on, and you did that little dance for me. I just wanted to go downtown."

"You did go downtown that night," Darla giggled.

They watched the sunset together in peace. A moment not shared by many.

Suddenly, they heard a scuffle come from the bushes, and the moans became cries for help. "Shut up bitch! Give me all your capsules!"

"Leave us alone you fucking lowlife!" A gunshot rang out and the mugger ran off through the bushes.

"We can't get any peace and fucking quiet anywhere around here."

"Forget it, Horsey, the sun's almost down. Let's just enjoy it."

"Maybe I'll just enjoy you." They embraced and watched the sun fall into the valley, ignoring the gurgling sounds coming from the bushes.

"Ah ... this feels good, Horsey. I wish I could hold you forever."

"You can ... I was thinking ... maybe we should go west and find a little place."

"Oh, good idea, like an ambush for the P.M."

"Not quite, more like settling down, somewhere away from all of this."

"Ha-ha! You're being silly. And let the P.M. win, right?"

Doyle swallowed his words. He wanted desperately to ask her to forget about the cause and to live in peace together, even if the risk was great.

Darla raised her head. "You're being serious, aren't you?"

Doyle leaned in and kissed the scars on her neck. "Nevermind, I was just thinking out ... that's odd. Does the sun look a little green to you?" Doyle observed.

"No, that's smoke coming from The Church down there."

"Green smoke?"

They both looked at each other and said, "Jack!" They sprang to their feet and ran down the hill toward the town.

The servant boy rushed through the door of Benny's bedroom. Benny had a woman tied up against the wall and was pouring salt in fresh wounds. Crude sex toys lined his shelves in perfect harmony with each other, showcased as if devices of deviancy were fine art.

"Master! Master! Come quick, something happened at The

Church."

"Does it look like I'm busy at the moment?" Benny continued to dispense salt as the girl moaned, a double-sided dildo fell from her crotch. "Shit, you're losing the moment."

"Some weird gas is spreading across the town killing people!"

Benny got up and walked over to the large picture window, ripping the silk curtains down. The green gas was hovering over half of the town. A person slammed against the window, tearing at his flesh, trying to get rid of the burning gas that had stuck to his skin. Benny watched the man melt away from behind the safety of the double-plated glass. "Interesting."

"Hurry up, we have to get Jack and get the hell out of here!" Doyle put on his suit and mask and then helped Darla into her gear.

People were running and screaming everywhere. A man fell down in front of them as his skin dripped off of his face like running water. The green cloud rushed forward, engulfing everything. Jack came running out of a large green cloud carrying Shawn on his back.

"What the fuck happened, Jack!" Doyle grabbed at Jack's suit.

"It was an accident!"

Darla jumped between them. "Come on boys! This is not the time or place!"

They took off running toward the front gate only to find it locked.

"Fuck! We got to climb over."

"I can't carry Shawn over the gate!"

"Who the fuck is Shawn? Shit man, you're compromising our mission!"

"Their Anarchy March, we can't leave 'em behind!"

Doyle watched Shawn's skin dripping off their flesh, exposing bone.

Jack's eyes bugged wild beneath his protective mask. "It happened so—"

The gatekeeper jumped down from nowhere to tackle Darla. He screamed in pain and tried to take off her suit. Before he could,

Doyle rushed over and kicked the gatekeeper off of her. He kneed him in the face and sat on his chest. "How do you open this gate!"

He gurgled as his skin started to deteriorate and his arm melted away.

An explosion destroyed the front gate from the outside. Doyle, Darla, Jack, and what was becoming less and less of Shawn, went flying into a nearby tent.

Through the smoke, four P.M. tanks emerged, led by the general and Lieutenant Bachmann. The general's one-hundred-man-strong unit, followed them, stomping in unison.

"They are here." Lieutenant Bachmann read from his holographic hand.

"Well, spread out and find those punks!"

The first wave of P.M. soldiers rushed in and was swallowed by the green gas.

"Stop!" Bachmann extended his arm, blocking the general's entrance to the town as he read from the digital data from his hand. "That's not normal smoke."

A few P.M. soldiers ran back out of the green smoke screaming, clawing at their eyes and exposed skin. A single frantic soldier ran up to the general as his skin dripped from his face. A swift kick in the chest sent the soldier tumbling to the ground as his bones disintegrated.

The desert wind kicked up and the green gas dispersed into the atmosphere, leaving a scene riddled with disintegrating flesh, skin, and bone.

The general kneeled down next to what was left of the dead soldier. He sunk a finger into his cheek, and some of the green gas clung to the general's hand. Feeling his skin begin to burn, he bit down on his cheek. "Find our old friend Benny, if he is still alive. I'm sure he has some answers."

The P.M. marched toward Benny's house, passing the tent where Doyle and the Anarchy March had fallen.

Doyle woke up bewildered. His ears were ringing as blood trickled out. He stood up only to fall again. "Darla! Baby!"

"She's over here." Jack pulled some heavy debris off of her.

Doyle rushed to her side and picked up her unconscious body. "Let's go! Get your friend."

"Oh fuck!" Jack peered at his friend's disintegrating body. "I'm sorry."

They bolted out through the rubble of the gate and ran back to the highway.

After a few miles of agitated hiking, Doyle put Darla down and leaned her against a tree. "Come on, baby, wake up." Doyle removed her gas mask and caressed her cropped hair.

Jack paced back and forth as tears rolled down his face. "I'm sorry, man, I'm sorry."

Darla opened her eyes and smiled at Doyle. Her body began to twitch, and she foamed at the mouth.

"Shit!" Doyle held Darla down using all of his strength.

"I need some help, Jack! Hold her legs."

Jack ran to her aid and held her legs down.

"You fucking idiot, what happened back there?" Doyle asked as he unzipped his suit and pulled out a Barbie doll arm, bitten with wear. He held down Darla's swinging arms and placed the plastic arm against her tongue.

"I'm sorry man, I was just having some fun, and I bumped into my old friend, we had some powder and—"

"Stop! I don't want to hear it. You fucking destroy half of that town and almost got all of us killed, you dumb fuck!"

"I know. I fucked up. I fucked up bad."

Darla's body began to relax. They both released her and fell back on the ground exhausted.

Doyle got up and rushed Jack. He ripped off his backpack and rummaged through it; he found one canister. "One! Fucking one left? Is this going to be enough, Jack? Have you forgotten the *importance* of our mission? How many Anarchy March have died for this? Your own father!"

Jack remained quiet as he stared at the ground, knowing it was his father's last work and final words.

Doyle put the last canister in his own backpack.

Darla coughed and woke up. She wiped the foamy blood from her mouth. "Did I have another fit?" she asked looking around, "Where are we?"

"I don't know, baby. We're off route."

Jack pulled out his map. "We're still only a two-day walk from the tunnels. We can't go back though. It's probably crawling with the P.M. by now."

Doyle convicted Jack with his eyes.

"Dude, I said I fucked up. I'm fucking sorry!"

Darla sat up and looked at the swampy forest ahead. "We have to go through the marsh."

"Fuck that! It's infested with Nukies."

"Well, Jack, thanks to you we have no other choice!" Doyle helped his fiancée up, and they walked into the thick marsh. A wild animal howled in the distance.

"You hear that boys, it won't be that bad. There's still life in the marsh." They then heard a loud, high-pitched squeal, as though the neck of the wild animal had just been snapped in two.

"Yeah, not bad at all. Just a little walk in the park."

They began their march into the bog and disappeared into the shrubbery.

The general and the small division of soldiers pulled up to the front door of Benny's home. The general knocked using his side arm.

The servant boy came to the door and peaked through the peephole. "Yes, how can I help you?" he yelled.

"This is General Stripes of the Prominent Municipality. We would like to speak with Benny Hall about the recent Anarchy March attack on your town."

The servant boy looked back at Benny, who waved him off and shook his head no.

"Sorry sirs, um, Benny is out of town at the moment. Can I take a message?" He looked again through the peephole in the door. His eyes widened, focused on the barrel of the general's gun.

The general shot the servant boy through the peephole and

then ordered his men to use the battering ram. The soldiers knocked the door down, and the general walked in. "Tell him that the general is here." He stepped over the servant's dead body and walked through the foyer into Benny's lounge area.

"How was your trip, Benny, back so soon?" the general asked, holstering his gun.

Benny sat still in a grand rococo gold gilt throne next to a masonry fireplace cupping his wine glass. "Don't you know it's so hard to find good help?"

"Benny, Benny, Benny, it's been a while. I trust you're well."

"I can't complain." His mannerism was most urbane.

Lieutenant Bachmann retrieved Benny's digital dossier from his hand.

"Looks like you're a little late on your payment this month. Is the Prominent Municipality not providing you with everything you need?" The general walked over to the *Mona Lisa* and studied it.

"Um, it, it has been rough in Savage Town, the arena's not making the profit that it used to."

"Is that a fact?" The general looked over his shoulder at Bachmann's digital readout blinking red. Bachmann confirmed with a strong headshake.

"I took all of your tests! Nobody is sticking anything into me ... unless, I truly want them to."

The general pointed at the painting and glanced at Benny. "She is sure an ugly woman, huh?"

The military personnel in the room chuckled.

"Actually, the *Mona Lisa* is said to be a self-portrait of da Vinci with female characteristics."

The general punched through the historic portrait. "You really like that faggot garbage, don't you?"

"What do you want?" Benny's hands began to shake as he tried to hold onto his wine glass.

"What do I want? I want to know the truth. Why are we here? What purpose does the man upstairs have for us? Very Augean questions, but I know an easy one for ya. Who was the A.M. that came through here, and what was that glorious weapon they had?"

Benny remained quiet.

"Don't play stupid with me, Benny. I'll have the Prominent Municipality erase Savage Town off the face of God's green earth. I know the Anarchy March came through here with their bioweapon and decimated half your town."

"I don't know any Anarchy March."

"Really?" The general continued to read from Lieutenant Bachmann's hand. "Two counts of conspiracy with Anarchy March, four counts of drug smuggling across Section borders for the Anarchy March, eleven counts of illegal technology trading with the Anarchy March. Shall I continue?"

"That was a long time ago. You know I take my orders from the Prominent Municipality now."

"You tell me all these answers, but you don't tell me the right ones. Now, I'm gonna ask you one last time. If you want to continue running your little operation in this shithole, I suggest you tell me who they were."

Benny's upper lip began to quiver, but he maintained his silence. He knew, once you gave the Prominent Municipality what they wanted, you may as well put a bullet into your own head.

"Wrong answer." The general grabbed Benny by the lapel and pistol-whipped his face, sending him reeling back against the wall. He pressed into the exposed button. The red cloth began to open from underneath the glass, revealing to everyone his Purgatory masterpiece.

"Holy Saint Mary and Joseph, Benny. You have been busy. You're a sick individual!" The general grabbed Benny and threw him at a military soldier. "Take him in. Book him for possession of art, under law: 8743987-7432883-234324-A and 748293748-234723-33742D, harboring known terrorists." The general stormed out of the house, and as he passed two armed military guards standing next to the front door, he ordered them, "Burn it down!"

Benny was handcuffed and thrown into the back of a jeep. He

watched the military use flamethrowers to burn down his house and all of his possessions. The jeep rolled back down the hill, separating from the other vehicles. Benny ground his teeth together and clamped down on one, setting off a homing beacon.

"Hey, you, turncoat, yeah I'm talking to you." One of the soldiers sitting next to Benny said, "I wonder what the A.M. is going to do to you after they find out you've been playing both sides."

Benny ignored the man.

"I'm talking to you, fag!"

"Hey, 69, do you hear a beeping sound?" A soldier in the passenger's side of the jeep asked.

Benny turned and looked at the man harassing him. "Your number name is 69?"

"Yeah, so. You find that funny?"

Benny chuckled and received a sideswipe across his mouth from the man's gun. Benny's homing tooth flew out next to the soldier's foot. He picked up the flashing red tooth.

"STOP THE JEEP!"

Something smashed into the side of the jeep, flipping it onto its side. The driver flew out and slammed his head against the hardened dirt. He was then ripped from the ground by an indeterminate force.

CRACK! The body fell back, broken in half, ripped in two at the spine.

"Boys, I would like you to meet Kongo."

The jeep's ragtop was ripped off and towering above them stood Kongo. Dark blue arteries were popping, and drool trickled from his mouth. He reached in and grabbed another body like a ragdoll and slammed it against the ground.

The general was walking on the side of one of the tanks leaving Savage Town.

"Sir, I can't get a read out in this Section, we are too close to the marshes' radiation."

"I guess it's an old-fashioned manhunt. Search the town and the outskirts. Don't leave any corner unlit. Rats hide in the dark.

Make the call and seal off the highways."

"What about the marshes?"

"If they go into that godforsaken place, let the war babies take care of them."

"The Nukies, sir?"

"Yes. Did I stutter?" The general passed the demolished church and saw a sign lying on the ground that read: Reagan's Children, see you in Hell tonight! The general spat, "History? Blaspheme."

Testament III

RHETORIC VERSUS REVOLUTION

Among the heavily guarded briefing room, the press's incessant chattering filled the space. The room buzzed with speculation about this unexpected call, and as the emergency president was introduced the room hushed. A nationwide broadcast of the president's speech was about to begin.

"Ladies and Gentlemen, please rise for 'Honest' Gabe Rover, the emergency president of the United States."

The president approached the podium with feigned poise laced with the occasional glimpse of uncertainty. His eyes darted around the room, never stopping on one person for too long. He took a few seconds to gather his thoughts as he breathed heavily into the microphone. "Mr. secretary general, Mr. vice president, distinguished delegates, ladies and gentlemen. Thank you for giving me the honor of addressing this General Assembly. The American people respect the idealism that gave life to this organization, and we respect the men and woman who stand for peace and human rights in every part of the world. Welcome to Washington, DC, and welcome to the United States of America." The emergency president rubbed at the back of his neck, relaxing his shoulders as the assembly of press and photographers clapped in approval.

"During my reign, um, excuse me, my term in office, we have overcome many obstacles and hurdles. I'm addressing this assembly because our beloved country has fallen on hard times once again. It has been one year since November Fifth, and terror is at an all time high from those radical, anti-American networks. Our nation is in a critical—"

"Cut the bullshit, Gabe!" a voice hollered from the back of the room.

The secretary general stepped up to the microphone, "Excuse me, you will address the emergency president of the United States with the utmost respect. Throw that man out!"

Two armed men rushed the out-spoken journalist.

"What happened to freedom of speech? All that nonsense you just said about human rights! I just have some questions that need to be addressed! You owe the American people here and all over the country!"

Gabe Rover looked at his secretary general and smiled, "Let him go."

The armed men released the journalist. As he regained his composure, he continued. "Mr. E.P., I just want some hard facts that the American people have been asking for, for well over a decade now."

Gabe Rover adjusted his tie and scratched his neck. Clearly the multitude of eyes upon him pressed hard.

"All this talk about peace and equality and in your reign, as you said earlier, you have done nothing but cause wars and separate nations. Now, how do explain that?"

"What is your name?"

"That is not important. I asked you a direct question."

"Well, if you have been paying attention to the state media, we are at war with terrorism and radical—"

"That you own and created, Mr. E.P. We are done listening to your paid off propaganda over the airwaves. I have documentation of your family's history that puts you in bed with these so-called terrorist groups. Oil and gas prices are through the roof, and I ask you, Mr. E.P., who owns these companies?"

"Next question please, this man is obviously a Liberal. He has nothing better to do than to incite fear of the government with these ridiculous conspiracy theories."

A reporter, sitting in the front row, raised his hand. Gabe Rover pointed at him, "Yes, Mr. Edgars, what is your question?"

"I want to hear your answer to this man's question. I think Americans deserve the truth, Mr. E.P. With all due respect, you have kept us in the dark regarding these wars."

The restlessness bubbled to the surface, and in agreement, hands flayed the air, voices rose in anticipation, urging the emergency president to engage in an honest dialogue.

"You want to know the truth? Our administration has been fighting for this fine country for our children and our grandchildren and our children's grandchildren so they can have a better life."

"Bullshit! Our children lie starving in the street due to this horrible economy that you created. There is a void where the middle class used to be. America was founded and thrived on the middle class, and you have taken it away. The average family goes starving because they don't have enough money. We can't get an education because our schools lost funding, and we can't go to work because the infrastructure of the roads and buildings are crumbling. We are back in the fucking Middle Ages! When is enough, enough? You keep talking about these goddamn wars that our children are dying in so you and your bureaucratic fat cats can feed your greedy mouths!"

"But the Constitution, but the war, but..." Gabe pleaded to no avail. He began to scratch his neck as the briefing began to fall into chaos. The press was now fueled by countless unanswered inquiries, and they erupted into frenzy and exploded with a barrage of questions that had festered in the back of the public's mind, questions forgotten through the years and which had never before — until now — been asked with such blunt conviction.

"What are you going to do about our failing education system, Mr. E.P.?"

"We now can arm every man, woman, and child but are unable to feed them. Who are these interest groups?"

"Why have we been at war with every country since your presidency?"

"What are we doing about our global warming or climate change or global climate disruption? Whatever you're trying to call it now. We need a real solution, not a redefinition of the crisis."

"Mr. E.P., where are all these weapons of mass destruction you talked about? And do they threaten us or you more?"

"The oil in the fields and offshore has almost dried up, what is your plan to fuel our vehicles, our everyday lives?"

"Can you explain why we have been in an economic depression for over a decade now and we're on the threshold of reaching a pentillion dollar debt?"

"Is this government responsible for importing illegal drugs into the U.S. then fabricating a war on drugs? One out of three Americans are addicted to at least one illegal substance, and I don't think I need to mention the questionable record-breaking profits of the 'legal' pharmaceutical companies."

"Is it true that there is a floating plastic island the size of Australia in the middle of the Pacific Ocean? Is it true that our fish population has almost disappeared?"

"Why are more and more sick and uninsured Americans dying in the streets, while corporate powerhouses show record profits? My uncle and my father passed away two days ago. The same treatment that could have saved their lives is offered for free to the people in your cabinet."

"What really happened on 11/11?"

"Hey! You know darn well what happened there," Gabe stated.

"No, no, no, I'm talking about in 1887."

"Mr. E.P.! Mr. Emergency President! Gabe! Gabe!" echoed through the briefing room.

"Everyone, calm down! This administration has—"

"Done nothing but fucked us! We are sick and tired of living under a rule of capitalism and so-called God-fearing Christians." The journalist stood up on the stage and walked to the podium, pushing the emergency president to the side. "The country has had enough of your lies, Mr. E.P. It's time for a revolution."

The crowd cheered as Gabe Rover looked around at the uprising. Lenses zoomed in and every camera flashed. The world was watching, judging. Gabe took a deep breath and stepped back.

"It's time to wake up, America! It's time that we all got together."

Just then a bullet ripped through the face of the outspoken

journalist, silencing him for good. His body wilted and fell off the stage, landing at the feet of Mr. Edgars in the front row. Behind the smoking gun stood the emergency president. He lowered his gun and looked around the room with a defiant stare. A hush fell over the shocked crowd as the armed men, standing guard, clinched tighter and cocked their guns. A sudden realization came over the press room that either they were with this tyrannical government or against it.

President Rover took a handkerchief out and wiped the blood spatter off his face and tie, "Are there any more questions?"

The crowd remained silent.

"May God bless you and God bless the United States of America. Good night and good luck." Gabe Rover holstered his gun and walked off stage.

"Wake up! Wake up!" Darla shook Doyle, trying to rip him out of his night terror. He jolted up and wrapped his hands around her neck and squeezed.

"It's ... me ... Dar ... la."

Doyle's eyes glossed over before he realized what he was doing and released Darla. Sweat beaded and trickled down his forehead. He took a few deep breaths and looked around to gather his surroundings. "I'm sorry. I'm so sorry."

Darla rubbed her neck, stretching it. "It's not your fault. There's nothing to be sorry about."

The night was pitch black with a few twinkling stars, barely visible through the thick coat of smog. Their small campfire had burned out, only a faint red glow remained.

"Are you okay, Horsey? Your night terrors are getting worse."

"I was at the Executive Judgment Speech."

"That must've been scary. Mom told me about that speech when I was a kid. I remember it was the first time I've seen her cry." Darla's head wilted as she struggled with the faded memory.

"I was in the front row. It seemed so real. I could smell the blood."

She embraced him. "Things will get better; they just have to."

He picked up a small rock and threw it at Jack. "Hey, wake up, fucker, you let the fire die out again!"

Jack ripped off his headphones, and bawled, "Huh? What happened? Man, I'm trying to sleep here!"

"Tough shit! You're the reason we're here," Doyle growled.

"Hey, take it easy on him, besides it's my turn to get the firewood," Darla said, squeezing Doyle's arm.

Jack turned over and said, "Thank you, Darla. You're the best." Then he readjusted the volume on his headphones and fell back to sleep.

"Be careful out there, babe. Just yell if you need anything."

"Oh, I'll yell, no problem. You'll hear me from Section C." Darla stood up and walked into the darkness carrying a small solar-powered flashlight and her handy knife.

"Jack!" Doyle poked at the dying fire with a stick, trying to spark a flare, "Jack, hey..."

"What?! I said I was sorry. Why can't you just let it go?"

"It's not that. Do you ever feel that, I don't know, what, well, what we're doing'll even make a difference?"

Jack sat up and took off his headphones, the dying fire reflected off Doyle's moist eyes.

"Why are you thinking about things like that? Of course it will."

"I love her so much. I don't want to lose her like everyone else." Doyle prodded the smoldering ash. A few sparks flew and then were extinguished by the damp air. "Sometimes I feel I should just run away with her to some abandoned section and live a peaceful existence."

"Stop talking like that, man. You know they'll never let that happen. That's fucking selfish of you to even say that. What about the next generation, and the ones after that? You know that's how this whole fucking mess began, people not caring about each other and ignoring the truth." Jack yanked out his wallet and searched through his makeshift photo album, there he found a picture of his father. "Would you tell him this?" Jack asked, pointing at his dad.

Doyle hung his head and prodded at the ground. He silently

shed a tear.

"I have known you all my life and we've been best friends forever. I'm telling you, we have to keep going, it's all we got. Just like the late and great Captain Sinbad used to say, 'I would rather die on my feet, than to have to live a lifetime on my knees.'"

Doyle stopped prodding the fire, "You're an idiot. First of all, Sinbad was a fictitious character in a book like Jesus and second, Emiliano Zapata, the Mexican revolutionist, said that."

"Whatever, man, you know what I mean."

"Yeah, you're right. Fuck the world!"

"F.T.W." they laid back down and stared up at the dull stars through the thick blanket of smog. "I wonder if any of those planets up there have the same problems we've got down here?" Doyle ruminated.

"I wonder if those alien chicks are hot. I would love me some green poon."

Darla searched around for firewood using her flashlight. She picked up a hefty log to replace the tiny twigs she had found. The narrow beam of light illuminated a clearing of grass. She pulled down her pants to relieve herself. She began to hum to quell the eerie silence, and through her tune she heard something rustling around in the bushes off in the distance. "Horsey, is that you?" She pulled out her knife, wary of the noise until she saw Jack approach. "What are you doing here? You left Doyle by himself?"

"He told me to check on you." Jack unfastened his safety pins and stood next to a tree.

"I'm fine. Can I get some privacy here?"

"I don't know, can you?" Jack stated, as he urinated on the tree. "Almost done ... oh, oh, ah! There it is." Jack shook and zipped as he walked away. "All yours."

Darla waited for Jack's shadow to disappear before she continued to relieve herself. She tried to ignore the terrible stench that Jack left and whistled to get the juices flowing. A low pitch whistled back at her with the same melody.

"Jack! Stop fucking around, I'm trying to pee!"

The whistling stopped and a deep groan came from the bushes. She pulled up her pants and shined the light in the shrubbery. Nothing but swaying leaves.

"Jack, is that you? Not funny, asshole!" She caught a glimpse of something with her flashlight, but it disappeared before she could make it out. She began to breathe heavily, her heart thumped as a cold gust of wind twirled around her. She heard the noise coming from all over, circling her, but could not pinpoint it. As she turned around, the light shone on the melted face of a pale, naked figure that towered over her. Its face oozed pale pink against red sinew from decades of radiation poisoning, exposing the creamy glint of bone.

She belted out a yell as the monstrous humanoid beast tackled her to the ground. Its cracked nails dug into her shoulders, pinning her down. She fish-hooked the creature's mouth in an attempt to get it off of her. The creature squealed and tried to bite down on Darla's thumb as the saliva dripped down her arm. The creature broke free from her hold and swung its swollen arms, striking her. She managed to knee the gaping cavity between its legs and push the creature away. She stumbled up but fell back down. She had a gash down her leg from the attack. Struggling to her feet, she limped back toward camp. Her flashlight highlighted the dead trees and disfigurements weaving in and out, closing in from all around.

"Doyle! Doyle!" she screamed. She slammed into somebody.

"Whoa! Whoa! It's me, Jack. We heard your scream. Calm down. What's going on?"

Doyle ran to them. "Nukies! They're everywhere!"

Another beast from the treetop swooped down and grabbed Jack by the head, pulling him up toward the smoggy, low-hanging clouds. Doyle jumped on Jack's legs as they played a tug-of-war. The creature bit into Jack's arm — blood gushed out. "Fuck!" he howled.

Another creature tackled Doyle from out of the shadows. Doyle flipped the beast onto its back and mounted it. He hooked his thumbs into the creature's jawbones and slammed its head against the ground. He then dug his fingers deep into the eye sockets as it shrieked and tried to buck Doyle off. Another creature jumped on Doyle's back. Darla jetted to the rescue and stabbed it in the ribs.

POP! POP! POP! Out of nowhere a fusillade of shots were fired. The quick flashes of light revealed a few dozen Nukies around the perimeter. Jack fell to the ground with the creature breaking his fall. The Nukies dispersed and the gunshots stopped. A flare lit up in a hand. Doyle looked up and saw some familiar faces with Anarchy March armbands.

"Got a little Nukie problem?" Maverick said, holding a night-scope equipped gun.

"Fuck you, what the hell took you guys so long?" Doyle stood up and helped Darla to her feet.

"Your transmission cut in and out. It was unclear where you guys were coming from, but you're welcome." Maverick threw a pack of food capsules at Doyle.

Jack got up and kicked a dead Nukie. "Fucker bit me! It better not have fucking POLPOX."[1]

"Jack! Long time no see, buddy. You still hanging around with this bum, Doyle?"

"Ha! Jack's like a fungus, he's hard to get rid of and just kinda grows on you." Doyle joked, pushing Jack.

"Hey, Maverick, you got some batteries I can borrow?"

"For you? No. So what brings you through this section?"

"We have a special delivery for Lee. Something that might change the fight to our favor."

"Well, I hope you weren't planning on going through the

---

[1] Manufactured in Section A labs, what's commonly called POLPOX is a viral germ that is highly contagious. It was designed to eliminate the infected and killed off the weaker of the subspecies, though the strong grew immune to the disease. When the disease enters the bloodstream, it destroys all motor neurons leading to severe flaccid paralysis and corneal ulcerations causing blindness.

tunnels," Maverick said.

"Why, what happened?"

"We lost the tunnels about a week ago. Fucking P.M. found out about it. The place is FUBAR, a fucking massacre."

Doyle bit into his food capsule. "That's not funny."

"We have a mole."

"Bullshit! Nobody would betray the Anarchy March," Jack affirmed.

"I wouldn't have believed it neither if I didn't see it with my own eyes."

"What did you see?" Darla asked, bandaging up her leg.

"They knew the tunnels like the back of their hands. There is no fucking way their shitty computer-generated map could have known every path to all the sections. I'm sorry, but the underground tunnels are no more."

"Great! Fucking great, now what?" Jack took his frustration out by giving the Nukie another solid kick.

"Maverick, do you have a vehicle with a P.M. clearance?" asked Doyle.

"We had one at the foot of the tunnels, but that's probably crawling with the P.M. by now."

"It's worth the risk. We have to deliver this package at any cost. I have a plan."

The small army of Anarchy March survivors accompanied Doyle, Darla, and Jack through the thick marsh as it came to an end. The land became hard, and they gathered their footing again after dumping the slush from their boots. They continued on until they reached the foot of the underground tunnel, burrowed into the side of an unassuming hill. The blanket of darkness allowed them to move into a close proximity. The entrance of the tunnel whistled as the wind blew through, bringing a stale smell of death and gunpowder.

"Shh ... down," Maverick said, as he heard chattering by the entrance. They crept through the shrubbery and saw three P.M. soldiers guarding the tunnel. One of the soldiers paced back and forth, mumbling to himself before he blurted, "Mad Dog thinks it's not fair, why do we get the garbage graveyard shift while Outfit Niner gets target practice of the rest of the A.M. captives?" Mad Dog groused while leaning against the wall smoking a cigarette.

"Fucking A!" said the soldier standing to his left as he lifted up his rocket launcher and pointed it to the top of the tree line.

"I wouldn't be complaining if I was you, Mad Dog. I heard the general cut out the tongues of a whole outfit for whining about clicks traveled. Listen up, this ain't no bullshit watch. Intelligence said that this is the only route back to Section X. So, keep your eyes peeled, Mad Dog. We might have a firefight on hand," the third vigilante asserted, as he peered over to the bushes upon hearing a noise.

"Whatever, no pussy-ass A.M. would dare step up to Mad Dog."

"Hey, Mad Dog, you always gotta refer to yourself in third person?"

"Mad Dog says yes," he laughed and walked away. "I have to drain the dragon. I'll be right back."

"Hey stupid, you forgetting something?" The soldier picked up Mad Dog's gun and threw it to him.

"Now don't go shooting your dick off!"

"It would have to be bigger than this to do that job!" He grabbed his groin and shook it at the two soldiers.

Mad Dog walked into the bushes and behind a tree. He began to urinate right next to an unseen Darla. The stream hit Darla on top of her head, and her face reddened with fury as she pulled out her knife. Mad Dog saw a shimmering reflection from the moon in the bushes. Before he could do anything, a quick slice cut off his member. Mad Dog shrieked and dropped to his knees. Darla swiped again, cutting his throat. He gurgled as his throat filled with blood.

"Yo, Mad Dog, stop fucking around!" yelled a soldier. "Yo, Mad Dog!" he yelled louder.

Something pelted him, bouncing off his chest. He looked down and saw the severed penis. Just then, from up above, Doyle and Maverick jumped down behind the soldiers, landing on them with blades duct-taped around their ankles. Doyle's blade pierced right through the skull of one, but Maverick's attack stabbed the other deep in the shoulder blade. He screamed and pulled the rocket launcher's trigger, shooting into the air. Maverick tore the blade from his ankle and straddled the soldier, stabbing him through his trachea. His legs twitched and went limp.

"You think anybody saw that?" Doyle asked, as he watched the stray rocket fly far away, sailing into the clouds.

Out of nowhere, a P.M. interceptor helicopter flew past them following the missile. "Come in, watch one! Come in! What did you see? Over."

Jack came out from the darkness and picked up the handheld transceiver from the dead soldier. "Um, thought I saw a damn A.M. radio-plane. False alarm. Over."

"Don't waste your ammo. We will not be supplied until 23:00. Over."

"Yeah, no problem. Fucking A. Over." Jack relished his improv response.

Darla slapped the handheld transceiver from Jack's palm, her nostrils flaring with anger. The helicopter came flying back overhead and disappeared into the clouds.

"That was a close one. You need to practice your ninja skills," Doyle cracked as he began to scavenge the dead bodies.

"My bad. Did you hear that though? This outfit is low on ammo, we can take 'em and gain our ground back."

Maverick picked up the rocket launcher, and they snuck into the underground tunnel.

Kongo was running full throttle on a dirt path, jumping and dodging every obstacle that lay in front of him. He lept over fallen signs and torched cars, a veritable junkyard in his path. An aimless rocket coasted high overhead, and he barreled down, attempting to charge faster.

"Are we there yet?" Benny asked, saddled on Kongo's back, holding on to his large shoulders. "I'd rather not get hit with any stray rockets today."

Kongo breached the tree line and into a clearing. The open, abandoned highways stretched as far as they could see. A thunderous storm approached as lightning struck in the distance, forcing Kongo to hesitate.

Benny tugged on Kongo's choke chain. "Well, what are we waiting for?" he asked.

Huffing hard, Kongo pointed out at the thousand of little red lights that lined the highways.

"Come on, you big oaf! It's only a few chaser mines." Benny jumped off of Kongo and pulled out a little L.C.D. beacon. "Look, right over the old 15, over there is where I parked the Mangler." Benny dug in his pocket, he pulled out a hypodermic syringe. "Now man up! And I'll let you ride in the back when we reach the vehicle." Explosions echoed in the distance. "If the P.M. wants this bioweapon so bad, I can use this to my advantage."

Kongo took a knee and Benny jumped on board. He injected Kongo in the neck with the syringe. His veins protruded out from his bulky mass as the adrenaline-enhancing drug pumped through his bloodstream.

"Ready, steady, go!"

Kongo jumped onto the highway, and the chaser mine lights turned green. Hundreds rose from the ground and zeroed in on any electrical devices that Benny was holding. Kongo jumped over the old discarded vehicles and fallen debris. 25, 35, 45 M.P.H., Kongo was a freight train. The chaser mines were not as fast and detonated as they lost speed. Explosion after explosion followed Kongo, shaking the ground as he jetted across the highway.

Benny mused, "It's not subtle, but effective!" He white-knuckled the chain around Kongo's pulsating neck.

Kongo saw a dozen chaser mines coming toward him, so he jumped over to an adjacent highway. The chaser mines rushed by them. They landed hard, and Benny's grip weakened; he began sliding off Kongo's back and grabbed at the choke chain again. Kongo jerked his neck to the left, and Benny went flying back up onto him.

"Whoa! Where are we going?"

"Short cut," Kongo grumbled.

Benny looked behind him and now saw thousands of little green lights chasing after them. Kongo began to breathe heavily as exhaustion was kicking in.

"Um, why do they look like they're catching up?" Benny noticed Kongo was weakening fast. He dug into his pocket and pulled out a few more syringes.

Kongo jumped over a downed highway sign, and the needles flew out of Benny's hand.

"Intolerable!" Benny wrapped his arms tight around Kongo as he saw the highway exit. "Come on! Come on! Move it, you oaf!"

Kongo's legs began to burn, and the veins in his neck burst, sending blood dripping down his exhausted body. 45, 35, 25 M.P.H. — the chaser mines were catching up to them.

"Jump!" Benny closed his eyes as Kongo jumped off the exit and onto a grass clearing. Benny flew off into the bushes and tumbled into a tree. The chaser mines relit to armed red, fell to the ground, and wobbled to a stop.

"Kongo!"

Like a dutiful pet, Kongo ran to his aid and helped him up.

Benny looked around and noticed the fallen exit sign reading: Exit 13A. "Wrong exit, oaf. How many times I got to tell you? It's B, B! Not A!" Benny stood in front of Kongo waiting and tapping his foot. "Well, I'm not going to get up there by my lonesome." Kongo kneeled down and Benny climbed onto his shoulders, and they trekked into the woods.

They came across a grassy knoll and Benny ordered Kongo to halt. "Over there, the fig tree." Kongo strolled up to the tree and Benny pulled on the fake tree branch. A secret door opened below their feet. "Come on, let's get you cleaned up, you look terrible." Benny went down the secret staircase. Kongo followed, huffing, panting, bleeding. They descended into a darkened room. Benny groped around, found a cord, and yanked on it. A generator roared to life and the lights turned on.

"Ah, there she is." Benny admired his 1965 mint El Camino. It was equipped with turbo boost and trimmed with weapons.

Two large Gatling guns mounted the sides, spiked tires, missile launchers set up on the roof, finished with a rear .50 caliber on a stand bolted down in the back. All encased in a matte black paint. "They don't make them like this anymore. Come to think about it, I don't think they ever made them like this," he surmised, patting the hood.

He walked over to some dusty shelves and pulled out a few bottles of wine. "2020, good year." Benny laid the bottles on the floor of the El Camino's passenger side then jumped in the driver's seat.

Kongo tended to his wounds with bandages he had grabbed from the shelves. His blood had soaked through the first two layers.

"What are you doing? We have no time for that. Let's go!"

Kongo grumbled in pain.

"Hey, it's not my fault that you decided to take that *short cut*. Maybe we should leave the thinking to me, huh?"

Kongo bandaged his remaining wound and jumped in the back of the El Camino taking a hold of the .50 caliber gun. Benny started up the car and revved the engine back to life. He picked up a bottle of wine and stuck it out the window. "Kongo, would you do me the pleasure?"

Kongo turned the gun, aimed it at the top of the bottle, fired one shot, and the bottle top shattered off. Benny took a swig from the broken bottle, cutting his lip. But he didn't care. Fueled with his drink of choice, he peeled out and drove up the ramp and out onto the dirt road. The roar of the engine caught the attention of a few wandering Nukies on the road, but Benny mashed the pedal flat and Kongo released a stream of bullets, ripping the Nukies to shreds.

"Dangle! I'm coming to get you!"

The small Anarchy March brigade hid in the shadows along a narrow corridor, treading lightly through the dark tunnels. The putrid smell of death and suffering lingered in the air. They walked into the huge underground tunnel that was laid with hundreds of miles of Light Rails shooting out in sporadic directions into other tunnels. Now that this fifteen-year-old secret was out, an uneasy depression and fear engulfed Doyle as he looked around at the bloody mayhem that covered the ground. He looked into a carved-out dwelling where kids had once played innocently; now a family of four were tied up with blindfolds, laying face down on the ground in an execution-style murder. The once beautifully nurtured flower garden was now a trampled muddy puddle containing a sole bud standing alone, clinging to life.[1]

"What happened here?" Doyle asked, breaching the silence.

"Like I said before, they just came from everywhere. We had no fucking warning."

Doyle stepped over dead bodies that had been piled up in preparation to be scorched.

"I don't like this, man. Where the hell is the P.M.? They just didn't leave." Jack observed, looking into a dark corner.

"Hey, Horsey, Jack's right. It's too quiet."

"Let's just keep our eyes peeled."

"Don't worry, we will get you safely to Section X." Maverick took point and his men followed.

"Maverick! Thank you, thank you for saving our asses back there." Doyle stated with sincerity in his eyes. Maverick nodded and led his men into the darkness ahead.

Doyle, Darla, and Jack trailed behind. The tunnel lights flickered off and on, and the ground shook every so often. A war was being raised in a different tunnel. They could hear the hellish sounds of wailing and mutilation, yet they were nowhere near the center of the Earth. They continued creeping into the unknown.

---

[1] Before the Anarchy March, there was a group of sound-minded individuals called The Displacements who built the light rails. Their sole purpose was to survive the threat of World War III. After going insane from living underground, they abandoned the incomplete tunnels and resorted to cannibalism. Since then, the Anarchy March had secretly maintained the tunnels in the effort to travel safely to all the Sections.

"At this pace we will never get there. We need a light rail." Jack said, as he dragged his feet on the ground.

Then they heard gunfire crackling ahead and saw flashes of light reflecting throughout the tunnel.

"Go! Go! Go!" Doyle commanded, as he ran to help out his brothers in need. He entered into a large cave posing as a makeshift train station for the light rails. The fires still burned, and smoke rose from the decimated structures. He saw Anarchy March huddled down behind a tipped over light rail. Maverick laid in the middle of the ground over a rail track, breathing heavily in a large pool of his own blood.

"Get down!" someone yelled.

Doyle jumped behind a fallen metal sign with Section S crossed out and replaced with a spray-painted Savage Town. Just then a laser shot ricocheted off the sign. "Laser sniper!" Doyle took out his handgun, checked his clip, and noted that there were only three bullets left.

Darla and Jack held back from entering the station.

"Hold on!" an Anarchy March soldier yelled and ran out to grab Maverick, dragging him to safety.

A laser streak zipped through his leg, almost severing it. The Anarchy March soldier fell by Maverick's side. Another soldier reared up ready to rescue both of the downed men.

"Stay the fuck down, they are just baiting us!" Doyle looked around for answers.

"Darla! Throw me your mirror!"

She peeked around the corner and threw her compact at Doyle's feet. He grabbed it just as a laser blast pierced the rock again. Doyle opened the compact, inside was an oval picture of Darla's mom. Her weary face expressed years of hardship, but he knew it was the only picture that Darla had left of her mother. He pocketed the worn photo and used the mirror to locate the sniper's position. His hand started to tremble, and he could not make out the location of the gunman. He held his wrist with his other hand and tried to focus his vision as it blurred. Another shot zipped through the compact and through one of Doyle's fingers. "Motherfucker!" he yelled. His middle finger fell to the ground.

The floor began to rumble, and at the end of one of the dark tunnels shined a light.

"Light rail coming through!" The train barreled down the same tracks the wounded men laid upon.

"Fuck this, I'm moving them!" the last uninjured Anarchy March soldier yelled. He rushed to the bodies in an attempt to drag them off the track, but a laser shot ripped through his neck, decapitating him.

As the light rail arrived, Doyle watched in horror as the elongated train crushed his comrades. The amputated arms and legs twitched along the side of the tracks as a metallic door slid open. Two sets of metal stairs emerged, unfolded, and assembled. Out stepped the general and Lieutenant Bachmann, both in fresh-pressed uniforms. A few dozen men marched out and lined up in formation.

"Amazing isn't it! Look what those little ants built. I'm growing fonder of this group, Bachmann. They were able to keep this a secret for so many years. We had no idea. Absolutely amazing, little ants," the general mused. He called over a random soldier. "Why didn't you know about these tunnels, private?"

"Um. Well, sir, I..." the nervous soldier stammered.

The general unholstered his gun and shot him in the head.

Doyle crawled around and flanked the light rail. He grabbed on to its side and signaled to Darla and Jack.

Lieutenant Bachmann opened up his hand, and a holographic image appeared depicting the whole underground tunnel complex. "Yes, they have been busy."

The laser sniper descended from the top of an empty water tower and ran to the general with his gun drawn.

"Sir!" the sniper saluted. "It's not safe around here. There's some A.M. hiding in here, sir."

The general looked around at the severed body parts strewn around the tracks. "Oh, that's gotta hurt," he chuckled while Lieutenant Bachmann covered his ear to listen in on a direct order from base.

"Sir, Command has called for a cease and desist. ... We are to take any survivors in."

"Alive?" The bewildered general acted like a child stripped of his favorite toy. "Fine, I had my fun. Attention! Attention! For any surviving Povs out there, please throw your weapons down and come out. I promise not to kill, maim, or destroy you ... until further notice."

"I don't think that is going to work, sir."

"What? Do they want me to beg for their surrender?"

"Move this piece of junk out of the way!" ordered the laser sniper.

The driver complied. He engaged the turbine engines. The light rail lurched backward.

Doyle climbed to the roof of one of the cars and held on. He saw Darla looking at him, and their eyes met.

Doyle read Darla's mouth: "Go."

He looked around at the hopeless situation and mouthed back, "I will find you."

"I love you, Horsey."

"I love you," Doyle mimed back.

The light rail whizzed away, gone from sight in seconds. The narrow corridor was now exposed as all the soldiers raised their weapons.

"Hell-oo! I said I won't kill. We're taking prisoners! Count your lucky stars!" yelled the general.

"What should we do?" Jack whispered.

"We give up."

"What! The P.M. doesn't take prisoners and you know that."

"Doyle said he'll find us. I believe him."

"Hello! Any Anarchy March in there." The general took a few steps, straining to see into the dark corridor.

"Fuck Doyle. He made it out! He is not coming back," Jack asserted.

"Hey, shut up and listen. Stay calm and follow my lead." Darla walked out with her hands up.

"Well, well, well. How do we find ourselves in these nasty predicaments?"

Jack followed her lead, reluctantly.

"If I remember correctly there were three of you."

"He died, in Savage Town."

"Oh, too bad. I wanted so much to meet that individual again. ... Ah, you two are in luck though. I have orders to take prisoners of war. This truly is a monumental occasion. Not in my thirty-five years of service have I ever taken a prisoner in, alive I mean. What has the world come to? They must have something planned for you two," the general mused.

Doyle rode the top of the light rail, straddling it as best he could. As it accelerated, it became harder to hold on. The wind beat on his face as his eyes watered. He lost his grip and slid back, falling down between the cars.

He slammed his head but rolled to safety into one of the back cars filled with boxes that read: Highly Explosive Material.

He stood up and ripped off a section of his T-shirt and bandaged his hand. He snuck his way through the car until he reached the engineer's compartment with the driver.

The driver focused on the rail and did not hear Doyle until it was too late. Doyle wrapped a knife around the driver's neck. "Shh ... Where are we going?"

"What? What is the meaning of this?"

Doyle began carving up the driver's throat, blood trickled down his neck. "You were saying?"

"Section W! We're going to Section W. Don't kill me, please."

Doyle inched the blade closer to the driver's jugular, "What's in Section W?"

"The brigade, I ... I'm to transport them to reinforce the area from the last fighting A.M. in Section X. Please, I don't want to die."

"Shut up!"

"I'm just a transporter. I never killed anyone. I'm just trying to survive, like you."

"You're like me, really? Then I should let you go, so you can continue your important work for this tyrannical government? Like me?!"

"I'm a family man ... just trying to survive."

"What the hell do you know about surviving?! And I don't have a family, somebody that loves me? Am I just insignificant in the grand scheme of things? Fuck you! And fuck your world!" Doyle spat in the man's face as the knife sliced into the driver's neck, he winced. "It's people like you who are afraid to stand up for yourselves, fucking cowards through and through."

"I don't have a choice."

"I have no pity for you!"

The driver pleaded, "I'm sorry!"

"Sorry? That's not good enough. There's a point in everyone's life where you have to face your demons. And buddy, I'm the devil!" Doyle flung the man out of the light rail, his body smashed against the tunnel wall.

Doyle took the controls as it sped down the tracks to its pre-programmed destination.

"Ill-educated asshole, trying to reason with me. I have no sympathy for that. Tell me, I tell him!" Tears of frustration streamed. He wiped them from his grimy face, smearing the dirt. He looked at himself in the reflection of the glass window and cleaned the dirt and blood off his face. "Don't worry, babe, I'm not gonna lose you too," he vowed.

Miles flew by in seconds as the light rail arrived at the pickup point and screeched to a stop.

"All aboard! Next stop, Section X!" he yelled out the window, careful not to show his face.

A few hundred P.M. soldiers, ready for battle, poured into the vessel. He reveled at their ignorance as he pulled on the accelerator lever, and the light rail shot down the tracks headed for Section X.

The display on the console destination panel blinked that Section X was near. He turned on the P.A. system to greet his guests.

"We are arriving at your final destination, Section X. Thank you for riding with the Prominent Municipality. I trust you had a fast and easy travel. But alas, this will be the end of your journey. I do hope it was worth it." He programmed the train for maximum speed. He then jumped out before the light rail sped off in overdrive.

"What a friendly conductor," mumbled a soldier as the train accelerated.

Doyle watched the light rail disappear down the long dark tunnel.

"Viva la Anarchy March!" yelled a man in a crowd of enraptured people amassed in a semi-circle, mesmerized by a powerful speaker.

His words echoed throughout the large, metal-encased warehouse that sat near the bordering wall inside the compound of Section X. Since Section X was the Anarchy March's stronghold, it was the site of initiation for new recruits.

The enigmatic speaker, an older gentleman with lines of wisdom etched deep into his well-weathered face, paced back and forth focusing on his words. "Now, you'll probably be asking yourself, 'Why am I here?' I can't tell you why, I can't speak for you, and I can't make any decisions for you. What I can do is tell you a little story about me and why I am here." His face collapsed into the palm of his hands and he closed his eyes. He exhaled, then opened his eyes. "I was an average Joe just like you. Model citizen, law abiding, a pillar of my community. After November Fifth, maybe you noticed a subtle change? I heard the stories about pollution in the air and in the water. 'Climate change' they called it, but I was just too busy to care, dealing with my daily grind, trying to do the best for my family. Between cheering for my team to win at the big game and binge-watching my favorite T.V. shows, I just didn't notice the sky getting darker. Yet the excuses were plenty; was it man-made or just Mother Earth shaking off her fleas? One day, while playing catch with my boy, I noticed he was coughing. Kids don't get emphysema." He shook his head with a disbelieving smile.

"A few of my neighbors began to move away, closer to their jobs. The gas prices never bothered me, until I realized that half of my check was going to travel expenses. Inconsequential businesses began to collapse like falling dominos, and before I knew it, I was out a job. No problem, I'm a well-educated man with tons of experience. Not good enough, our company is downsizing after the merger. Are you willing to work for free to gain experience here until further notice? You'll feel pride and security knowing the company's bottom line looks better, and yours will look better too. These were just some of the many explanations for why I could not find a living wage. Our population was at an all-time high and jobs were few and far between. But it's not the end of the world, right? Now the government has started another unpaid war with another country over land ascendancy, the most expensive one in American history.

"Then the stock market crashed. Corporations turned to government funding. Jobs were plenty now, in the government. Something in my gut told me this was not the path I wanted to take, but my boy got sicker and my back was against the wall. So, I took that government job in hopes of saving my boy. Little did I know, I was just the cause of other people's suffering. And that ate at my soul. So, I walked away, as did my wife. When times get rough you really find out how strong your wedding vows are. I was by my son's side in the hospital when the government first announced their new bill called The Government's Rights. The G.R. card, you might have heard of it? It wasn't long after that they announced a group called the Prominent Municipality who would enforce this bill.

"Sure, we were in troubled times, and hopefully, this group could set things right, right? We were wrong, terribly wrong. The G.R. card was released, and with a limited supply of cards, they were expensive and wanted by all. Only the few could afford it. That night I experienced firsthand what that card was all about as the P.M. stormed the hospital and booted everyone out that did not have this elusive card. All government services were now paid on demand. After a brief encounter with these enforcers — keep in mind that I was not a fighter — I walked home with a broken nose and my sick son in my arms. I kneeled at my bed pleading to God for an answer, but the only replies I got were draft letters in my mailbox.

"All my neighbors had moved to the Midwest for any opportunity and to try to keep on living. I remember looking out my window as a fiery glow came closer to my house, and it dawned on me. We are being exterminated, like fucking cockroaches. Why? Because I didn't have stocks or money? Because I wasn't somebody important? Because I didn't want to join the wicked? Is the human race really that ignorant that we will destroy ourselves just to not be proven wrong? I lost everything I ever cared about and loved, for what? So politicians and the wealthy can buy that second yacht for their summer homes?"

The man paced back and forth across the stage. He looked up at the lights burning down on him as he spilled his heart out to those who would listen.

"After I buried my son in the backyard, I abandoned my house and moved here to this barren wasteland we used to call Oregon. Sections have replaced states and names with numbers. Some of you might know this history, while others have been blinded by the Prominent Municipality's propaganda. They started to erase all history: libraries, books, art, et cetera ... There was a thing called the internet where anyone could reach for any information they desired. Knowledge is power, right? Oh, the P.M. put a stop to that early in their reign. I'm sorry for the bleak image that I have drawn, but I remain optimistic and so should you."

The candid man tightened his grip on the microphone. The crowd stood silent, mesmerized. Empathy consumed them.

"Slowly other people came here with similar horrific stories of injustice. I now know some of you are here because you were able to hang on longer to the little bit of humanity you had left and finally accept the truth. Who is to blame and who can we exculpate? Whom do we point the finger at? Religion, politicians, The System? I impute their claims and their rigid grip on this world. They called me an Anarchist for not believing in their lies and not living in their world. So, I started the Anarchy March. We are carpenters, doctors, accountants, husbands, wives, mothers, and fathers. Not fighters, but we've learned. Together we will stand up and say, 'Never again!' And together we can march against injustice, we can march against this oligarchy and the absolute corruption that plagues us, we can march for equality, but most of all, we will march for humanity!"

The crowd erupted, tears of elation streamed. They had hope for the prospect of a good life.

"Now, if you are here and your story is similar to mine, I can tell you that you now have two choices. Go back to where you came from and work for the killing, greedy, inhumane machine, or you can stay here and fight to bring back a future we once had!" The man jumped down off stage, "Together we pave a path to the future of humankind!"

A loud explosion jerked the metal warehouse, and the shockwave ricocheted everything back and forth.

"Lee! Lee! We lost contact with our soldiers in the underground tunnel!"

Lee raced out of the warehouse and scaled the bordering wall. He peered past the tops of trees at the horizon, where a large mushroom cloud dwarfed the mountain that housed the underground tunnel.

"They are nuking the tunnels, clear out a five-mile radius from the entrance," Lee ordered, jumping off a ladder. He bolted toward the warehouse, as a hand grabbed him by the shoulder, jerking him backward.

"No, it was me," Doyle announced.

"Who are you?" Lee asked the bruised and bloodied patriot of the cause. "Do you have any idea what you have just done?"

Doyle smiled, "Yeah, I just won the war," while holding out the cylindrical, faded green canister.

Testament IV

GREEN HELL

Apocalypse conveniently forgotten and hopes revived, Section X was the last place I could find the almost extinct middle class. People lived in a mutualistic community. I rub your shoulders, you rub mine. Trees were plenty and green, and the air was fresh with an unusual sense of peace. Much different from the outside terrors that the resistance and I were used to. It was the first time I stepped foot on this ground and marveled at the imprint the grass made. It wasn't soggy, it did not wheeze under foot. It didn't glow an unnatural color and shrapnel did not protrude from the soil. It stayed virtually undisturbed. I always had visions of what Section X would look like: the structures, the people, and to tell you the truth, I found myself gazing through the looking glass at a kaleidoscope of hyperbole. It was the stronghold of the Anarchy March, but I couldn't help but wonder where the Anarchy March went.

Lee took Doyle for a stroll in a park. Lush greenery surrounded them, and Lee savored the smell of fresh-cut grass.

"So, what Section you say you're from?" Lee asked.

"I'm from Section Y. The Anarchy March has been trying to reach you for over a year now, but our messages didn't seem to get through. It's important, so that's why I'm here ... and where is here?" Doyle's eyebrows furrowed while he watched a cottony, white dog playing fetch with its master.

"That's strange. I'll have our intelligence check that out," Lee said, watching a low flying bird.

"There have been extreme casualties in the Sections. Why haven't we been putting up a counterattack?"

"I have never heard about this. You know, you should expect

losses; after all, we're at war, son."

Doyle waved away a bee. "I understand that, but is it me, or is the Anarchy March backing down?"

"I assure you that the A.M. is strong, and we are moving forward, progressively," Lee said, as he looked into Doyle's restless eyes.

"I'm sorry. I'm just a little frustrated. It took a few months to get here, and I lost my whole crew. My fiancée has been taken prisoner, and so has my best friend."

"What is so urgent that you had to travel here, risking your life and your loved ones?"

Doyle handed Lee his last canister. "This right here can change the war. It's a new bioweapon."

Lee examined it with skepticism, trying to decipher the faded stenciled lettering.

"It was made by the late Dr. Jack Foster. He was killed by the P.M. after they discovered his lab ... are you listening to me?"

"I'm here. Continue."

"Anyway, he gave his son a map to his hidden compound. After the P.M. left, his son and I went to look for it and found this along with some radiation suits."

"Where is the son now?"

"Jack was the one captured along with my fiancée. He doesn't know anything, and I'm afraid that they will kill them if they don't talk."

"What's so good about this weapon?" Lee held the canister and caressed its side, thumbing the rim.

"We've seen it in action. It's a deadly gas that can level cities. In the letter, it said that if anything should happen, find you and your research team in Section X to continue Dr. Foster's work. Maybe what's in this canister can end this war by force. Once and for all we can rid the world of Section A."

"A treaty in a can?" Lee scoffed and handed the canister back. He turned to admire the low soaring birds in formation as the sun penetrated through their translucent feathers. "You see those birds up there?"

"Yeah, so."

"No, really look at them, and tell me what you see."

A reluctant Doyle looked up and stared. "What am I supposed to be looking at? They're just fucking birds flying around, so what?"

"Were there birds in Section Y?"

"No, the P.M. killed them all! Are we gonna use this bioweapon or what?"

"There are birds here because I was able to keep away the Prominent Municipality through diplomacy. You can't just jump into war and jump out. It takes delicate negotiations."

"What the fuck are you talking about? We've lived under their iron rule for too many years now and look where we are. There is no reasoning with the unreasonable."

"You're young and so vigorous, full of hate. I don't understand the punk generation and never will. Son, listen, this is the way we win. Look around."

Doyle looked around at the verdant setting. The trees offered shade, grassy meadows lined small lakes with swans and ducks paddling along. Lovers held hands and laid around absorbing the sun's rays in search for the perfect bronze skin tone. Peace and love were on display, but it was only a hollow throwback to a past, recreated by false hopes.

"Don't get me wrong, Lee, I appreciate what you have done with this Anarchy March stronghold, but this is a bubble about to pop. It's great here, but it's horrible everywhere else. We need to end this regime, so this happiness can be experienced by all the Sections, not just here."

Lee shook his head in disapproval as he called over an attractive young girl. Her long, blonde ringlets were swept off her tawny skin. She wore a woven two-piece bathing suit with a sheer pastel pink wrap.

"This is Sunshine, she will escort you to your chambers and be your personal guide through Section X."

"I don't want a tour guide. I want to save my girl!"

"I totally promise I don't bite if you just give me a chance." Sunshine bit down on her lip.

"I know you've been through a lot. Let Sunshine take care of you, and tomorrow we will address this matter. But for now, get a good night sleep and a good meal. I'm sure you are sick and tired of those chalky food capsules."

Sunshine took Doyle by the hand, a small needle protruded out from her fingers, injecting Doyle as she led him out of the scenic park.

"Take good care of him, Sunshine!" Lee winked.

A defiant Doyle peeled his hand out of her grasp.

"O.M.G., so you're, like, a V.I.P. from another Section?"

"What did you say?" Doyle rubbed his head, his legs began to wobble, his vision blurred.

"You know, like, numero uno and stuff. I overheard you say you're totally, like, important."

"Where are you from? You talk funny."

"As if." Sunshine rolled her emerald green eyes. They continued on toward a majestic wooden house, carved out of an ancient oak tree. Panoramic glass windows reflected a large clear lake. Sunshine escorted him to the front door and opened it. "Is there, like, anything I can do for you?" Sunshine asked, cocking her head to the side.

"Hey, I'm sorry. Maybe I just need to lie down for a moment, to gather my thoughts." Doyle looked inside the beautiful and spacious house — it had all the trappings. A carved wooden staircase spiraled up from the foyer to the second floor. From the vaulted ceiling hung a chandelier made from etched bone, casting an ebullient glow, inviting guests into the living area. He walked in amazed. Things he had almost forgotten about, that he hadn't seen since his childhood, sat on a glass and oak console. "Is that a T.V.?"

"Um, yeah! I, like, totally love that machine. We have a V.C.R. also." Sunshine turned on the television.

"What's a V.C.R.?"

"Um. Visual, camcorder, reviewer, duh."

A dizzy Doyle laughed as he sat down on the overstuffed couch.

Sunshine put in a tape and pressed play. A made-for-television movie flashed on the screen: *Columbus, The Prince of Tides*. He wrote in his diary in the bow of a boat as a voiceover played out in the background. *These people are very unskilled in arms. With fifty men, they could all be subjected and made to do all that one wished.* The movie was interrupted by the breaking news as a clean-cut anchor with a dismal demeanor appeared on the television screen. "It's, like, um, old propaganda and stuff, back in the late nineties. News, they called it. I like watching the commercials though, they're all, like, flashy and junk."

"I feel really, really good right now ... like I'm on a fluffy fucking cloud." Doyle stared at his blurry hand as he opened and closed his fist.

"Oh, it's probably just the serum."

"The what?"

"The serum, silly." Sunshine's smile drooped and melted into her neck.

"You sir, are a horrible ... person."

Doyle slumped to the side of the couch.

"Lee told me to calm you down, so I secretly injected you with some Happy 77 serum.[1] Here, let me make you feel more comfortable." Sunshine unbuckled his spiked belt and pulled off his muddied jeans. Doyle's hand fell slack and his engagement ring slipped off and clanked onto the floor.

Darla woke up in a panic, she felt naked as she rubbed the smooth void around her ring finger. Hundreds of little red lasers scanned a square room and its contents. Her wild eyes searched the room as one of the red beams crossed over her eyelid, lighting up her

---

[1] Happy 77 Serum, a euphoric concoction developed in the labs in Section X was known to keep the peace and numb its users depending on its doses. Side effects may include: Headaches, stomach cramps, anal leakage, sneezing, blood clots, cough, fever, irregular bowel movements, dry skin, runny nose, nausea, diarrhea, stiffness in joints, rash, shortness of breath, sudden loss of taste, blurred vision, hives, projectile vomiting, amnesia, watery eyes, stroke, night terrors, cancerous tumors, balding, colored urine, swelling of the face, lips, tongue, or throat, severe dizziness, mild thoughts of suicide.

normally dark brown irises. She blinked hard attempting to gather her bearings and inspect her surroundings. She sat in the middle of a dimly lit room with mirrors for walls. She focused on her reflection and saw the constriction of leather binding her to a chair and the warm ooze of blood dribbling out of her mouth.

She regained her voice, "Let me out of here!" She struggled to get free.

From behind the mirror lay a multitude of operating systems reading her vitals. A computer downloaded her every evidence of existence, from DNA to dental and fingerprints. The computer also detected two life forms.

"Ah, look at that, she is carrying a little Pov," said a voice from the darkness in the corner.

She began to bite at her straps.

"I wouldn't do that if I was you." A deep voice pierced through the room from a loudspeaker in the ceiling.

"What do you want with me? Where's Jack?"

"You are prisoner 3459320532, arrested for conspiring with a known terrorist group, the Anarchy March."

"I have no idea what you are talking about."

"I was hoping you were going to say that." A door opened, and in walked the general with his hands behind his back. "Now we can begin our interrogation."

Darla stared at him as he cracked a half smile and took a seat in front of her. He adjusted his chair to sit aligned with her head and crossed his leg.

"I do admire you people. Complete dedication to your cause. Shoot, if I had half of you in my army, we'd probably own this planet." He stood and revealed the book he held behind his back. "I know all educational books are banned and punishable by death under code 128987-3437745-34555432-L, but Lieutenant Bachmann said this was a must read for me. God bless his soul. Guilty as charged."

She looked at the cracked spine of the book, worn with age and use, hoping it was a children's story meant to lull her to sleep.

"The author's name and publication date have been erased, of course. But the subject matter intrigued me."

The general pointed at the vade mecum titled: *It's a Tortuous World After All: The Complete History of Torture Methods and Devices*. He sat back down and put on his reading glasses. He cleared his throat and began. "'Chapter one, Extraction. Sometimes referred to as Exodontias, was a method of torture to obtain forced confessions in the 14th century by extracting teeth from the subject's mouth.' Yes, that's a nice one."

The general continued flipping through the dog-eared pages, his eyes widening. "Oh, listen to this one. 'Chapter four, Human Branding. It is a process in which a hot or cold iron is forced onto the subject's skin, scarring them for life. Runaway slaves were marked with an F for fugitive.' I bet you didn't know about that interesting tidbit, huh?"

He continued, oblivious to Darla's hate-filled stare, "The list goes on: De-nailing, Electric shock, Flaying, Knee capping, Sensory deprivation, Water boarding. Oh, water boarding? Do you know what water boarding is?"

"Yeah, my mom used to take me and my sister water boarding all the time out on the lake when I was young."

The general stood up and walked to the other side of the room and whispered into the two-way mirror wall.

"I'm ready to die," she said.

He strolled back and took his seat.

She observed his spotless, shiny patent leather shoes.

"You might be ready, but is your son?"

Darla stared at him and then down at her stomach. She thrashed at her restraints.

"Oh, you didn't know. How sad, now I'm going to ask you again and if I don't get the answer I want, so help me God, I'll be forced to end your and his existence. Where is the Anarchy March and that new bioweapon?"

Darla spat in his face.

He sprang up and kicked over the chair, and it skidded across the room into the mirrored wall.

The door swung open and Lieutenant Bachmann along with

three other soldiers rolled in a large metal bed with hand and feet restraints. More personnel followed with a fountain-like pump filled with water. Behind them came a person with an electric generator. They all lined up on one side of the wall and began to set up a deviant device.

Darla watched as the men set up the unconscionable equipment.

"Hurry up, I don't have all day." The general glanced at his watch while he tapped out his frustration with his foot.

They grabbed Darla and strapped her to the metal bed as she flailed. Her mouth reached out to one of the men's ears in the struggle and she bit down and took a small chunk. He winced, then backhanded her face, sending the bit of flesh flying across the room.

They tied her down as the general approached. "Quite the fighter. Careful, though, she's with child," he quipped. He began to read the book out loud to Darla's stomach as if he were reading a bedtime story. "Now, it says here: 'You must cover the interrogatee's mouth with plastic wrap.'"

"Check!" Lieutenant Bachmann walked over with a sheet of plastic and wrapped it around her mouth and head a few times.

"Okay, comfy?" the general asked.

She sucked the plastic in and out, attempting to breathe.

"Now, 'Tilt the bed back where the interrogatee's feet are in the air.'"

Lieutenant Bachmann pushed down on the bed and it reclined, "Check!"

Darla started to pound the back of her head against the metal bed, trying to knock herself out.

Lieutenant Bachmann responded by tightening the straps to prevent her from moving.

"Now, I'm gonna get creative. Bachmann, hook up the electric generator."

Bachmann grabbed the two wire clamps. "Where does it say to put them?"

"Hold on." The general thumbed through a few pages. "Ah! 'The nipples,' of course. I should have thought of that."

Bachmann ripped open the plain jumpsuit she was dressed in, exposing her breasts. Darla struggled to no avail, the straps only dug deeper into her flesh. Bachmann attached the clamps with steady hands.

"Now, 'apply water.'" The general stood up and moved the water pump over her face. He looked at her tearful eyes. "It says here that 'most interrogatee's talk within fourteen seconds.' Shall I proceed or did you have something you want to tell me?"

She closed her eyes and the tears gushed down her shaved scalp.

"Perfect." The general turned on the water pump and brown, gritty water dripped down upon her face. The water sought out her nasal cavities, a drowning sensation overwhelmed her. Her gag reflexes spewed out bloodied water from her nose.

The general shut off the machine. "That was about five seconds, how do you feel?"

Her face lost all color.

The general turned on the pump again and pressed the red button on the electric generator.

Her body convulsed as seemingly every muscle contracted.

After an eternal ten seconds of agony, the general turned it off. "I got an idea. Bachmann, pull down your pants and relieve yourself in the water."

A reluctant Bachmann looked sheepishly at the wall of mirrors, he pulled down his pants and stood over the water.

"What's wrong, Bachmann? We are all waiting."

"I can't urinate with everyone watching me," he mumbled.

"Oh, for God's sake! Get lost! Go check on our other prisoner!" The general unzipped his pants and pissed into the pump's tank; he shook it to and fro, "Good to the last drop! ... I have to do everything my damn self." He zipped his fly and walked back to Darla. "Alright, where were we — oh yeah! Mommy's going for the record here, twenty seconds."

Bachmann walked down the faintly lit hallway watching his every step, as the fluorescent bulbs skipped on and off. He counted his steps and kept his shoes inside the linoleum squares, framing each footstep in an attempt to distance his mind from the passing interrogation rooms where agonized prisoners were pleading their cases.

"Lost everything. Why can't you understand that? I was just trying to feed my fam—"

"Don't know the Anarchy March, I said! And if I did, I ... just kill me and get it over with."

Bachmann reached the room called: Rehabilitation. A gunshot echoed from an adjacent room. Opening the door, he found Officer Walton wearing an oversized uniform that draped over gangly wrist. He snapped to attention.

"Officer Walton, good day. What happened to your medals?"

"What do you mean? I polished them early today. They're perfect!"

"They're upside down."

"How can you tell?" Walton scanned his chest, dumbfounded by the variety of stripes and colors. "Let me help you, sir."

On an operating table lay Jack, who was only now waking up, one eye at a time. The room was pure white with men in bleached lab coats holding shiny instruments. They huddled around Jack poking and probing at him as if he were an animal.

"Hey! What the fuck is going on here, where's my player box? Let me go!" Jack yelled. He tore at his straps.

"Sir, his anesthetic wore off earlier than expected," one of the men said, pulling out a large hypodermic needle.

"It will be fine, 78934758007532. Continue with the procedure," Bachmann ordered as he put on a white lab coat.

The only scientist in the room greeted Jack. "Hello there! My number name is 78934758007532 and you have been chosen by the Prominent Municipality to participate in our new personality correction program."

"Wait, what? I like my personality. Let me go, you fucks!" Jack kicked and punched the air, attempting to hit all of them.

"If you don't calm down, I will be forced to sedate you."

"I'm not scared of your fucking needles, man!"

78934758007532 pulled out a folded metal baton and swung it

open.

"New personality, huh? I can probably use another one."

"That's better."

Jack laid his head back and attempted to relax on the uncomfortable metal bed.

"It's for the better. Soon you'll be part of a normal society, functioning like a real human being. Job, God, and taxes. Doesn't that sound grand?"

Jack ground his teeth, "Is it gonna hurt?"

"Like hell," Bachmann assured.

A compact machine was wheeled over and 78934758007532 hooked up a few wires to Jack's head. "Now, you are going to feel a little pinch," the scientist warned as he pressed a button on the device. Small scalpel-sharp needles pierced Jack's skull.

"Fu-u-u-ck! Small pinch, my ass!" Droplets of blood crawled down Jack's face.

"Oh-oh, he's a bleeder," the scientist observed. "Don't move! Basically, these little metal probes are sticking in your brain right now, and if you twitch, they will leave abrasions on the surface of your brain causing a hemorrhage."

"Is that good or bad?"

"What do you think?"

"I don't know, doc, that's why I'm asking you."

"Well, luckily the personality change will also bring up your Intelligence Quotient and allegedly your vigor, but don't quote me on that, we are still working out the kinks."

"Kinks? Whatever, man, do your worst. I just want to let you know that I am a strong-minded person and I don't think any—"

78934758007532 again activated the device, and imagery projected deep within Jack's psyche.

"What program are you using on him?" Bachmann asked.

"It is really early in the testing, so we don't have an official name, but my colleagues have been jokingly calling it red, white, and ruse."

"Cute."

"The hallucinations he is seeing are a mixture of righteous

wars, unadulterated religion, and a resilient discipline with just a hint of espionage."

Jack's body convulsed as his brain was filled with unspeakable images of the past. Death, war, societal despair while a scratchy audio broadcast of F. T. Marinetti played out in the background. *... Destroy the museums, the libraries, every type of academy ... the great crowds, shaken by work, by pleasure or by rioting ... We will glorify war, the world's only hygienic answer — militarism, patriotism, the destructive gestures of freedom, bringers of, beautiful ideas worth dying for.* Flash after flash polluted and indoctrinated his mind with venomous rhetoric.

"How long will it take? I need him to infiltrate as soon as possible."

"I'm just hoping he lives, the last six hundred and sixty-five died on this very bed."

Blood spewed out of Jack's ears, foamy drool ran down his chin, and his eyes glazed over.

"No! No! Not again!" The scientist activated the escape command, and the device stopped.

Jack's head slunk to the side as blood rolled down his face from his eye sockets. One last breath and then, nothing.

"I need the defibrillator!"

The medical staff burst through the door and went to work, trying to resuscitate Jack. "Clear!" The jolt caused his body to reel up. They checked for a heartbeat. "Hit him again! Clear!" Another jolt, but nothing.

"Come on, clear!" They paddled Jack again, there was a response on the heart monitor.

Jack opened his eyes and looked around the room.

"Undo the straps." Bachmann commanded.

"Um, sir, I don't think that is—"

"We don't pay you to think, now undo the straps!"

78934758007532 unbuckled the straps, and Jack sat up and looked at Lieutenant Bachmann with an empty, robotic glare.

Bachmann smiled, "Gentlemen, we have ourselves a soldier."

Doyle woke up from his forced sleep feeling a little queasy. He found himself staring at the ceiling with a large Anarchy March sign carved into it.

"Oh, my head, where am I, is this heaven?" Doyle massaged his head and looked around the room at all the beautiful flower arrangements.

"O.M.G., you're finally awake, sleepy head." Sunshine brought Doyle a crystal-clear glass of water.

"How long have I been out?" he asked as he sipped on the purified water.

"Um, like, one week. No, two weeks tops ... no wait, does like Tuesday follow Thursday?"

Doyle spat out the water, "Two fucking weeks! Where is Darla?"

"I don't know any Darla ... no wait, I do know a Marla, very nice, but not too bright. She totally likes to talk and ramble on."

"Stop talking! I need to get to her and Jack." Doyle scanned the room, searching for his clothing and saw his gas canister sitting on a pale oak side table next to a vase of blooming cyclamen. "Has Lee researched anything with that bioweapon?" Doyle pointed at the canister.

Sunshine picked up the bioweapon and laughed. "I was wondering what that was. I totally thought it was like your hair dye and junk. I was gonna surprise you and everything and freshen up that gross puke green! How do you open this silly thing?" Sunshine began to prod the canister, and Doyle ripped it from her child-like hands.

"Hey! You almost broke my nail. You need to relax, take a chill pill. You know what your problem is, you're not spiritual and stuff. Here take one of these." Sunshine opened up her hand, revealing a small blue pill.

Doyle slapped the pill from Sunshine's hand, it flew across the room. "It was a mistake to come here. What was I thinking?" He sprang to his feet, throwing on his clothing while he stumbled out of the house.

"Hey, where are you going? I just made breakfast! Shoot."

Doyle snooped around the compound where everyone milled

about making small talk with one another. Two men looked as though they were approaching him. Wanting no part of that, he leapt into the yellow flowering bushes to avoid any contact.

"I hear that our bees are on the rise. Good thing, though, I need that honey to cook my special honey casserole."

"I would literally kill someone for that recipe, but I know you would give it to me if I asked enough." Both of the men enjoyed a good laugh as they continued down the road.

"What the hell is wrong with this picture? Don't these people know that we are at war?" Doyle jumped out of the bushes and walked up to a man with a long gray and braided beard feeding gold- and mauve-colored finches with fresh bread.

"Excuse me, can you tell me where I can find Lee?"

"Why would you want to find someone on this magnificent day?"

"Well, um, I have a few questions I need to ask him. It's a matter of life and death."

"Nonsense, we are all safe here in Section X," the man said staring through glazed eyes.

"Yeah, I can see that, but what about the other Sections? People aren't so lucky."

"What people?"

"Look, are you gonna tell me where I can find Lee or what?"

"You're a strange bird. You talk a lot more than the others."

"What the fuck is this town on! I'm an Anarchist, motherfucker, not a bird!"

"Alright birdie, fly away. If you really want to see Lee, just fly to Woodstock Lane, last house on the left."

Doyle stormed off, kicking up the manicured grass. He reached the house as an old El Camino pulled up and two familiar faces climbed out. Doyle took cover behind a tree. Benny and Kongo entered Lee's house. He snuck around the side and looked through an open window. A heated conversation had erupted inside. He moved closer so he could hear what was being said.

"I don't care about Savage Town, alright. It's filth, nothing but debauchery and crime!"

"Hey, that was my town, alright. When we made this deal, you got this Section and I got Section S. Now because of some punk kid from the Anarchy March, I lost everything. I want half of this town."

"It's not my fault that some kid took my words literally and destroyed your town. I have created a peaceful haven here in Section X, a place that escapes the terror of the outside world. I'll be damned if you try and bring crime and gambling and whatever else you degenerates do. Here, have a pill."

"I don't want your damn drugs. I need to find this Dangle kid and the bioweapon!"

"Dangle? We just let someone in named Doyle that fits that description, ranting and raving about his captured fiancée. He is sleeping in our guest quarters."

"What! He's here? Bring him here. He has a new bioweapon that the P.M. is looking for. We can probably strike another deal with them if we deliver it to 'em."

"What about the kid?"

"Fuck him, hand him over to the P.M. Let them deal with him appropriately."

A hand wrapped around Doyle's mouth from behind.

Kongo heard a rustling sound from outside the window. He walked over and looked out.

Doyle and the stranger took cover right underneath the windowsill.

The door swung open. Sunshine was out of breath. "I, like, totally lost him, like, before breakfast, O.M.G. fer sure."

"Somebody please explain to me what she just said?"

"He's gone!" Lee exclaimed and ran out of the house, followed by Benny and Kongo.

After the coast was clear, the stranger released his hand from Doyle's mouth as they stood up.

"Who are you? What the fuck is going on?" Doyle demanded.

"You're Doyle, right?"

"Yeah, who the hell are you?"

"Is it true that you are holding a weapon that could end this war?" the stranger asked.

"Where did you hear that from?"

"Word travels quick on low frequencies, but you should know that." The stranger dug inside his jacket.

Doyle jetted toward him and ripped open his jacket: inside was a first aid kit.

"Take it easy, I'm here to help." The stranger pried Doyle's hand away and opened up the first aid kit, he handed Doyle fresh bandages for his head wound.

"Thanks ... I have something, but I don't know what to do with it or who I should trust with it ... what's going on here?" Doyle studied the man's face, unsure whether he could reveal himself. "What happened to the Anarchy March? This isn't why I joined. Section X is supposed to be the stronghold of this establishment, not a fucking hippie compound."

"I'm sorry to inform you that the Anarchy March hasn't been the same for years now. The leaders have sold out for a piece of the pie."

"This can't be. We have been fighting—"

"For yourselves. The cause has died away, man. The shit is corrupt everywhere."

Doyle looked around in disbelief. He stared hard at the stranger who talked and acted like he should be in his early twenties, but a harsh life weighed upon his wrinkled brow.

"Don't worry, comrade, there are still people like us that are willing to die for the cause. We have factions set up in the east sections, on old Indian reservations."

"Who are you?"

"My number name is 6869656, but my friends call me Six."

Doyle pulled out his knife and despite his weakened state, forced it against Six's throat. "You're fucking P.M.!"

"No, no, I've been discharged and exiled from Section A. I joined the Anarchy March over five years ago. Can you put your knife down, please?"

"I don't trust you. I don't trust anyone anymore." Doyle pressed harder against Six's neck. A thin trickle of blood fell past the man's Anarchy March neck tattoo. Seeing this, Doyle eased off.

Six wiped the blood from his neck and pointed to his tattoo. "Maybe you can trust in the ink. You know for sure they would have me terminated for this." Six dug in his pocket and pulled out a photo of him and his family.

"This was my wife, 847365 ... I mean Anna, and my little baby boy, William." Six's eyes welled up.

Doyle lowered the knife and withdrew his hand from Six's neck. Six patted at the cut and examined his bloodstained fingers as he lapsed into distant, more pleasant memories.

"I had it all, I knew what was going on behind the Great Apartheid Wall, but my family came first, just like everybody else thought. Ignorance is bliss, right? My wife kept books in the attic that her family had passed down. Just a bedtime story, but it always made William happy. A spying neighbor saw the book one day and reported it to the P.M. I was a goddamn dedicated soldier for them! It didn't matter. They raided my house and tied all of us up. They said they would make me a deal since it wasn't my books. Eliminate the art and its readers, and I can walk away. How do you kill your wife and child? What human can do that?" Six put the photo in Doyle's hand, "But I did. I knew the P.M. would kill them anyway and then me for not taking orders. I'd rather they die by my hand than those filthy animals. I did walk away but with a promise to come back and end this madness."

Doyle stared at the picture. He became lost in the photo of a young family all dressed in blue jeans and crisp white T-shirts. The man he looked at now was weathered and despair wore heavy in his eyes, but they held fast a determination that only those willing to fight against the corruption could hold.

"You say you have a weapon that can end this? Then, Doyle, I will stand with you and we will continue this march." Six wiped the tears from his beaten face.

"I'm sorry for your loss." Doyle offered the photo back but was denied.

"No, you hold on to it. My family's memory is in your hands now. I didn't track you down for pity. I know someone in Section

Z that can make that bioweapon into something that the P.M. will fear."

"Alright, let's go. We need to act fast." Doyle pointed out Benny's El Camino.

They snuck up to the car and jumped in. Six grabbed control of the .50 caliber in the back.

Doyle hotwired it, and the engine roared to life. "Hold on to your asses." He slammed the gas pedal to the floor, and they peeled out toward the town's open gates.

Doyle and Six zipped by, waking up the gatekeeper. Groggily, he asked, "What, what's going on?" But as soon as he had awakened, he lowered his head and fell back to sleep as Doyle and Six roared down the road.

"Where are we going?!" Doyle yelled.

"North! Stay off the highways! I'll keep the Nukies at bay!" Six fired some rounds at suspicious movements in the distance.

"How well do you know this guy in Section Z?"

"I met him once!"

"You're joking, right?!" Doyle looked at Six and swerved off the road.

"Watch the road! Don't worry! He is the man to go to with our situation!" Six shot a few Nukies as they tried jumping on the passing car.

"How can we trust someone we don't know?"

"Don't worry, he's eccentric!"

Doyle shook his head and prepared for the worst.

The sun set over the hills and only gunfire could be heard echoing through the valley. The long ride to Section Z to make contact with this so-called eccentric guy, who could save the world, bothered Doyle. Darla passed through his mind every other second. Where is she now? How is she? How am I going to save her? Questions that time may solve, but time did not care about Doyle or anyone. What had seemed like an eternity of contemplation ended as they reached a compound hidden deep in the mountains. A large camouflage fence surrounded the perimeter.

"Stop here!" Six yelled.

Doyle parked in front of the fence, and his attention diverted to the piles of dead, burnt Nukies that lined the perimeter. Doyle looked closer. Electricity arched from link to link. "Tight security. How we getting in?"

"He told me when I brought you, he would know."

Doyle and Six stood around and waited. Doyle's contemplation began to creep back from the deep recesses of his mind, and he shook off the ensuing thoughts eager to get moving again. Exasperated, he blurted through the silence, "This is stupid! I don't have time for—" The fence slid open and a bright, blinding light hit them.

"Are you the Seeker?" the amplified voice coming from the light asked.

Doyle raised his hand in front of his face, trying to shield his eyes.

"My name is Doyle. I'm a member of the Anarchy March from Section Y."

"So, you're not the Seeker."

"I don't know what or who is a Seeker? I came here to see—"

"I only deal with the Seeker!"

Doyle turned to Six. "I thought you said you knew this guy?"

"I don't know. Tell him that you're the Seeker."

"Oh yeah, you mean, the Seeker ... I'm him. Can you help us?"

The bright light shut off, and there stood a naked old man covered in grime holding a bullhorn. He walked up to them, his aged penis swinging back and forth, slapping against his thighs. He stopped in front of Doyle, elated to see him, and jumped into his arms and hugged him tight. "Oh, Seeker! I knew it. Name has been waiting for a long time for you."

"Excuse me, who are you?" Doyle asked.

Name continued to hug him. "Name is named Name, by default. Quick, come inside." Name whispered, letting go, he hurried back into his compound.

"This is weird, how is this guy gonna help us?"

"Trust me, he is a brilliant man. One of the last of his kind. I found a beacon a while back on the networks I was hacking into. The message was encrypted so intricately that not even P.M. scientists could break it. I didn't try to break it, I just tracked it down, and it led me here."

"Come quick! We have a lot of work to do." He pushed his way through the bushes and onto a hidden path. Six followed, but Doyle hesitated. He took a deep breath and started down the beaten path.

"I don't know, Six. This one's kinda out of his mind. How exactly is ... whoa!"

Doyle and Six walked into a clearing and marveled at a giant satellite dish next to a functioning and ecologically sound house. Old cans, tires, car parts, anything Name could get his hands on were locked into place to make the awe-inspiring habitat. Attached to the gable was a large weathervane in the shape of an atom spinning points posed as electrons.

"I told you, man, this guy might be fucking looney tunes, but I think he was part of the A.I. Society."

"I heard stories about the Dream Children. Is it true?"

"You tell me. If it's true and the P.M. doesn't know his location or even if he exists, we have a great shot at attacking them where it hurts: technology."

"Wow, a real-life Dream Child."

"Come here, Seeker, I want to show you something. Quick, quick!" Name wiped off the hardened dirt on the side of the giant satellite. The embossed patent label read: Artificial Ice Nucleation for Weather Modification.

He pressed a few buttons on the dish's console. The saucer rotated and pointed into the heavens. A red glow illuminated around the tip of the four protruding metal beams that connected at its middle.

A loud laser beam shot up into the sky, knocking Doyle and Six to the ground. The red beam disappeared into the thickness of the clouds.

"Holy shit!" Doyle stood up and stared. The clouds were now electrified, and within seconds a storm erupted. Rain beat down on them. Doyle opened his mouth, drinking in the cool water. "I can't even remember the last time it rained. Can you?"

"It's been a few decades at least." Six cupped his hands and splashed water onto his face.

Name operated another lever, and the clouds overhead became much darker. Little drops of ice and snow fell to earth. Thousands upon thousands of pieces of ice pelted down as Doyle and Six took cover under a tree. Name pulled the last lever and a crackling thunder boomed from the clouds and echoed throughout the valley. A lightning bolt struck a hillside in the distance, and the flash stretched across the land.

"Seeker! It's for you, now the gods will fear us as if they were mortal. Did you bring me the medicine I require?"

"Um, yeah," Doyle looked at Six and shrugged.

Name jumped down from the console and faced Doyle.

Doyle looked around, dug in his pocket, and pulled out the first thing his fingers settled on. That old chewed piece of bubble gum he had saved since his childhood.

Name grabbed it with a gleam in his eye and popped it in his mouth.

Doyle and Six watched the man chew on it, then swallow it.

"I'm cured! Cured! Now I can continue my work!"

Doyle pulled out the gas canister. "Can you make more of this?" he asked.

Name grabbed the canister and smiled. "Anything for you, Seeker. But for now, we celebrate! Bring out the dancers!" Name clapped, and a machine hidden in one of the tall trees emerged. Just like that, a dozen dead Nukies, hung up by chains, dropped down and danced around from the machine, acting like a human marionette show. Old organ music blasted from hidden speakers as Name danced around the Nukies in absolute happiness.

Doyle and Six looked at each other in disbelief, then, joined in on the festivities.

"You're right, Six! He's a crazy son of a bitch, but I love him!"

"I told you, he's just a little eccentric."

Testament V

RE-RIGHTING THE WRONG

hunter's moon they call it, but I do believe the blood moon suits it best. With enough light, the Nukies invaded small pop-up tent towns and dragged off unsuspecting victims. The screams ... I remember the screams echoing out from the middle of the night and how it would wake me up from one nightmare to another. I could never sleep on nights like these, one eye open and one knife in hand. Even in this barricaded fortress owned by a strange naked man, I feel less at peace after my dreams were shattered by Section X reality.

Where did it go wrong, and how? Is everyone looking for a way out, fucking over the next to find one's own salvation? Where has the empathy gone and where is the camaraderie? It makes me think about the Grey Wolves of the past. The near-extinct Canidae that used to prowl and dominate these woods until displaced by man. Another conquering and eradication of a species that just wanted to live, to survive. I had read about these types of dogs who traveled in packs, kept to their own, and would die for one another. This type of communal organization I expected from Lee and Section X, but I was left to find my own way. Now I'm the one that roams in this Dog-Eat-Dog world where the Grey Wolf becomes my meal of the night. I'm envious of my food and what it used to stand for, but rest assured I will not choke on their bones.

The full moon laid its murky glow on the decimated trees that littered the landscape, accenting the whisper-quiet night; only a wisp of the wind could be heard disturbing the moonlight. Doyle climbed on top of Name's house and sat on the roof made of sea-softened glass bottles and rubber strips. He stared off into the glittering sky thinking about Darla. He hung his head and kicked some debris from off of the roof. He heard a noise coming from behind him and quickly pulled out his knife. "Oh, it's just you," Doyle said, loosening the grip on the handle and putting it away. He continued to stare off at the moon.

Name slipped up to Doyle and plopped himself down too close for Doyle's comfort. He studied Doyle, his hairless brow, furrowed with worry collapsed into his pale scars.

"I couldn't sleep," Doyle said, inching away. "I have so many things on my mind."

"Seeker, you're a wise lad. Why do you find happiness in loneliness?"

"Well, um, Name. Your observational skills are a little off. Do I look copacetic? I'm fucking miserable. Everything I've ever believed in is false. I don't know where the hell I'm at and where I'm going. My best friend is probably dead for all I know and Darla, I ... I don't even want to think about it."

Name put his head on Doyle's shoulder to comfort him.

"And now I'm telling my life story to an old, naked crazy man."

"I was in love once. She was a stunning woman and smart. I thought we would spend our whole existence together."

Doyle looked up at Name in disbelief that he had made a coherent statement. "What did you say?"

"You heard me. It was a long time ago, back in the A.I. society."

"I heard all these crazy stories about that, so is it true? The cryogenic experiments, the virtual reality, the ship? Was there really a spaceship?"

"Ha, it's funny how top secret we were supposed to be. But I now know that we were foolish to believe the Prominent Municipality."

"Wow! A real Dream Child," Doyle marveled. "So what happened?"

"Her name was Ursula; she was a German scientist. When she first came to our lab, I swear I heard angels sing every time I saw my polymath beauty."

"I know what you mean," Doyle nodded.

"My background is in geo-engineering, and she was a brilliant astrophysicist. We worked so well together and discovered so many important scientific truths through our enhanced Gedanken-experiments. One of our most important discoveries was an exo-planet in the Gliese system, a Super-Earth."

"You found a new place to live?" Doyle's eyes beamed with hope.

"Yes, however, the only problem was that it was a few billion light years away. Our intelligence was not at the proper level to solve space-time travel yet. Just thinking about it gave me a headache. The Prominent Municipality was not going to accept that as an answer, though. They told us that they had been secretly working on a brain enhancing microchip. They discovered this technology from a crashed unidentified flying object."

"You're fucking kidding me, aliens?"

"I said, unidentified. Could have been from the Russians as far as we knew. Nevertheless, who would not want to be more intelligent? She was the first to volunteer, and I quickly followed."

Doyle for the first time appreciated Name's brilliance.

"It was beautiful! Just in the first few months alone we had advanced technology a hundred years. Virtual reality, population, global warming, disease, oil, you name it. We had the answers for it all. The P.M., however, was uninterested. They did not want to fix the troubles; there would be no monetary gain, the price was costly and timely. Instead, they just wanted to run away, namely to this new solar system. They had us working like slaves on a space program to build a ship when I accidentally opened up an electronic mail.[1] We all had our doubts and raised a few questions that fell on deaf ears. When Ursula's eyes started to

---

[1] The electronic mail was the only form of communication for the populace until a powerful government interest group began to intercept the digital words. They read and compiled incriminating data on the people, and the justice system used this to purify Section A inhabitants. The intrusion of privacy caused the masses to reinvent the pen and paper.

bleed, the program was cancelled. It read that the A.I. society had shown recent signs of rebellion toward the end of their life expectancy. Terminate the society and bring in the new batch. We were expendable, and it was all a lie. The brain implant worked by accelerating the thought process and eventually aging one's brain. Six months was the life expectancy."

"What did you do?"

"For some strange reason I did not have the symptoms like Ursula and the others did. They bled from all orifices from the neck up: eyes, ears, nose. It was horrific. We were being watched like hawks, so I started putting red dye in my ears and eyes to not attract attention while we worked. Ursula was the first to die. Her last words to me were not scientific research or data based. It was *I love you*, and then she died in my arms."

"That's horrible. I'm sorry, man."

"Don't be. The very next day I set the whole wretched place ablaze. All the records were destroyed, and all the bodies were burned beyond recognition. It never happened, and I never existed."

"So, what is your real name?"

"Tell you the truth, I can't remember ... and I figure Name is better than Test Tube Baby."

Doyle sat silent for a moment, then he reared up with an epiphany, "You're not crazy, just insanely smart."

"Anonymity and deception is the game. Show your enemy your face cards, and never let them know you have an ace up your sleeve."

"You're right." Doyle stood up, strengthened by this knowledge.

"You see that full moon out there? Right now, its gravitational pull is stretching the Earth a few inches. And since you are grounded, it pulls you too. You're literally taller right now than you have ever been before. Stand proud, Doyle, there is hope."

"Fuck yeah, let's go kill some P.M!"

"Ha! We have a demanding day tomorrow, rest up."

Doyle listened to Name's bare feet patter against the smooth glass roof as he walked away and climbed back down.

The morning collected the water's dew on the dead Nukies outside the perimeter. A breach of sunlight moved down Six's face as he slept peacefully. A cold bucket of water slapped his face.

"Up and at 'em, sleep is for the tired. We have a lot of work to do." Name walked away to refill the bucket.

Six yelled out through chattering teeth, "That's cold! What the hell, couldn't you just've shoved me or something?"

Name came back into the room with another bucket full of water, perplexed by Six's comment. "If I shoved you, there would be no guarantee you would wake up. Decanting a bucket of liquid, chilled to fifty-five degrees Fahrenheit would eliminate any—"

"Alright already, I get it."

Name went over to Doyle and held the bucket over his head.

"Don't even think about it, old man," he said, one eye open.

"Ah, not to be snuck upon, huh?"

Doyle grinned.

"Well wake up, I have something to show you."

Doyle arched and stretched and looked around. Six was fast asleep on a wet bed, shivering and talking in his sleep. Doyle got up and followed Name to the back of the house. The closer they came to the back, the more Doyle could see his breath. He felt the sudden drop of temperature. They stopped at a large metal door that had a digital security lock on it. Name put in his passcode and the door slid open. The entrance led to a huge lab. In the center, a coffin-shaped glass cylinder lay on the floor. The six-foot glass was filled with a familiar green gas.

"Is that the bioweapon?"

"Indeed. I was up all night running some basic analysis and came across this." Name flipped a switch. Tiny sparkling flakes filled the cylinder. The green gas turned a deep purple.

"That's great, I'm very glad you're able to turn the green gas purple. What next, water into wine?" Doyle smirked.

"Patience." Name flipped another lever, and the glass cylinder opened, letting the gas out, filling the room. "Uh-oh, wrong switch! Run for your life!" Name took cover behind a desk.

Doyle panicked and tried to run back out the door, but it was locked. The gas surrounded him, he screamed and tried to take cover diving onto the floor. "It burns! It's ... it tastes good?"

Name laughed and walked through the gas cloud, helping Doyle to his feet. "You should have seen your face, ha!"

"Ha, ha, very funny. I nearly shit my pants." Doyle licked his lips, "It tastes like, raspberries?"

"Boysenberry, more precisely. I was able to convert the poisonous gas into a harmless inert compound so it can be transported safely. Undetectable as a toxin, with a hint of boysenberry fragrance."

The reversal of the HVAC system sucked the gas through the vents in the ceiling and the floor; then it was injected back into the glass cylinder. Tiny flakes littered the ground. Then it returned to its original molecular structure and green color.

"I don't see how your boysenberry gas is going to help us."

"You are an impatient one." Name grabbed a balloon and blew it up. He twisted and turned it, until it resembled a dog.

"I thought you were just acting like a crazy person. I'm starting to second-guess myself."

Name rubbed the balloon against a shaved section of Doyle's head while Doyle stared at him.

Name walked over to the cylinder and reached out to the glass with the dog balloon. The static electricity sparked, and the ignited gas exploded, shattering a layer of the double-paned glass from the inside.

"This gas is also very sensitive to electricity, and equal parts of gas can duplicate a blast that rivals a nuclear bomb. I'm calling it Boysenblast! All you have to do is deliver this byproduct to Section A."

Doyle cocked his head. "That sounds easier said than done."

Name picked up one of the canisters. "I designed a special canister that can be used in the water lines which run to every house."

"Including the C Street House?"

"Naturally. If you can deliver this gas to those lines, the

boysenberry gas will rise through the drains. And now the best part. With my weather producer, I can create an electric storm over Section A ... and BOOM!" Name mimed the formation of a mushroom, "and simply let the rain wash away the filth."

"Yeah, but wouldn't that kill innocent people too?"

"Not one of those people are innocent. They are all nuts and bolts that keep the machine running!"

Doyle walked up to the cylinder and touched its smooth glass surface. "I don't know. I just feel that there is still hope for some people. They just don't know the truth."

"This is neither a fair nor a pretty war. It is time to fight fire with fire."

"Don't get me wrong, it's a novel idea. But, is there any way we can divert the gas to just the bad guys?"

"If you must, I can coordinate another plan. It will, however, take more preparation ... you mentioned your fiancée, time is not on your side, Seeker."

"That proves my point further. I don't know where she is. Blowing up their world would leave no survivors. It's the right thing to do for Darla and the people caught in the middle." Doyle contemplated this whole surreal scene: the lab, the old man, the situation, and his thoughts. "You did this all in one night?"

"I told you I have been waiting for you. They did not call us Dream Children for their own amusement."

An alarm sounded and red lights flashed all over the lab.

"What's going on?"

"Intruders!" Name ran out of the lab to his monitoring room, and Doyle followed.

Six sat up and stumbled out of bed dripping wet. "What's happening?"

He saw Doyle running across the hall into another room.

Name sat at his huge desk. L.C.D. monitors lined the walls, a tight security system equipped with infrared tracking and heat sensors adorned part of the console. A computer screen flashed *Warning: Perimeter Breached*.

"Look! They're everywhere." He pointed at the screen; the

enemy had surrounded the perimeter. The screen displayed the datum of each encroaching figure, reading *Unknown*.

"We are surrounded, what kind of defense do you have here? Grenades, guns, missiles?" Doyle looked around the room for an answer.

Name stood up and pulled an old Indian spear from the wall. "Those are weapons of a Scaramouch."

"Are you crazy, old man, those guys have guns out there?"

Name ran out screaming his war cry as he passed Six entering the room.

"Are we under attack?"

Doyle pointed out the hundreds of people surrounding the perimeter on the monitors.

"No wait! They're with me." Six ran after Name, trying to stop him.

Name burst through the front door; his raspy scream strained his vocal cords. He charged toward the front gate aiming his long spear, but he tripped up on a rock, and fell face first. He looked up at the people surrounding him, guns drawn. "So, you give up, or do I have to get rough with every last one of you?"

The intruders burst out laughing as Six and Doyle came running from the house.

"Hey Six, there you are!" the group's leader, covered in bright tattoos, with mottled, red spiky hair said. He stepped over Name to give his comrade a big hug.

"It's alright, Name, this is the last of the real Anarchy March from Section X. I told them to come here."

A few members of the Anarchy March helped Name up and brushed him off. A teenager handed him his broken spear.

"Here you go, mister."

"Give me that! Thank you for telling me we were expecting guests!" Name stormed back into the house, brushing the dirt off his bare ass.

"Hey Doyle, I want you to meet Cole and his younger brother Cutter, a.k.a. Thunder and Lightning."

Doyle shook their hands.

"Six radioed us that we have a new leader for the Anarchy March, it's a pleasure meeting you, sir."

"Wait, what?" A confused Doyle looked at Six.

"You're the one, Doyle. We need you. The Anarchy March needs you. Lee has sold out to corruption, and we need someone like you to bring it back to what it originally stood for. Freedom, equality, and humanity. What do you say?"

Doyle looked around at the army and their hopeful but lost faces. Their eyes pleaded for someone to shoulder them. "No, this is a collective coalition. No gods, no masters." Doyle took a gun from Cole.

"Okay, what should we do first then, sir?"

"First off, don't call me sir. There's no hierarchy here, just brothers and sisters. Second, that fucking hippie compound and Lee has to go. Who wants to take back Section X and reestablish our strong hold?!"

They erupted in a cheer as they banged their weapons together in comraderie.

"What's the game plan?" Cutter asked.

"This isn't no game, and I have no plan. War Tactics are for the P.M. ... I say we go in tonight under the cover of darkness in a frontal fuck-you assault, punk style, hit them hard and ... Sunshine is that you?"

An Anarchy March patriot in the front row looked up and tipped up her hat brim. "Hi."

"What are you doing here?"

"I want to, like, fight for the cause and stuff."

"This isn't T.V., this is a real war. You could get hurt, even die."

"I'm sure. I can totally take care of myself."

Doyle smiled and threw her a gun.

"I don't have to kill anyone, do I?"

"You know what, I got a job for you." Doyle took the gun back and handed her a two-way radio. "Take this and stay with Name here, call me if anything happens while we're gone."

Cutter grabbed Doyle's shoulder as he walked out the front gate. "No offense, but the 'punk attack' is not a strategy I can send them to die for."

"Oh? So you have a better *game plan?* Who's gonna score the big touchdown then, sport?"

"I'm just saying, Doyle, my brother has the schematics of Section X's compound. With a little time, we can find a weakness and prepare better. Have a smarter warfare."

A man ran through the crowd, "Cole! Cole!" Out of breath, he said, "Lee knows something is up and he's preparing for an all-out war!"

"The early bird gets the worm, it's your call." Doyle knelt down to tie his shoelaces in a knot. "We don't have the time. In a day or two they can fortify that compound and make any type of assault impossible."

Cole searched the skies for an answer as a raindrop fell on his forehead. "This is reckless."

"Recklessness leads to destruction and correct me if I'm wrong, but isn't that what we're doing here ... destroying to create?" Doyle walked away with gun in hand.

The sun had set, and the frantic pace inside Section X stirred up the usually placid dust. Heavy footsteps and loud alarms had everyone on edge; the tension was palpable knowing their protected fortress was threatened. A long table was set up inside the warehouse loaded with automatic weapons, grenades, rocket launchers, protective gear — everything for a full-scale ground war. Lee and Benny handed out the weapons to the followers while Kongo stood tall with his arms crossed.

"They are trying to take our freedom, our homes, everything that we worked so hard for and built through these troubled years. We must come together and fight this mutiny. The Anarchy March will prevail and continue on against this threat and anybody else that would oppose us." Lee leaned over and whispered in Benny's ear, "They are like goldfish, keep feeding them and they just can't get enough." Lee held up some camouflage clothing and a metal jar filled with small syringes. "Get your fatigues and war jar! The purple needles are your Phencyclidine, you will need this in the heat of battle. The red needles are your Fentanyl, when you get shot, this will relieve you of your pain so you can carry on the fight! I want multiple guns in the two towers to release every soul that comes near those front gates! If it has a Mohawk, shoot it! If it has tattoos, burn it! This is a purification of the 'Other.' Fight for us!"

"You really think that piss-ant is coming back here?" Benny picked up a jar and examined the syringes inside.

"I don't know, and I don't care. I worked too hard to build this community, and I'm not letting some punk kid come here, pushing his idealism around," Lee said as he loaded his gun. "I want at least one squad covering the back gates in case they try to flank us! Move your ass, Betsy. All women are to report to the ammo cache for rapid reload! And I don't have to remind you, if you get caught, the needles that are marked black is your Zyklon Z."

Yawning with flagrant exaggeration, Benny patted his mouth and let everyone know, "War bores me. I'll be over here working on my tan." He pointed to a pile of tires by the entrance gates.

A guardsman, standing at one of the two towers on either side of the main gates, sounded a horn jolting everyone to attention. "They're here! Everyone to the wall!"

"I want suppressive fire in those trees, ASAP! Weed them out in the open and shoot them down like the dogs that they are! Go, go, go!" Lee grabbed his gun and ran to the near-finished fortified barrier. He climbed up a ladder to the upper deck that overlooked the battlegrounds. One hundred strong, Doyle's Anarchy March stormed the gates and opened fire upon the fortress. Bullets darted past Lee's head as he took cover, returning fire through the gun slits at the top of the three-story wall.

Kongo jumped up into the east tower and saw a guardsman who was reluctant to return fire with the mounted Gatling gun. He stepped up to the guardsman and smiled down on him. "What are you doing?! Grab a weapon and return fire!" Kongo grabbed the guardsman by the face and threw him over the wall. He ripped the mounted weapon from its position and cradled it, unleashing a storm of bullets upon the oncoming Anarchy March soldiers — the spent cases bounced of his emotionless face.

Benny grabbed a discarded woven chair and sat down by the gates of the fortress as chaos and mayhem surrounded him. A soldier fell down from the upper deck and died next to Benny's feet. "Hey, watch the shoes! I traded some valuable pieces for these." Benny moved his legs away from the blood pooling in the dirt. He looked up and saw a stray bullet pierce Kongo's arm. He stopped shooting, and his eyes turned red with hatred. "Oh, I would hate to be that guy," Benny remarked as he watched Kongo's veins expand and pulsate.

Kongo stormed over to another mounted Gatling gun and kicked away the gunner, ripping the gun from its base. With a Gatling gun in each arm, he jumped down on the other side of the wall. Three dozen Anarchy March soldiers charged forward. He swung the massive guns around, smashing soldiers over the head, cracking their skulls open. He then mowed the others down with dual fire from both weapons. The first wave of the Anarchy March defeated, the survivors ran for cover behind trees and shrubbery.

"Kongo win!" he yelled as he relaxed his trigger fingers; it was quiet for a moment. Just then, the El Camino broke through the black smoke of gunfire and crashed head-on into Kongo. He flew back into the gates and fell to a knee. Kongo's seven-foot stature now imprinted into the solid metal entrance.

"Ha! Got that fucker!" Doyle looked out the broken window from the driver's seat.

Kongo stood up and stared back at Doyle. He took a deep breath, his nose flared, a trickle of blood pooled around his bullring. He kicked up dirt as he dug into the ground and planted his feet.

"Oh shit." Doyle shifted into reverse and whipped the car around.

Kongo roared and grabbed a handful of syringes from his war jar, jabbed them into his neck, and charged after the fleeing car.

"Doyle! That monster is gaining on us and he looks pissed!" Six yelled.

"Fucking shoot that bastard!"

Six turned the mounted gun toward Kongo and fired. The fast pace and bumpy road caused Six's aim to be off target. Kongo gained on them, snarling, saliva and foam drooling from his mouth. Before long, the engine choked and sputtered.

Doyle looked down at the gas meter. "Hey! I have some good news and some bad news. Which do you want to hear first?"

"Good news! Definitely good news first!" Six shot down a tree, creating an obstacle to slow down the raging Kongo.

"We don't have to run from this monster anymore!"

"Really? What's the bad?!"

"We must have taken a bullet in the tank, it's dropping fast!"

Kongo broke through the fallen tree as if it were a pile of toothpicks.

Six's Gatling gun smoked, and the barrel spun empty. "Well I have some worse news. We ran out of bullets!"

"Fuck, hold on!" Doyle spun the car around and floored it, charging Kongo head on. "Let's play a little game of chicken with this fuck!" Doyle white-knuckled the steering wheel.

Kongo lowered his shoulder, aiming at the speeding car.

"Hey Six! You think this is gonna hurt us?" Doyle looked back at Six, who had just jumped out of the El Camino. Doyle's attention returned forward, and Kongo's bloodshot eyes were the last thing he saw as the car slammed into Kongo. The impact threw Doyle through the windshield. Like a ragdoll, he flew into a clearing, tumbling over and over to the ground.

He laid motionless and bleeding. The El Camino had wrapped itself around a tree with Kongo pinned between the twisted metal and the thick tree trunk. His arm had been severed and laid on the ground next to him. His inflated pumping veins began to deflate as blood pulsed out of his mangled flesh.

Kongo roared as he forced the car off of him and stumbled over to Doyle's unconscious body.

Six ran toward them from the road. "Doyle!"

Kongo wrapped his large hands around a boulder, raised it over his head, and looked down at Doyle.

"Doyle!"

Suddenly, a rocket-propelled projectile whizzed past Six and hit Kongo in the chest. A chain net expanded out and lifted Kongo off the ground and threw him back, strapping him to a tree. The net chains tightened and ripped through his flesh, snapping his bones one by one. Kongo took one last breath before he fell, shredded in pieces.

Six looked back and saw a man holding a rocket launcher, gray smoke misted from the barrel.

"Bam! Jack's back, motherfuckers!" Jack dropped the weapon and ran to Doyle.

Six sprinted to Doyle and opened his first aid kit. He examined Doyle's vital signs, and satisfied that he would be okay, he began to bandage his wounds. "Who are you?" Six asked as he applied direct pressure to a large gash on Doyle's forehead.

"I'm the guy you owe your life to. How is he?"

Six looked Jack up and down. "He'll live."

Six wrapped gauze around Doyle's head wound.

Doyle jolted to consciousness, spitting out some blood and a few teeth. He struggled to get to his feet.

Six and Jack held him down. "Relax," they both urged. "Jack ... is that you? Where's Darla?"

"They captured her, man. They captured us both. They're shipping her off to Section A."

Doyle tried to stand again but fell back down. The bone piercing through the front of his lower leg caused excruciating pain. "I think my leg is broken."

Jack took off a P.M. jacket he was wearing and tied it high around Doyle's leg to slow the bleeding.

"And how did you actually escape, again?" Six asked.

"Who the fuck wants to know?"

"It's alright, Six, he's with me. Me and Jack go way back, he can be trusted."

"We have to get you to Name's place and fix you up."

"Fuck that, we got a fight to finish, splint this fucker and let's go."

As Six straightened his leg, Doyle screamed in agony. "Bite on this." Six placed a piece of wood in Doyle's mouth and splinted his leg, wrapping it in layers of gauze. Doyle wrapped his arm around Jack and limped to his feet. Leaning on Six and Jack, they pressed onward.

Doyle's Anarchy March gained ground on the warfront. Lee was losing men fast, forcing them to retreat into the compound.

Lee returned fire at the approaching Anarchy army. "Come on! Get some! Yeah!" He looked back and realized that he was the last man standing at the wall defending it. He saw Benny guzzling a drink, his legs kicked up on a tire.

Benny yanked out his homing tooth and threw the dead, red beacon away as a single tear rolled down his face. "This one's for you, old friend. May the heavens be kinder to you than this world had."

"What the fuck do you think you are doing? We are at war!"

"I'm over it! We have lost. Time to use a different weapon, our words."

Lee slid down the ladder and rushed over to Benny, kicking him out of his relaxed state.

"I'm not talking my way out of this. We're going to fight till we can't fight anymore."

Benny spat out dirt and wiped his mouth. "Save your speech for one of your followers. I'm going to sit right here and reason with Dangle. He's just a punk. He can't match wits with me."

"You're a sniveling coward and a stupid one at that. I'll see you in Hell." Lee ran off leaving Benny surrounded by discarded bullet casings and bodies.

Most of the gunfire had stopped, only a few sporadic shots could be heard in the distance. Benny set up his seat again and sat down, waiting for Doyle. An explosive was set on the metal gates, and the blast took the gates off their hinges. Finally, the Anarchy March secured the compound. Doyle limped in with Six and Jack by his side.

"Dangle! How the hell are you? Oh my, might want to get that leg looked at." Benny brushed debris from his slicked hair.

Doyle put his gun to Benny's head. "Where is he?"

"Who may I ask you are looking for?"

"Don't fuck with me, Benny. I'm in no mood. That fucking politician, Lee!" He pushed the barrel of the gun into Benny's forehead.

Benny covered his face with his arms. "Whoa, whoa, what is with all the hostility? I come in peace."

"He asked you a question, fuck-face." Jack pushed Benny with the butt of his shotgun.

"He left. Took a jeep out the back gate, something about Section A. I stayed here to reason with you. After all, if we can't talk, are we not civilized?"

"That's going to be your last mistake. Six, can I see your shotgun?" He then pointed both barrels at the bridge of Benny's nose.

"Hey, wait a minute! It's because of you I'm here. Did you forget you and your friends destroyed my beloved Savage Town?"

Jack chuckled.

"You find that funny, boy?"

"So, you're Benny Hall! I heard all about Savage Town and the games you put on." Six's eyes lit up with excitement.

"You see, Dangle, even your friends think I'm a good guy. And if I remember correctly, Darla was always a special fan of mine. Now tell me, does she still do that little trick with her tongue?"

Doyle smacked Benny with the shotgun, breaking his nose. "Shut the fuck up! Don't you dare talk about her like that. This man right here is a liar and a traitor to the Anarchy March. Don't be fooled by his forked tongue. He is in it for himself and doesn't give a fuck about anyone else." Doyle shoved both barrels into Benny's mouth. "I'm going to ask you again, where's Lee and where is he going?"

"Don't be an idiot, Dangle. I know you and what you want," Benny mumbled.

"You don't know me." Doyle pulled the trigger and the hammer clicked empty. "Now you know me. Without your bodyguard, I'm sure the Nukies will have fun with their new playmate." Doyle jammed the butt of the shotgun down on Benny's fibula, snapping the leg bone in two. Benny squealed. "And my fucking name is Doyle! Now get lost!"

Six kneeled down and tore the Anarchy March armband off of Benny's arm.

"Wait? Out there? You can't do this to me. We have a history!"

Doyle pointed the shotgun at Benny's belly. "Crawl, mother-fucker!"

Benny shook and trembled as he groveled on all fours out the gates. The gurgles of the Nukies reverberated on the outside of the compound as they gnawed on the dead. The back gates slammed shut, leaving Benny to meet his fate.

"Why didn't you kill him? He could run back to the P.M. and tell them everything."

"You have a gun; you can kill him. Trust me, the less people I kill, the better," Doyle snorted.

"Trust? Well maybe you should look a little closer to home then." Six glanced at Jack.

"You got something to say to me? Don't beat around the bush, step up and be a—"

"I don't like you or trust you; captured by the enemy and magically you escape. A feat that no man has even come close to before. All of a sudden you show up at the perfect time at the perfect place with a rocket launcher. Give me a fucking break, I smell a rat."

"I don't have to explain myself to you. Right, Doyle?" Jack looked at Doyle for approval, but Doyle ignored him as he searched the pockets of a dead body.

"What?! What is this bullshit? The Anarchy March pumps through my veins." Jack slapped the bulging veins in his arms.

Doyle nodded in agreement. "Maybe Six is right, brother. We fought for many years together, and more and more I find that people tend to hide their real intentions. Maybe we need an explanation."

"You're gonna side with a guy that has a number name! Fucking fine then! After you left your fiancée and me to die, they caught us. They fucking interrogated us with torture tactics, and after I thought I couldn't bear living anymore, they threw us on separate trucks, probably taking me to a shallow grave! Being a badass, I escaped by deceiving the P.M. like we were trained to do! I took out the soldiers and stole the truck, where I got my fucking ear shot off!" Jack turned his head to one side and revealed a bloody flap of skin where his ear used to be. "It was an ammunition truck, that is where I got the fucking rocket launcher before it ran out of gas. I footed it to Section X where we were supposed to be going before we got separated, and I heard the fighting. I saw Kongo about to kill you, and I saved your fucking ass! Is that a good enough story for you?" Jack raised his arms in frustration and stared at Six.

"Where is this truck now?" Six asked.

"I can take you to it if you want, princess."

"Just calm down, Jack. We're all a little on edge right now. Let's just go to the truck and grab the weapons inside. Cutter! Where are you? Cutter?!"

Cutter trotted up to Doyle. "Yes, sir."

"Damn it, Cutter. Knock that sir shit off ... What's our count?"

"We took a beating. I have about forty men wounded, a few dozen or so uncounted for, and I'm still waiting."

"Who can fight?"

"Right now, I say maybe ten."

"Alright, have them stay here and seal those walls and let's start the rebuilding process." Doyle walked out of the compound, leaving Six and Jack in a stare down.

"After you," Jack said, forcing a smile.

Six holstered his gun and followed Doyle.

The Anarchy March walked along the road past Kongo's corpse, the demolished El Camino, and the soldiers who had been mercilessly gunned down. They came to an abandoned P.M. truck.

"Wow, would you look at that. Bullet holes and everything," Jack smirked.

"Sir, take a look at this," a soldier said, climbing into the back of the truck. He opened up the tattered tarp revealing two dead P.M. soldiers and wellspring of ammunition. The Anarchy March cheered, no longer low on ammo.

The hodgepodge of weapons and ammo lit a beacon of hope. They began to load and stock their found treasure.

"You're welcome," Jack huffed.

"I'm sorry I doubted you." Six reached out his hand. Jack extended his arm but at the last second pulled it away.

"Psych!" Jack walked off laughing.

"Forget about it, that's just Jack's way of saying it's cool." Doyle gave Six a pat and followed after Jack.

Jack stopped and stared off into the rising sun, barely visible through the polluted sky. Doyle stood next to him, and they observed a moment of peace.

Doyle put his arm around him and said, "It's good to see you again, Jack."

"It's good to be seen," Jack replied.

"Do you know where they're taking Darla?"

"I was blindfolded, but I heard some of the soldiers speaking while I was being transported. All woman prisoners of war are to report to Section A for some kind of experiment."

"We don't have much time left. Let's go." As Doyle walked off, Jack tugged on his sleeve.

"What, are you crazy? You just can't walk to Section A. It's thousands of miles away, and even if we make it in a few months, it's still Section A! You know how heavily guarded it is? The C Street House, forget about it. Nobody has been in or out of that place in nearly forty years."

Doyle looked around at the few dozen remaining Anarchy March. "Six!"

Six ran over. "What's up?"

"Do we have access to any vehicles and more people?"

"It's hard to say. We have been out of touch with the other Anarchy March since the tunnels went down. I really don't know who is left or what is salvageable."

Just then they heard a loud explosion in the distance.

"What was that? Oh shit, that came from Name's place."

Doyle saw a small mushroom cloud form over the fortified compound. He grabbed the two-way radio and called, "Sunshine! Come in! Sunshine!" Nothing but static. "Let's go!"

They took off, racing to the only hope they had left.

Testament VI

RED, WHITE, AND RUSE

*A*sshole! Doyle's inner thoughts derided him. *Stupid jerk, how could I've been so naïve? Everything could be lost, and for what? So I could beat my chest full of pride, to avenge? I'm not strong, I'm not smart, only luck has kept me alive. I'm no better than Benny. He might have been corrupted, but aren't we all? Don't we all have demons, fears, skeletons that drive us to do acts we'll regret? Take these bodies for example, badly decomposing and tossed on the side of the road like trash; a family that runs together, dies together. Did I do this, or did the Nukies get 'em? Who's the real monster? It was probably the child's ringing toy that attracted them.* The thoughts of doubt penetrated my skull as I stopped and knelt down at the man's feet. The woman posed as a cover for her child, clear by the laceration across her back. This is my fault, their death. I recognize his face, a Section X defector, torn apart by an infiltration that I led. I can't stop thinking about every horrible thing that has happened because of my principles, my justice. All this guy wanted was to have a happy life with his family, and my interference ended his happiness. Why is my judgment final, why did I deem that on myself? I'll get everyone killed, Name, Sunshine ... my Darla ...

"Doyle! Hurry up! What are you doing?" yelled Jack as he stopped and looked back at his friend hovering over a dead body.

Doyle rummaged through the dead man's pocket holding his breath from the foul stench of death. He pulled out the man's valuables and then he caught up to Jack. "What? Thought I knew him."

The Anarchy March reached Name's place to find it in complete shambles. What was left resembled a garbage heap. Shards of glass and contorted metal twisted against uprooted trees. The monumental weathervane was the only recognizable ornament, and it was lodged upside down in the dirt.

"Name! Name! Where is that old man?" Doyle sifted through the debris around the perimeter of what was now a smoldering crater, expecting the worst. "Name!"

He could hear a low-pitched moan from under some rubble. Doyle rushed over and pulled off a door pinning Name to the ground.

"Seeker, I don't have much time ... you must..."

"Who attacked you? Was the P.M. here?"

"You must ... must..."

"Where are you hit? Can I get some help over here?!" Doyle desperately yelled as he held Name in his arms.

"It's ... it's ... it's my penis ... my penis hurts ... I need someone to rub my penis." Name laughed as he pressed a button on the remote-control device hanging from his neck.

"What is this?" Doyle blurted.

The image of destruction pixilated and disappeared. Name's house reappeared intact.

"You son of a bitch!" He pushed Name off of him. "I fucking hobbled my ass up here! Motherfucker, I thought you were dying." Doyle leaned up against a tree and collapsed. He adjusted his leg splint and shook his head in disbelief.

Name burst with uncontrollable laughter. "You should have seen your face!"

Sunshine came out from hiding, she could not control her laughter either.

"You assholes! I would expect this from him, but you, Sunshine?"

"He, like, totally made me do it." She covered her mouth in a futile attempt to stifle her giggles.

"I'm sorry, Seeker. I just wanted to show you this decoy hologram device in action. They're great for diversions. I think you might need it on your journey to Section A."

Jack whispered in Six's ear, "Who is this guy? And why is he naked?"

"That's Name; he's one of the last of the Dream Children," Six replied.

"Ah! Wait, really?" Jack crossed his arms. His pupils dilated and fixated on the old man, studying his every move.

"I've also taken the liberty to gas up the last known bio-diesel carrier in existence." Name pressed another button on his universal remote and what appeared to be a tree was just another hologram that cloaked an enhanced armament truck, equipped with an SA 20 grenade launcher, S1HB Browning machine gun, and anti-CED wheels.

"Crazy old man, did I tell you I love you?" Doyle marveled. The deep tread of the tires could climb the most difficult terrain; its heavily armored body was crafted with rivets and camouflage. Doyle's naturally relaxed posture swelled with a deep breath, and he exhaled. Victory might not be a fleeting thought anymore. They now had a fighting chance.

Name stood up and studied Jack with scientific interest. "What is that?"

"That is Jack, and he has fought with the Anarchy March since the beginning, and he's my childhood friend," Doyle said.

Name crept up to Jack and circled him, sniffing, poking, observing, utilizing all of his senses.

"I didn't know today was don't trust Jack day?"

"Name, calm down, he's cool." Doyle tugged at Name, whose aggressive sniffing rivaled the most ardent tracking dog.

Name jumped back and snapped, "Okay! On to more important matters: dinner! Let's feast tonight in celebration of our victory against the Prominent Municipality!" He skipped and danced away.

Doyle followed Name, stopping at a large pile of debris. "Hey, Name! You forgot to switch off the last hologram. What's hiding underneath this trash pile, utopia? Ha!"

Name stopped, turned, and took on a serious state. "That is not a hologram. That is my interplanetary craft I'm working on. You think it's trash?"

"Oh, I'm sorry. I mean, looks great. I'm sure it flies."

Name skipped into the house ranting and raving about the nuances of space travel.

"That guy has one too many loose screws. Does he even know that the battle is yet to come?"

"Our road led us here, Jack. And we really don't have any options left." Doyle shadowed Name into the house, Six trailed behind.

They left Jack standing by himself. He felt a tap on his shoulder and turned to find a smiling Sunshine gazing at him.

"Like ... what do you want me to do?" she asked.

"Why you asking me? I don't know? Like go service the men or something," Jack quipped as he walked into the house.

Sunshine's smile turned upside down, her mouth dropped open, "Eww, so gross. What a, like, horrible person. As if." She shuddered at the thought and then walked off to help the injured crew.

Name led them into the basement of the house. He turned on the lights, highlighting a chair hooked up to a large printing device positioned in the center of the room. A console lined the left wall with two monitors and a plethora of buttons in multiple rows. At the far end of the room was Name's workstation, an L-shaped table was covered with books and papers. Odd graphs and charts written in cryptic mathematical formulae held the secret of Name's research.

"What is this?" Doyle asked, scrutinizing the mass of buttons and wires on the central device.

"Seeker, how did you hurt your leg?"

"I tripped, what you think happened?"

Name kneeled down and examined Doyle's leg. With a short jerk, Name snapped the bone back into place.

Reeling in pain, Doyle howled, "Fuck you! That hurt!"

"But necessary, Seeker. Now you will have plenty of time to heal on your journey and beyond." Name handed Doyle some painkillers he had stashed in a drawer over-stuffed with multicolored pills.

Doyle warily pocketed the medication. "What are you talking

about now, old man? Beyond what?"

Name sat down in the chair and put on a headpiece that had thousands of tiny intricate wires attached to the machine. "Could you flip that switch for me, over there?" he asked, pointing at the console to the left. "When I'm strapped in, I want you to push that red button."

Jack leaned into Six and whispered, "Maybe this device will fry this crazy bastard."

Name strapped himself into the chair. "I might be a little crazy, but I'm not deaf, bilker. Why don't you come over here and secure the last of these restraints?"

"With pleasure." Jack walked behind Name and pulled extra hard on the last straps.

"When you're ready, Seeker."

"Is this going to hurt you?"

"Imagine, if you will, a dream world that you can live and breathe in. Everything you touch, you can feel; everything you eat, you can taste; and everywhere you've been, leaves footprints. Trust me."

Jack huffed, growing tired of the pall of mystery, "Sweet dreams, you old wacko. Seriously, I need the drugs this guy is on." He sifted through the pills in the drawer.

Doyle pushed the red button, and the surge of electricity dimmed the lights. A second, more potent surge hit, and the room went dark. When the emergency backup lights came on, Name was slumped, unconscious.

"Is he dead?" Jack walked up to him to get a closer look.

With a quick jolt, Name sat up and went into a momentary violent convulsion. Then his hobbled body fell limp again; an eerie silence engulfed the room. All of a sudden, his eyes began to roll under his eyelids, and he fell into a deep R.E.M. state.

"Check it out." Doyle pointed to the gears; they were moving.

They all stared in amazement as ink-jet needles drew a vast design onto a rolling sheet of paper. As the image became more intricate and clearer, Doyle recognized the diagram from past stories — stories that would not travel far and that few would repeat. "It's a graph of Section A." The machine spat out a detailed image as if it had known the place, inside and out.

"Huh, is this some kind of joke?" Jack scoffed, "*This guy* has the answers we need? Bullshit!"

"Shut up, Jack! He's the last of his kind. You know their story. His dreams could have all the answers we could ever hope for."

"It's a fucking fairy tale is what it is." Jack circled the room, surveying Name's workstation and the console depicting an obscure computer language.

The graph was near complete as the tiny needles began to draw again while Name ground his teeth, chipping one.

"What's happening? Jack, what did you touch?" Six ran to Name, "Stop it! Turn it off! Doyle! Do something!"

Doyle pressed the red button over and over again, but the machine did not respond. It was out of his control. The monitors were flashing indecipherable binary codes. "I'm trying!" The needles in the machine sped up and inked with uncontrollable intensity.

"Six! Wake him up!" Doyle yelled.

Six grabbed Name and shook him. He pried opened Name's eyes. His pupils were dilated, engulfing the white.

Jack stepped up. "Move over Six. I got this!" He raised his fist.

The machine stopped and Name woke up, blurting out a horrific scream that turned into a monstrous belch blowing into Jack's face.

"Eh! You disgusting old bastard!" Jack wiped his face as the odor seeped into his pores.

"Yummy, I love bacon bison burgers. Would you be kind enough to release me from these straps?"

Jack swatted the air trying to wave the smell away. "Do it your damn self!"

Six helped Name out of the chair and to his feet.

Doyle grabbed the large detailed printout and laid it out across the workstation. "Is this what I think it is?"

"Yes, Seeker, you now know your enemy's home field."

An astonished Doyle admired the printout. "So, you have been there?"

"Only in my dreams." Name gathered everyone close. "This road — and only this road — is the way into Section A." He ran his finger along the lines that stretched five miles east and stopped at the end of the printout, which was blotted out by a circle of black ink. "The road magnetically scans all transports every half a second, so you will need a licensed Prominent Municipality vehicle."

"And how the hell are we supposed to get that?" Jack asked.

"I'm pretty sure that's a M1199 truck model A outside, right?" Six pointed out.

"At least someone is paying attention," Name said. "Now, right here, a few miles down, is the first of the impregnable obstacles in your path. These sturdy guard towers are fully equipped to take out any approaching armies. Only highly authorized V.I.P.s are allowed to enter and leave Section A. You will need a pass card."

"And I'm sure you have one of those just hanging around here," a defiant Jack said with folded arms.

"Jack, shut the fuck up and just listen," Doyle scowled.

But Jack's anger would not be quelled. "Fuck you," he bellowed. "You know what, you can listen to this guy and get yourself killed if you want. I'll be outside punching myself in the face. It'll be more productive than *this*." He stormed off.

"Sorry about Negative Nancy, he gets real animated sometimes," Doyle explained.

Name walked over to his desk and opened up a drawer, pulling out a pass card.

"So, you do have one hanging around."

"No, this is a pass card to Area 31. My old workstation in Section V."

Doyle took the card. "Area 31? Why does that sound familiar?"

"You're thinking about Area 51?" Six asked.

"Area 51 has made news and has been in the public eye many times in the past. What people don't realize is that Area 51 is just one of the last hidden bases. I worked at Area 31, which had a lot more, well ... There's a reason you haven't heard of Area 31. Deep inside you should be able to find an old pass card that can get you in through the first gate in Section A."

"Why can't we go off the road to the side? It's a straight shot from here." Six traced a line down the map.

"You see those little red dots around the perimeter?" Name pointed out thousands of points that almost bled into one another lining the magnetic road. "Each one of those chaser mines contains a nuclear warhead. Unlike normal chasers, these are more deadly and will explode up to two hundred yards away from a precise target, ending all life within a twenty-five-mile radius outside of the walls."

"What about an aerial assault?" Six posed alternative options, ones less dangerous than knocking on the front door.

"Not possible, inside the rotating walls. There are miles of anti-aircraft laid out across the land. No one enters, no one leaves."

"What? Rotating walls?" Doyle inched his finger across the blueprint following the large circular section that covered nonexistent states.

"The Great Apartheid Wall has three reinforced titanium steel rings, towering over two hundred stories high that rotate accordingly. One rotation takes up to a year to go around Section A. Each wall has an opening, which only comes together on the Twenty-fifth of December, like a key lock. I'm not sure what time this happens or for how long it remains open."

"December Twenty-Fifth? Why on Christmas?"

"The Prominent Municipality believes that their front is so unbreakable that even when Jesus returns, he will not be able to get inside."

"Jesus fucking Christ?! This shit sounds fucking impossible to get in. Is there anything else we need to know? Is there a fucking three-headed hydra as well?" Doyle voiced his frustration, reaching the end of his patience.

"Well, since you asked. Once you get inside the rotating walls, you will be faced with your worst fears — the unknown. I can't even mentally penetrate those walls with my dreams."

Doyle walked away confounded. "It looks like another damn Panopticon." Doyle flinched as a memory flashed in his mind of a time when he had escaped from a prison with a towering spotlight, sirens blaring, and dogs chasing him.

"Doyle? Are you okay?"

"Yeah, yeah, I'm fine. It's just a lot of information. Okay, so you're telling us that once we're inside, there is no coming back until a year?"

Name rolled up the printout and handed it to Doyle. "When you insert the gas into the pipes I will know, and I'll take it from there. I wish you luck." Name extended his hand to Doyle. Their firm handshake sealed their bond of allegiance and their fate.

"Thank you, I will bring back peace and equality to this land or die trying. I promise." Doyle walked away with a sense of hope, but the feeling was interrupted when he heard Name say, "Catch! This handheld nuke is for you."

Doyle almost dropped it, fumbling it around before managing to cradle it in his arms. "What?! Where did you get a Class A weapon from?"

"Ah, it's been lying around here for years now. It's fairly dangerous, so do be careful with it."

Doyle nodded, and the group left the house. They met up with Jack, who was digging inside the armament truck.

"Hey! What is this, a joke? There's no ammo in this bucket of Section A scraps," Jack complained. "Awesome! Did you get a fucking fortune cookie too, Doyle?"

Doyle ignored his sarcastic comrade. He envisioned that Jack popped into the world, fell off the obstetrician's table headfirst, and flipped off the doctor on the way down. A preemie sold on the black market, he never trusted anyone until he met Doyle as a young boy; the Anarchy March were their only parents.

"Alright, how many people do we have left?" Doyle asked.

"I'm only counting two that can survive this journey, just Cole and Cutter."

Sunshine tended the wounded but overheard the conversation and approached them. "Hey, mister man, what about me? I can, like, fight and stuff!"

"Okay, okay, you're right. We need all the help we can get."
Doyle added with his fingers how many would march with them,
but he stopped counting when he reached his missing finger. He
stood and stared at the emptiness. "So, there are six of us to take
on the whole P.M. empire."

Everyone took a deep, collaborative breath.

"I like those odds!" Doyle boastfully yelled.

"Yeah, me too! F.T.W!" Six wrapped his arms around Cutter and
Cole.

"Let's do this." Cutter cocked his shotgun.

"Well, Hell, if everyone wants to die, I'm driving then," Jack
said as he stepped up into the truck.

The six of them took the road less traveled, sure of their united
mission. They set off for Section V through the unfrequented Area
31. Jack drove while Doyle stared at the wasteland forgotten by
time; structures that barely held on to their foundation reminded
him of what old America used to be like. Structures that were built
on a foundation of lies were all he could visualize. A beheaded
statue of a former president, a farm littered with shattered solar
panels left in the wake of the coal industry's last-ditch effort to
level the playing field. He saw landfills full of dismantled satellite
dishes, once used for entertainment and internet access before
it became known as a G.P.S. tracking device to oust the Other
as a part of a treacherous deal struck by Nielson. He snapped
out of his reminiscent daze when he heard Sunshine whistle an
unsettling tune: The Star-Spangled Banner.

"What the fuck are you whistling?"

"Huh?"

"I said, what the fuck are you whistling?"

"Um, I don't know. I heard, like, this catchy song on a broadcast.
Why? Do you not like it, I can totally stop."

"No, it's nothing. Sing what you want, whatever makes you
happy." Doyle's patronizing was lost on Sunshine, and he
wondered if she even knew the history of that song and how it

might be the cause of her status right now.

Sunshine continued to whistle the tune but choked on a passing puff of smoke that spewed out of the truck's exhaust stack. Doyle took aim through the scope of his sniper weapon at a few Nukies in the distance. He watched them, studied them. The Nukies saw the armament truck and ran off in fear. Doyle lowered his rifle. The truck climbed over a few hills and into a murky sunset. The dark nights turned into day and the long days dimmed into unforgiving darkness. The long journey began to weigh on the Anarchy March.

"Doyle, Doyle!" Six was in the back of the truck. Doyle was focused on the mission ahead and did not hear him.

"Hey, Doyle, I think Six is calling you," Jack said, keeping his eyes on the road.

"Huh?" Doyle climbed to the back of the truck. "What's up?"

"We've been traveling for days now. I think we need to stop and set camp for a while."

Doyle's dedication to the mission put him at odds with his comrades. They had stopped only to add rubbish for fuel and to change drivers, nothing more. And after being tricked by a band of vagabond bandits, posing as people in need, he deemed it unsafe to stop in hostile territories.

Cutter was on an old CB radio calling out for any response. "Echo, echo, come in. Rats have escaped the sewer, over. If anyone can hear this message, please respond, over. Rats are hungry and looking for a new hole, over."

"Cutter, heard from anyone yet?" Doyle asked while he applied fresh bandages to his leg. He then popped a few of Name's painkillers.

"Not yet, sir, nothing but dead air. I'll go at it again after we clear these mountains."

"No, do it now, keep trying." Doyle secured his bandages with a safety pin and crawled to the front of the truck.

"Doyle."

Doyle stopped. "What is it, Cutter? A response?"

"Sir, we need to rest."

"I'm not stopping now; we have to keep moving. It's too dangerous at night. We will break at dusk."

Six stared out the window at the passing abandoned cars and homes. He fixated on the glowing rubble lit by smoldering fires. A few gunshots rang out in the distance, but Cutter would rather take his chances out there than to be cooped up like clipped pigeons in a steel cage.

"Is that alright with you?"

"Whatever you want, sir."

Doyle staggered to the front, "And for fuck's sake, stop calling me sir!"

"What is wrong with Cutter and Seven, I mean Six, whatever his number name is?"

"They're just tired, Jack. We all are."

"Yeah, well, no rest for the wicked, right?" The truck's headlights beamed on a lone man carrying a woman on the desolate road. Jack slowed down and honked as he steered past them.

"Just fucking drive, I don't want to hear your shit right now." Doyle stared ahead, spinning the phantom engagement ring missing from his finger.

They passed a large apotropaic cross piercing the earth, and Sunshine began humming again finishing the last stanza of The Star-Spangled Banner. Doyle scoped out the horizon with his binoculars. A tall chapel and some dilapidated structures surrounded it; its steeple pointed toward the heavens. He scanned across the cracked walls and saw a tattered poster that he remembered from childhood. The unmistakable bust of Uncle Sam's taunt: "I Want You" in vivid red, white, and blue had a different meaning to him now. Not just an old man with a funny looking hat ordering you. The hat was shredded, and the patriotic colors faded by time and conflict. "You want me to what? Die?!"

"I said I could stop singing." Sunshine's voice trembled, her eyes wide like a scared rabbit.

Jack slowed down, "You're losing it, man. Maybe we should pull over."

"No! We keep moving."

Without warning, the truck's engine sputtered and died and the Anarchy March lurched. Smoke billowed from under the hood as they coasted along.

Jack slammed on the brakes. "Come on! What now?"

Doyle jumped out of the truck and lifted the hood. A cloud of white smoke engulfed him.

Six got out and stretched but was quick to raise his weapon after hearing a guttural moan in the darkness.

"Looks like we blew a radiator hose. It's hard to tell though. I can't see shit." Doyle looked around at the dark and dismal surroundings. "Fuck, guess we're staying here tonight."

Sunshine got out of the truck; shivering, she wrapped her arms around herself. She strayed away from the truck, ignoring Doyle's warning not to venture too far. She gathered sticks and any other objects that could be used for kindling. Jack joined Doyle and Six as they looked over the engine. Another disturbing moan radiated their ears through the cold black night.

"Sounds like a great place to stop." Jack pulled out a pack of roll-ups and lit one.[1] Doyle and Six stared at him. "What? Did you want one?" Jack extended the pack of smokes.

"Where did you get those cigarettes?" Doyle asked.

"Off a dead body."

"You've never smoked before; when did you start?"

"Right now," Jack replied as he walked off taking a deep drag from his cigarette.

"Whatever. We're going on shift watch, and Jack, you're up first." Doyle pointed to a moonlit high peak that jutted from a cliff in the distance.

---

[1] Corporate powerhouses and lobbyist controlled the plentiful supply of cigarettes, a.k.a. Success Sticks. They fed them to the addicted populace for pure profit regardless of the monumental heath risk it caused the residents in Section A. Deemed only for the rich, and a status signifier, roll-ups now have a total of 600 extremely toxic and addicting ingredients with the recent addition of Dextromethamphetamine. The infamous propaganda posters read: The more, the better!

"I've been driving the whole fucking time; I need some me time. Why do I have to go first?"

"'Cause I said so! Now take your damn roll-ups and get the fuck out of here."

Jack took a defiant drag and then threw his cigarette to the ground, it landed on a red anthill. The ants attacked the glowing roll-up, charring themselves in the process.

"Hey, it's not all doom and gloom. Name wanted you to have this." Doyle threw him a cassette player with headphones.

"Gee, thanks." He gathered up his pack and a two-way radio and headed to the cliff.

"So it looks like we're coming up on the southeast end of Section V, in close proximity of Area 31." Cutter said, pointing to an area depicted on his map.

Doyle, always being one step ahead, inched his finger along it to measure how far Section A was from their location.

Sunshine returned and sat on the ground, she bundled the wood in a neat pile and struck a match.

Not pleased, Doyle nodded at Cole.

Cole walked to the small fire, smiled at Sunshine, and then stomped it out.

"You jerk! I'm freezing!" Sunshine stomped off to the other side of the truck.

Doyle popped open the glove compartment and dug out an emergency kit. He removed a little round cylinder and brought it to Sunshine, who sat alone in the dark. He placed the round cylinder in front of her, twisted its knob, and a soft light glowed, heat radiated out.

"Here, this will keep you warm, and the soft light won't attract any Nukies."

"Thanks," Sunshine pouted, wiping away her tear and stared mindlessly at the cylinder.

Doyle sat down next to her.

Cole came around and sat on the other side of Sunshine. They all enjoyed the warmth.

She rolled her eyes and scooted away, turning her back to him.

"I'm sorry, alright?" Cole offered her his musty coat.

"As if." Sunshine looked at Doyle and batted her long eye lashes. "Do we, like, have any food left? I'm so starved."

Doyle handed Sunshine a food capsule. "That is the last one, so eat it slowly. I'll tell you what, we're gonna need to find some friendlies soon or we are all gonna starve."

"What are we supposed to do if we don't?" Cutter asked as he sat down to enjoy the warm gathering.

Doyle looked at everyone's disheartened expressions and felt their morale dropping fast. He thought of Darla and how she could cheer him up so easily with a few simple words: "Hey! Who wants to play a game?" he asked with as much enthusiasm as he could muster.

The tired and travel-worn crew looked at him as though he were crazy.

"Come on, it'll take your minds off of things. There's a little game Darla and I would play every time we were in a bad situation. It's called, 'Why?'"

"And, like, *why* do you want to play this game?"

"Because, Sunshine, if we don't, we'll likely kill each other. Then when hunger sets in we're liable to eat one another. No offense, Sunshine, but those scrawny legs of yours aren't gonna feed anyone." Doyle said, cracking a smile.

"I second that," Cole blurted.

"The point of the game is to really get to know each other, eliminating any doubt, so you can trust one another. I'll start. Why do you have that tattoo on your arm, Cole?"

"'Cause it's cool."

"That's it?" Sunshine asked.

"Yeah, it's cool, so it makes me feel cool. And other cool people can recognize my coolness." Cole caressed his tattoo of a scantily dressed woman pleasuring herself.

"I don't think it's cool, it's totally lame, does that make you not cool?"

"I don't care what you think is cool or—"

"I have a few tattoos," Doyle interrupted, "so I know what Cole is talking about. To me, my tattoos show the trials and tribulations throughout my life. It shows what I've been through and where I want to go." He pointed out gravestone tattoos across his bicep. "These are for all the people I cared for that died fighting the good fight." The amateurish drawings were elegiac, though not the most attractive to look at.

"Yeah, I mean that too. I got this one right here to show my love for the Anarchy March." Cole unzipped his jacket and revealed his large Anarchy March insignia, tattooed across his chest. "I feel that this can shield me from any bullet, and it reminds me every time I look in the mirror of who I am, and knowing that makes me feel worthwhile."

"Nice, and that's how you play, why? Since I choose you Cole, it's your turn."

"Okay, this one is for my dear brother." Cole grabbed Cutter's leg with a vice-like grip. "Why ... did you fuck Melinda?"

"You knew about that?" Cutter asked.

"We're brothers after all."

"Who is Melinda?" Doyle inquired.

"She was my first love — my everything!"

"No she wasn't. She just popped your cherry."

"Doesn't matter, I felt love. My question is, why?"

"You really want to know? Fine, I, I just thought she was no good for you. I went out to prove it."

"That's so not a cool thing to do to your, like, brother," Sunshine opined.

"I didn't want to see him get hurt, cause I ... I, um, I love him," Cutter mumbled through his teeth.

"Well, I love you too, bro." Cole reached over and put his arm around his brother. "I didn't really care for her anyways, I heard she had case-four herpes."

"Fuck you."

Doyle and Sunshine laughed.

"So, what is your deal, Sunshine? Why are you even here?" Cutter asked.

Sunshine's laughter transformed into a serious moment. "I

don't know. I, like, have been asking myself that a lot since the beginning of this trip. I just think it is the right thing to do."

"Bullshit." Doyle blurted.

"Um, excuse you, what did you say?"

"I said bullshit. I know why you are here. You had a nice little life back in Section X, but that is gone now. You saw an opportunity to come and find that again. Let me tell you something, honey, that life you had was a lie, a sugarcoated bubble that finally burst. You're just trying to hold on to the last familiar thing you have left, your life."

Sunshine folded her arms and gawked at Doyle, "And what about you, Mr. Anarchy March, with all your barbaric killings and righteous war, why are you here?"

Doyle scratched at his facial scars. "Because I didn't have a fucking choice to be born."

The cylinder's battery life waned. Doyle laid down and closed his eyes. The conversation was over, and everyone sat silent concentrating on soaking in the cylinder's last bit of the heat. Their eyes glanced off each other.

The wind delivered the cold, and night engulfed the land. They slept close to the truck and close to each other, but none of them fell into a truly restful sleep. The moans and groans in the darkness kept the small crew wary.

Six sat up, a bright light from the cliff stirred his attention. He shook Doyle. "Doyle, Doyle, wake up."

"What's happening, what's going on?" Doyle sat up expecting to see the worst.

Six pointed at the cliff where Jack kept watch. "Look." A fire illuminated the jagged rocks.

"What the fuck?" Doyle grabbed his binoculars and focused in.

"What do you see?"

"Yeah, it's Jack alright. What is he doing?" Doyle dropped the binoculars down and groaned, "Oh ... I didn't need to see that."

Six took the binoculars away from him and laughed, "Ha, does he really need a fire for that?"

Doyle grabbed the two-way radio. "Hey! What are you doing up there?"

Doyle and Six snickered while they waited for Jack to respond.

"Jack, come in. I know your hands are full right now, but we can't have that fire. You know better, it will be Nukie central if you don't put it out ... copy?" Silence. "Jack! Come in!"

"He must have turned off the radio." Six grabbed the binoculars to take another look. "Oh shit."

"What? What is it?"

"He's got company."

Doyle picked up his sniper rifle and focused in the scope. A Nukie was stalking Jack from behind. He took aim and waited until the Nukie was well lit by the fire. Doyle's shot whizzed past Jack and hit the Nukie between the eyes. Jack let go, looked back, and stumbled to his feet. His widened eyes glared at the dead Nukie. He picked up his radio, still panting, "Hey ... thanks."

"Don't thank me, thank Six. Fuck Jack, you are supposed to be watching our backs, come on! Put out that fucking fire and pull up your pants."

"I'm, I'm sorry. Um, you didn't see anything did you?"

"No, Jack, there wasn't much to see." Doyle and Six couldn't help but laugh, close call or not.

Cutter and Cole ran up. "What happened? We heard a shot," Cutter said.

"Nothing, it was just a buffoon acting like an idiot. Now let's get some shut eye, we have a long day ahead tomorrow." Doyle put his weapon to rest and laid back down. They all tried to go back to sleep.

The night disappeared as the sun breached the hilly terrain. The strong smell of sizzling meat woke Doyle from his slumber. He rubbed his eyes and there was Jack, cooking a small animal, rotisserie style, over an open flame.

"What time did you get here?" yawned Doyle.

"I've been here for awhile. I figured I'd cook breakfast for everyone for fucking up last night."

"It's alright, I know it's been a tough trip so far," Doyle acknowledged with a friendly pat.

Sunshine strolled up and marveled at the small critter Jack had caught. "Eww, like, what is that? I don't eat anything that might have a name."

"Then you don't eat." Jack seasoned the undersized animal with a few weeds he had gathered.

"Sorry, Sunshine, but Jack is right. This is all we got."

Jack took the feral animal from the open flame. He blew on one of the ears and then bit into it, tearing it off. "The ears are the best, a little chewy. I'll save the other one just for you, Sunshine."

Sunshine began to dry-heave and ran off to the other side of the truck.

"Not an ear person, I guess. Fine, I'll save you the tongue!" Jack chewed on the rubbery meat.

Doyle packed his backpack and slung it over his shoulder.

"Where are you going? Did you want this other ear?"

"I don't fight on a full stomach." Doyle grabbed his weapon and hiked toward the cliff to get a better view of the area.

Cutter and Cole stopped him. "What do you want us to do while you are gone?" Cole asked.

"Secure the perimeter. Only shoot when necessary, we need to conserve our ammo." Doyle patted their backs and headed for the rocks.

Doyle returned a few hours later and joined Jack and Six, who were hovering over the truck engine. "Did you fix it?" he asked with urgency.

"Nope, just remembered that I know nothing about engines," Six admitted.

"Come on, Jack. You must remember how to work on a vehicle." Doyle leaned in and glared at the radiator hose; it was a poor patching job.

"Here's your problem..."

Jack and Six looked closer.

Doyle pointed at the radiator hose, which looked like it had been patched with chewing gum. "Name is a hell of a scientist, but a mechanic he is not." Doyle pulled a roll of e-tape out of his backpack and leaned in to reinforce the patch. He then poured water into the radiator. "Alright, give her a rip!"

Jack jumped in the driver's seat and turned the key. The engine roared to life.

Doyle closed the hood and cautioned, "We have to take it easy on her or she will—" At that moment, the truck sputtered, coughed, and died, again. Doyle popped the hood and gave it another look-see. "Fuck, I hope it's not the fuel pump relay."

"What is that?" Six asked.

"Ah, it's this little bastard-looking fuse." Doyle lifted the housing's plastic cover; a fuse was missing. "Huh, that's odd?"

"What's wrong?"

"The relay fuse, it's not there."

"What do you mean, not there?"

"It's not here, as in it is missing."

"Did it fall out or something?"

"Impossible, relays don't fall out."

Jack jumped out of the truck and walked over to the engine. "What's wrong now?"

"I don't know. But we need to figure it out quick. I was watching a group of Nukies just over that hill and they disappeared somewhere ... I have a task for you two."

"Oh, finally, some action. What do you want me to kill? Just name it."

"Forget about it, Jack, this is a stealth assignment. These Nukies are different. They follow patterns and congregate."

"Yeah right. Nukies are as dumb as Section A dirt. I once saw a Nukie drown by holding its mouth open when it rained."

"Anyhow, they're in our way. Over those hills is Area 31, and it is infested with them. I'm gonna cause a diversion to lead them away, so you guys can sneak in and get the pass card."

Six grabbed a backpack. He placed wire cutters inside next to a nylon rope and a crowbar, and hiked off toward Area 31 with Jack. Doyle looked perplexed as he watched them disappear over the hill.

"Like, what do you want me to do?" Sunshine asked with a

bright smile.

"You want something to do? Here, take this and figure out different ways to kill someone with it." Doyle handed her his knife.

"Um..."

"You said you wanted to fight, so here you go. If you can't defend yourself and others, you're as good as dead."

Sunshine took the knife with a serious face and swiped at the air.

"Hey, keep your smile on and they'll never see it coming."

Sunshine practiced with the knife as Doyle watched, admiring her tenacity.

"Did you see Cutter and Cole anywhere?"

"Yeah, they are, like, shooting at helpless Nukies. Told them to stop it, but they totally didn't listen to me."

Doyle heard a distant gunshot and walked off down the road to see Cutter and Cole lying in a trench with their new sniper weapons, taking aim at Nukies that posed no threat.

"I see it! I see it!" Cutter took aim, "This one's for Stitch." He shot at the bobbing Nukie, hitting it in the arm. "Damn it!"

"Man, where did you learn to aim?" Cole grabbed the gun and zoomed in. He took his shot at the injured Nukie as it hobbled off, severing its head from its shoulders. "That's how you do it. Did you see that head fly?!"

Doyle jumped down in the trench behind them and kicked them. "What are you two doing? I told you shoot only when threatened. We have to save our ammo for when we really need it."

"It's alright Doyle, we got it under control." Cole peered through his scope and saw an elder Nukie pop its head up. "Just a little bit of revenge for..."

While taking aim, a white blur covered the scope. Cole looked up to find himself face to face with a Nukie. The snarling pale face blended into the brown saliva dripping off his ravenous teeth. Cole jumped back as he realized Nukies were surrounding them with guns.

Doyle threw his weapon down and raised his hands, urging everyone else to do the same.

The sneering Nukie ripped the sniper weapon from Cole's hands and pointed the barrel of the gun inches from the white of his eye. The Nukie pulled the trigger, shooting Cole point-blank in the face.

Cutter charged forward, but Doyle held him back. "Not now," he urged.

A Nukie was dragging Sunshine by the hair and threw her at Doyle and Cutter's feet. The well-equipped beasts hovered over them stationary and expressionless. M-16s and grenade launchers were pointed centimeters from their faces.

A Nukie aided by a cane stepped forward. It wore a cotton vestment and had a hangman noose as a belt. It cracked open the side of its disfigured mouth as the lips appeared to be melted together. "May Jesus forgive you while your flesh burns in Hell. Take these blasphemous sinners to the prophet Coe!"

"This is a mistake; we meant no harm. Get your hands off of me! We just want to pass through your land!" Doyle pleaded.

"This is not my land, it's God's land," the Nukie said as he raised his cane in the air.

The Nukie army tied up their captives, chain-gang style, and hauled them off to God knows where.

Testament VII

AN INVOCATION FOR ALL ATHEISTS

ttired in holy robes and hooded cloth, my mind wanders ... I never understood the meaning or purpose of religion. Maybe because I was never indoctrinated or raised to believe in fictional characters. Most of those books were categorized under Sci-Fi or Fantasy in our library. I did read up on the facts, which were far and few between. Over five thousand ingredients of truths all claiming to be the correct recipe for accessing God.

I believe Sigmund Freud said it best when he wrote, "America is the most grandiose experiment the world has seen, but, I am afraid, it is not going to be a success." One man saw an ominous future and had incredible insight, he knew traditions wrapped tight in lies offered a bed of comfort, which became truth as time passed. Stories were rewritten and prose was cemented in stone, fabricated to fear the unknown.

For me, it was always the action that spoke louder than any word. The killing for one God over another never made any sense to me, and what always seemed to follow: war, cruelty, famine, death, and destruction in the name of God. What kind of person believes in something so vehemently that they will destroy all that is not familiar to them? Only the selfish and foolhearted put that much time and effort into whimsical fairy tales, especially when you are of sound mind. Nonetheless, I find myself bound, tied up like an unholy animal to be sacrificed in the name of God. They pray for my death. I hear them through my hooded cloth, the jeers anointing me as the devil, the bad guy. Am I so wrong I should be snuffed out, my ideas dismissed? Is my thought process so evil that merely just the words I say are condemned, demonized as false, forever? What if I do have a God, a faux religion that suits my needs and my God tells me to kill, ain't I just like you? This game is a deadly conundrum that should be put to rest once and for all, and if my God of Anarchy tells me to do so ... so be it.

The Anarchy March struggled to free themselves of their restraints. Crudely woven fabric wrapped tight around their heads made it difficult to fully grasp their surroundings. The only sound that encompassed the prisoners was the Nukies' grunts and heavy breathing from years of inhaling polluted air. They pushed them into an underground dwelling.

Doyle managed to spy through a small opening in his coverings a collection of handmade crucifixes covering the compound. Another rustic sign caught his attention that read: Area 31.

"Where do you think they're taking us?" Sunshine whispered.

"I don't know, but if these Nukies can speak, they must have a hierarchy." A butt of a gun hit Doyle in the back of his head.

"Shut up, sinner!" the Nukie yelled. "God did not give you a tongue to speak evil."

A door slammed behind them, and they were pushed to the floor. "Kneel before the prophet Coe!"

Their coverings were removed, and they were forced to kneel on the ground.

A decaying nave came into focus. Images and statues of Jesus Christ covered the walls like centuries-old fungus. Rows of pews fell one upon another, bowing forward to worship their idol. An old man deformed by a crooked spine hobbled out from under a ray of holy light breaching through the cracks in the ceiling.

"Are you the leader of this hellish brigade?" he asked.

"My name is Doyle and I'm the leader of— "

"Your name is Satan! Why did you come to this Holy Land of peace? Is it to spread the word of the devil with your immorality?"

"I'm the leader of the Anarchy March and I—"

"The leader of Satan's army!"

Cutter blurted out, "Fuck you! You killed my brother!" A guard struck him in the head.

"Only speak when spoken to by the prophet Coe!"

"I can explain why we are passing through your Holy Land," Doyle said, getting to his feet.

"Can you explain this?" The prophet waved over a group of Nukies.

They carried a limp body. Fresh blood trailed in a pool from multiple bullet holes. One of the many victims Cole shot.

"He would do it again if he were alive!" Cutter yelled. Another crack to the back of his head silenced him and he slumped to the ground, unconscious.

"That was a mistake," Doyle warned.

A young Nukie boy came out with tears in his eyes. He fell next to the dead Nukie's body and hugged him.

"Now, now young one, your father is with God along with your mother. It's time to make your choice. Do you want to continue on, Christian Soldier, or be with your family?"

The young, innocent child continued to cry, unresponsive to the ominous question.

The prophet signaled a Nukie guard. He pulled out his pistol and shot the child dead.

Coe ordered some Nukie guards to remove the bodies and explained, "God only wants the strong minded to fight his war."

As they dragged the bodies away, he made the sign of the cross over each one, and through oozing eyes, looked at Doyle. "Their blood is on your hands sinner, a mistake you will pay dearly for. Repent!"

"I hate to break the news to you buddy, but there is no God." Doyle's patience had reached its limit.

"You're an atheist? Heretic! I said pray to God for forgiveness!"

Sunshine clasped her hands together to pray out of fear. "Okay! Okay, you just put your hands totally together and, like, cry, right?"

A gun butt smacked the back of her head, and she fell unconscious next to Cutter.

"God is not to be mocked, and you wouldn't want to feel his wrath. Lucky for you, sinners, I can't kill you until you know the name of God, and only then will he judge your fate." The prophet raised his hands up to the sky and spoke in tongues: "*Domini meus pasto est et nihil mihi ... Potentia tua gloria vera est regnum ... Et sanguinem, Christus Dominus noster corpus et spiritus est nobiscum!*" He then fell to the ground and went into a convulsive state. His body flopped around, and as his eyes rolled upward, a yellow film replaced his black pupils.

The guards began to shout in tongues as well. The loud prayer echoed inside of Doyle's mind as he covered his ears. The room began to spin in brilliant colors, kaleidoscopic, stained glass; Doyle watched the surreal events in horror.

The prophet then stopped and stood up. "Jesus has spoken to me, and he wants you to follow in his path of righteousness. This is truly a blessed day, hallelujah."

"Hallelujah!" The Nukie guards rejoiced.

The prophet spoke through a vacant stare. "We will lead you to the lord or die trying. Your path to purity begins now."

Instead of seeing the holy light, Doyle saw the butt of a rifle just before it knocked him unconscious.

Doyle and Cutter woke up in a large, honeycomb dome-shaped sacristy. Free from their restraints, they were propped against a wall in plain view of the center of the dome. A crudely constructed stage stood in the center where the prophet Coe was conducting a sermon from a lectern. He wore a large, gold-threaded robe with white miter that blended well with his melted features. He spoke grave and stern words to an audience circling the stage.

"Only God can show you the right path, only God knows what is expected from you. We were selected as God's soldiers to continue on spreading the gospel. But we were punished and punished harshly for our sins!" The prophet opened his robe, showing his grotesque body, distorted by nuclear waste. "But the time has come, my brothers and sisters, for the Holy War to reclaim this land in Jesus's name!"

Doyle looked over the faces of the Evangelical Nukies as dozens prayed to God for forgiveness.

"This place freaks me out, bro," Cutter said as he felt the clotted blood on the back of his head.

Doyle surveyed the surroundings and saw an unmanned door behind him leading out of the dome. He stood up and crept backward.

"You in the back!" the prophet yelled. "Where are you going? You of all people should hear the word of God. Do you want to burn in eternal Hell till the end of time?"

The circle of praying Nukies looked back at their prey, fixating on Doyle.

"Sorry, I already paved the road to Hell, might as well ride it down!" Doyle retorted.

"Lost souls can be found if you ask for forgiveness. Don't you want to be saved?"

"Saved from what exactly?" Cutter asked. He was sick of hearing the forced preaching shoved down his throat.

"Well, damnation of course; the pits of Hell are not a good place to spend eternity. The prophet has spoken, and God has a plan for you. Come here."

"Fuck you very much, we have to go." Doyle and Cutter tried to push the door open, but two imposing figures held it shut. Escape was still beyond their reach.

"You are going nowhere until you've seen the light. This right here is God's land, and we took the oath. If we ever forget that we are a nation under God, then we will be a nation gone under!"

Doyle and Cutter walked through the indoctrinated crowd of Nukies trying to avoid their piercing, judging eyes.

"Today will be your baptism."

A bowl of water sat on a pillar next to the lectern, Doyle chuckled, "Don't worry, Cutter, we're just going to play their little game here until we can leave."

"I'm not going anywhere till I kill every last one of these motherfuckers. Cole will be avenged."

"In due time." Doyle walked up on stage and raised his hands. "Okay, I am ready to be saved!" Doyle put his head close to the water, ready for his cleansing. "When you dunk my head, could you be careful with my hair? I just had it dyed," Doyle joked.

"Today we baptize another sinner that rages war against God. With the Holy Ghost on his side, he can do no wrong again!"

Doyle knelt down in front of the bowl of water. Two Nukies grabbed his arms and held on to them.

"I really don't need any help doing this."

A door across from the stage opened, and two hooded Nukies brought in a branding iron shaped into a large, glowing red cross. Doyle smiled at Cutter, whose smirk had turned to fright. He looked back and realized the brand was for him. He struggled to get free as Cutter jumped up to rush the stage. A few Nukies grabbed him and held him down. "Do not fret, it will be your turn next," they said to Cutter.

The Nukies ripped off Doyle's shirt, his body rivaled their own unsightly man-made disaster. His chest revealed a war-like scene; bullet hole scars covered burn scars and knife wounds that had been badly stitched shut.

"Wait! Wait! Let me go, you crazy fucks!"

They pushed him against the cistern of water. The branding iron sizzled into Doyle's flesh. He screamed.

"Suffer for Jesus as he suffered for you!"

The branding rod was pulled away and dumped into the abstergent water, steam flowing across Doyle's face.

They dragged him to the side of the stage. A few Nukies grabbed Cutter, forcing him toward a searing iron rod that two more hooded figures presented to the prophet.

"Let me go!"

"Don't you want to go to heaven, son? These are the steps to righteousness."

"You can shove that righteousness right up your ass!"

The Nukies propped him on his knees and ripped off his shirt. The large, cross-shaped branding iron held behind him, glowed orangy red.

"In the name of Jesus, take this sinner and make him reborn!" The prophet twisted and contorted his body as he blared out in tongues. *"Christus Dominus noster corpus et spiritus est nobiscum!"*

Suddenly, a loud alarm went off, startling everyone. Doyle took advantage of the distraction and jumped up to grab the branding iron. He swung the rod, cracking it across the Nukie holding down Cutter, knocking him out.

"Get the infidels!" the prophet yelled as he loped off behind the stage.

The Nukie guards stormed through the doors and began shooting erratically toward the stage. Doyle and Cutter jumped for cover as the bullets ripped through worshippers.

"Sir, we're pinned down, what do we do?"

"Looks like Jack and Six made it inside, let's go!" Doyle took off running to the door across from the back of the stage. Bullets flew past him as he jumped through the door, and Cutter popped up and took off running after Doyle. As he reached for the door, a bullet hit his thigh, sending him falling at the door's edge. Doyle pushed over a large statue blocking the door's exit. Helping Cutter up, he wrapped his arm around him and they stumbled off.

Sunshine woke up in a large, transparent plastic room set outside on the ground level of Area 31. The space had been left over from the old radioactive testing rooms. The relentless sun pounded at the sloping walls, creating an insufferable heat. Tiny air holes lined the arches of the plastic dome, though they allowed only a minuscule amount of air in.

She saw many other similar rooms around her with Nukies pacing about. As her eyes focused, she homed in on a little girl peacefully drawing at the far end of the room.

"Hello, little girl!"

The girl continued to draw and did not respond. Sunshine walked up to her and noticed that she was drawing crosses upon crosses over and over again. Startled, the girl turned around. Liquid dripped from her every orifice, a side effect of radioactive poisoning.

"Hi, I'm sorry. I totally ... totally didn't mean to scare you. What ... what is your name?"

The little girl's stare unsettled Sunshine. She patted her ears, indicating she was deaf, and flipping her paper book over, she wrote: My naMe iS MarY.

"My name is Sunshine. Can I draw with you?"

Mary snapped her single black crayon in half and handed the piece to Sunshine.

"Oh! Thank you, Mary. Um, like do you know why we're in these rooms?"

Mary wrote: yOu hAve siNNed, likE uS. God No LikE siNNer.

"How sad. How in the world did a little girl like you sin?"

The young girl flipped over the paper book and continued to obediently draw out her crosses.

Sunshine noticed reddish swells of skin, as well as purple and green bruises running up her arms and legs.

"Mary, how do we get out of here?"

The girl held up her drawings of multiple crucifixes and beamed an innocent toothless smile. Sunshine knew that escape would soon be impossible.

Nervous, Sunshine ran up to the plastic wall and banged on it, "Help! Help me! Someone help!" Her screams went unanswered and ignored, as other Nukies in the plastic rooms continued to pace and mumble out prayers. "...Help me!" She crumbled to the ground in despair.

As the sun continued to beat down on the plastic room, Sunshine began to feel lightheaded; sweat poured from her forehead and soaked her. A song radiated from another plastic room as a few Nukies began to sing; it parasitized Sunshine's ears. The other surrounding rooms joined in on the repetitive hymn.

"*God is good, God is great, lessons learned seals our fate. Save us soon, save us now. Here I come, Kingdom come. God is good, God is great...*"

"Can you stop singing, please!" Sunshine blurted out in frustration; she pressed her face against the air holes.

Mary stared at Sunshine's back and tilted her head in confusion.

"When do they feed us? You know, eat." Sunshine gestured indicating that she was hungry.

Mary wrote: tWo WeeKs of fAstEnig foR God.

"Two weeks! I can't, like, do that!" she cried out hoping someone would hear her plea. "This is so a mistake. I don't want to be in here. I'm, like, not into this religion stuff." Sunshine frantically banged her fists on the plastic walls in a feeble attempt to escape.

Mary wrote: aCCept hiM aS youR lOrd aNd savior aNd yoU wiLL be fRee.

"No, no, no honey. I, like, totally don't know if there is a guy up there. But if He or She is real, this is totally not what it would want. A little girl like you should be, like, playing in the fields and stuff, sneaking kisses from cute boys, living life. This is so not a free life."

Mary ripped a piece of paper out of her book and gave Sunshine a crooked scribbled cross.

"What a world." A dejected Sunshine hung her head in worry.

A door swung open on the other side of the room, and a figure dressed in a white cloth, head to toe, walked in. The grotesque old woman removed her hood and stared. Her hairless head had few distinguishing features. She hobbled on one leg; the other had been severed at the knee. The door slammed shut behind her.

"Hello, my name is Mary and the lord told me I should pray for you," she gurgled out.

"Another Mary, as if, I don't need your prayer. I need to get out of here."

"And where will you go? Away from God? He will always find you because he is deep inside your heart."

"This isn't happening, I'm just gonna wake up and everything will totally go back to normal." Sunshine closed her eyes then one at a time reopened them hoping her wish had come true. She sulked to the other side of the room, her wish unanswered.

Mary followed and knelt next to her. "Oh Lord, I pray to you to help my friend here. She is lost, my Lord, and I know only you can save her from eternal damnation, my Lord. In Jesus name I pray, *Potentia tua gloria vera est regnum. Et sanguinem, Christus Dominus.*" Mary fell into a trance of tongues. A loud alarm went off, and all of the doors in the plastic rooms swung open.

Sunshine realized the opportunity and pulled out Doyle's knife. "Back off, I have been practicing, and I know how to use this thing."

Mary stepped out of Sunshine's way as she bolted out of the room. "He will follow you, wherever you may go, he will follow you!"

Six and Jack reached the outside of the barbed wire fence. Six pulled out a cutting tool and cut the fence enough for them to squeeze through. They saw some Nukies walking in formation and fraternizing with each other.

"Un-fucking-believable. These disgusting animals are talking." Jack spat on the ground.

"Let's just get in and get out, that building over there has the ventilation system."

Six and Jack crept low as they jetted across the compound to their destination. Six pulled out a crowbar and jabbed it into a thin opening in the vent cover and pried it off. They crawled inside the narrow ventilation shaft that led them deep inside the compound. Six led the way, but as he came upon a four-way split of the shaft, he stopped.

"Why do I have an ass in my face?"

"Hold on!" Six held up his hand feeling for airflow. "This way, I think."

"You think? Move over, I'm taking lead."

"And how are we supposed to do that?" Six asked, gesturing at their confining surroundings. "Why don't you think before you speak?"

"I think when we get out of here, I'm gonna hurt you. No, I take that back, I know I'm gonna hurt you," Jack retorted.

"We'll see." Six took the path leading to the right, and Jack followed, reluctantly.

They came across an air vent. "Look," Six said.

"All I can see is your ass, move!"

Six pressed himself into the wall of the shaft so Jack could see.

"Shit, they got Doyle." They watched Doyle being dragged away and cringed when they saw the huge welt in the shape of a cross-branded on his back.

"We have to go get him," Six stated.

"No, we have to move on." Jack urged.

"It's Doyle, our leader!"

"He told us to go get the card. We all risk our lives here. Doyle would do the same."

Six reflected on Jack's words and then moved on. The airflow became stronger as the shaft led to a large open space with a spinning fan underneath them.

"I see a door over there, we need to pass this fan and—" Just then, Six slipped and slid down the angled shaft toward the ominous rotating fan. Jack caught his arm, struggling to hold on to him.

"Pull me up!" a terrified Six yelled.

"Only if you say the magic word."

"Asshole, pull me up, I'm slipping!"

"I don't believe that asshole is the magic word."

"Please! Fucking, please!" Six yelled.

At that, Jack pulled him up and bellowed out a sadistic laugh.

Six regained himself and punched Jack in the face. "After this mission, I don't want to see your fucking face ever again." Six stood up and walked across a small beam above the revolving fan.

Jack licked the blood from his lip. "A simple thank you would have been nice."

Six reached an emergency door as Jack caught up. He peered through the window on the door and saw an empty room. Large burgundy drapes let in a fraction of sunlight that beamed onto a statue of Jesus on the cross.

"Okay, this door should lead us to Name's old workstation." Six opened up the door, and a loud alarm went off.

"Huh, the alarm still works." Jack bolted through the door. Upon entering, they saw a naked boy with welts on his backside, praying on his knees at the foot of a statue of Jesus Christ. Iron shackles bruised his wrists and ankles; he was chained to the floor. The small boy turned around and revealed a drooping eye socket with skin melted into folds exposing sinew and bone.

"Who, who are you?" the trembling boy asked.

"I'm Jesus, kid. Your Lord and savior. Who did you expect?" Jack did his best pose of Jesus on the cross.

"Shut up, Jack. The kid's scared shitless, can't you see that." Six took a step in front of Jack and kneeled in front of the boy. "He is not Jesus, but Jesus did send us. Do you think you can help us find something?

"Anything for Jesus. I've been praying, I've been a good boy like the prophet told me to."

Jack strolled around the holy asylum littered with medieval whips, sadistic torture devices, and shattered mirrors lining the walls. Candles burned throughout on shelves covered with religious paraphernalia. Mugs, plates, candelabras, and clocks all held religious depictions of the birth of Christ, God on the mountain, and the Virgin Mary.

"We should burn this place." Jack searched the shelves, dropping a Virgin Mary on her head.

"We're looking for a card, kinda like this one. Have you seen one?"

The boy tilted his head like a dog trying to understand and reached to touch Six's face; he caressed his crow's feet. "Can you take me with you?"

"Fuck! It's not here," said Jack as he rummaged through some dilapidated drawers.

Six grabbed the candelabra and started to strike the boy's chain.

"Hey! What are you doing? We didn't come here to save the children." Jack pushed Six aside and grabbed the kid by the throat. "Where's that pass card you little fucking freak!"

Six jumped to his feet and tackled Jack to the ground as the truck's fuse relay fell out of Jack's pocket.

Enraged, Six burned a stare at Jack, and they waited to see who would flinch first.

Doyle held up Cutter as his bullet wound saturated his leg, leaving a trail of blood.

"Wait, stop! Put me down. I'm slowing you. Leave me."

"Fuck that, don't be stupid." Doyle set him down and ripped the sleeve off his shirt. He used it as a bandage to stop the flow of blood.

Doyle heard footsteps from around the corner. He grabbed Cutter and hid in a dark spot. The prophet jumped out from the hallway. Doyle stuck his leg out and tripped him. The prophet fell flat on his face, breaking his nose.

"Was that a fall from grace, prophet?" Doyle asked as he ripped the prophet from the ground. "Cutter, can you walk?"

"I don't think so, sir."

"Alright, I'll be back. I'm gonna use this prick as leverage." Doyle picked up a piece of sharp glass on the ground and pressed it to the prophet's throat. "Come on, Holy Man, you have some Nukies to preach to."

He held him close and reentered the room. The armed Nukies watched as Doyle walked in holding their prophet hostage.

"Hold your fire!" the prophet ordered.

"What's wrong? Don't you want to be with your God?" Doyle asked. "Now, tell them to drop their weapons."

"My Christian soldiers, please relinquish your weapons. Your judgment is not final. These sinners will feel the wrath of God."

"Shut up! You know what, I'm sick and fucking tired of hearing you talk. In fact, I want you to tell these naïve Nukies that God did not do this to them, it was the government and their nuclear bombs."

"You may do to me as you will, but I'm not giving up the only faith these people have."

"A forced religion is not faith. You people make me sick; you have the answers for everything, don't you! Tell them that there is no God, the truth, or I'm gonna fucking jab this glass in your throat and watch you bleed to death!"

"We are with you, prophet, we will continue on with God's will," an armed Nukie promised, pointing his gun at them.

Doyle dug the shard into the prophet's throat.

"Okay, stop! There is no God, like he said."

"Tell them that religion was made up to control the masses out of fear."

"It's true, everything he said."

The Nukies lowered their weapons and stood agape. The prophet broke free and ran over to the Nukies' side, ripping a gun from one of their hands.

"Now you die, infidel."

Doyle put his hands up, "So you've just proven that you are a liar and a cheat, not even willing to die for your faith. I don't know what you have been preaching here, prophet, but I think the jig is up."

The prophet turned around and saw that the Nukies' guns were pointed at him.

"What are you peasants doing? Do you want to burn in Hell! You will obey the will of God! Damn you people! Listen to me, I am your prophet anointed by Jesus Christ, our Lord and Savior. He is coming soon! And he will only save people with the Holy Spirit!"

One of the Nukies grabbed the gun from the prophet's hands. "For too many years we have been obeying you, prophet, without question." The Nukies pulled out a book that had never before graced their eyes, The Holy Bible. "This is the book you say you preach from, but nothing you say comes from here."

"Where did you get that? You were in my Holy Sanctuary? This is heresy! You're all going to burn in Hell!"

"Only after you," a Nukie vowed, and they pounced on him like starved ravenous animals. They ripped at his flesh, blood gushing everywhere as they mutilated his body.

Doyle slowly backpedalled toward the exit, careful not to disturb the onslaught, but he accidentally kicked over a bucket of holy water, spilling its contents. The Nukies looked up at him, covered in the blood of the prophet.

Doyle nodded and proceeded back into the hallway where Cutter sat.

"Did we win?"

"What do you think? Let's get out of here before they change their minds." Doyle picked up Cutter and carried him out on his back.

Finally reaching the outside, they were blinded by the bright sun. The two trekked across the upended compound, and a loudspeaker overhead ordered all Nukies to the front gates and delivered the news of the demise of their faux prophet. "All outsiders may leave unharmed."

They came across a vehicle that had not been touched in years. Doyle put down Cutter. "Let's see if this car has that fuse." He was able to scrounge up the needed missing part, and they left the compound.

Halfway back to their campsite, Doyle grew weary and had to rest. Off the beaten path was an old gas station. He put Cutter down and propped him up against a gas pump in shade. Cutter buried his head in his bloodied hand and wept. Doyle did not say anything. He knew his loss, and he knew a good cry uninterrupted was sometimes necessary.

"I'm sorry, I just need a few minutes." Cutter stared at an oil stain on the broken concrete. "Fuck!!! We were supposed to be Thunder and Lightning, how's there gonna be thunder without lightning?" Cutter swiped at the tears on his face.

"You don't have to go, Cutter. But don't let your brother's death defeat you."

Cutter nodded and covered the oil stain with dirt, he stood up on willpower alone. "No, let's go, it's getting dark."

Doyle and Cutter reached their campsite and found it in shambles, someone had rummaged through it. "Where are the others? Have they not made it back yet?" Doyle asked. He checked around their pillaged campsite looking for any of their comrades.

Cutter stumbled to the truck and opened up the door. There was Sunshine, hiding under the dashboard. "Found one!"

"Took long enough, where have you guys been? I've been hiding in here for, like, over an hour, you know!"

"I'm glad to see that you are safe, too. Any word on Six and Jack?" Doyle helped Sunshine out.

"Not yet. Wait? Who's that coming over the hill?" Sunshine pointed at a single figure walking toward them.

"It's Jack. But I don't see Six anywhere."

Jack jogged up to them out of breath, "Good, you guys escaped. Fucking crazy Nukies, huh?"

"Where's Six?" Cutter asked.

Jack hesitated then replied, "He didn't make it."

"What do you mean, he did not make it? Where is he?"

"Do you really want me to draw you a picture? He didn't make it! Man, I'm sorry. But I got this." Jack pulled out the pass card.

Doyle grabbed it then paused to take a moment of silence for another fallen friend. "Six died for the cause, and his last mission was completed. He can rest in peace." Doyle walked over to the truck, opened the hood, and replaced the lost fuel pump relay. "Jack, give it a little gas!"

Jack jumped into the driver's seat and started up the engine. It coughed as a puff of black smoke escaped from the muffler. The engine struggled at first but ran.

Doyle slammed the hood shut and jumped in the passenger seat. "Come on everybody, Section A bound."

Sunshine helped Cutter into the back of the truck. The remnants of the Anarchy March drove past the compound. Doyle reflected on the intelligent Nukies. He saw them unrobing their sin-covering clothes, while others unearthed and discarded wooden crosses buried deep in the dirt — an Acephalous community seemed to be inevitable.

"Look how far a species can go in the wrong direction when shown a crooked path."

"So, what were those Nukies, some kind of religious freaks?"

"No, Jack. Just lost and ill-informed people looking for an answer. Everyone needs something to believe in."

Doyle continued to stare at the Nukies' compound as the disillusioned milled around in what seemed like mindless circles.

"Is there, like, any chance for them? I mean, you know, survival and stuff?"

"I don't know, I guess it's up to them now, it's really none of our concern."

Sunshine nodded as she tended to Cutter's bullet wound. Passing through the last part of the compound, she saw a little girl walking along the side of the road. It was little Mary, her head slumped away from the town.

"Stop! Stop the truck!" Sunshine yelled as she climbed to the front.

"What's with this chick; we ain't stopping for nothing."

"I said, stop!"

Jack slowed down, and Sunshine jumped out and knelt next to Mary. "Hey Mary, where are you going?"

Mary pointed down the lonely road to nowhere with tears in her eyes.

Sunshine clasped Mary's hand and led her to the passenger side of the truck as it rolled slowly down the road.

"We can't just, like, leave her like this, you know?"

"It's not our problem," Doyle said firmly.

"It's not our problem, but it is, like, totally our fault. I'm gonna stay."

Doyle stretched his leg to the driver's side and mashed his foot on the brake pedal. "Do what you have to do, Sunshine. If you feel this is your path."

Sunshine handed Doyle's knife back to him, "This is what I care about, not this."

Doyle took the knife. "Cutter!"

Cutter jumped out of the truck and stumbled forward.

"I want you to stay with Sunshine and protect her."

"What about the mission, sir?"

"You can barely walk or fight for that matter. Jack and I can handle it. Heal up and help Sunshine with this Nukie society."

"And what about you?" Cutter asked, thinking that sometimes Doyle's heart was bigger than his brain.

"What about me?" Doyle motioned Jack to press forward.

The truck sped away as Cutter, Sunshine, and Mary walked

back to the compound.

Jack adjusted the rearview mirror. "Eh, we're better off without them. Back to the triumphant trio, Jack the Ripper, Doyle our intrepid leader, and Darla..." Jack stopped his boasting, realizing that there was an important person missing.

"Darla the Daring! We're coming baby, I'll see you soon," Doyle vowed.

Testament VIII

TILL DEATH DO US PART

Another etching on the wall indicates my time in this prison. I am forced to eat ants, beetles, centipedes, roaches, and spiders — the only source of protein I get in this hellhole. One meal a day to share, a form of mashed-up meat that I believe is from other prisoners who could never survive this place. One scream silences another, and like a revolving door in comes another meal. I cannot figure out why we are here and what they have planned for us. In this cellblock, all the prisoners have nothing in common other than gender. My first cellmate only lasted a week before I woke up to find her swinging from the tightly noosed sheets, and it took another week for the guards to remove her dangling body.

Suicide should never be an exit, and I never got to know this woman, her fears and her failures. I began to call my dead cellmate "Sue," Swinging Sue. It was only on the second day while she hung, I noticed a wedding band sliding down her emaciated finger. How will her husband feel when he finds out, if he finds out? Should her death be a secret? Or should I make a story of her being a martyr so her kids join the fight against tyranny? It makes me think about Doyle and how our future will end.

The only thing that is guaranteed in this place is a hypodermic needle at noon every day. They are injecting us with something that makes us feel euphoric, but the cell bars kill the high every time. It makes me feel numb to the world. I cannot feel the cold concrete under my feet, and my words spew like a power-slick politician. In this daze I did something I'm not proud of, but when you are a caged animal, all bets are off — and so was Sue's ring finger. I have been slowly sawing it down. Her bone will become a tool of escape, a shank to freedom. Our next visit from a guard will be his last.

A prisoner in discolored garb ran across a prison cell, slapping her bare feet against the cold concrete. Her scraggly hair had not seen a comb in months, and her face was drenched from fear. "Darla, Darla, wake up. I hear footsteps coming," she whispered.

"Not now, Zee, I'm having a nice dream for once." Darla pushed Zee away and rolled over on a flea-infested blanket.

"I think they're coming to this cell. Whatever happens, you have my loyalty till the end."

"Why do we have to go through this all the time? Those idiots don't know the difference between their ass and a hole in the ground."

"Oh no, this is it! They know everything; we can't hide anymore." Her whisper began to rise to a squeak. "We're doomed. They are going to feed us to the dogs."

"Please, Zee. Just calm down."

A group of military personnel passed by their cell in single formation. Zee hid in the corner, rocking back and forth with her sheets over her head, peeking out as Darla was calmly on the ground.

"Are they gone?" Zee asked through the sheets.

"Long gone."

"That was a close one. I think I saw one look in as they passed. He looked very suspicious of us."

"You know what your problem is, you think too much. You have been in here for what? ... About a week now and all you talk about is getting caught. Look around! We are caught! Those are bars and this is a cell. Let's think positive, alright? Let's think about our families, our loved ones, and how great it would be to see them again."

"I don't have anybody. I mean besides you and the Anarchy March now."

"Shhhh." Darla motioned with her eyes at the ceiling reminding her cellmate that big brother was listening.

"What do you think they have planned for us, Darla?"

"I wish I knew. It's unlike the P.M. to take prisoners. It's always kill first, ask questions never. All I know is that my Doyle is coming, and that keeps me alive." Darla looked down at her bare ring finger, reminded only by the pale band of skin.

"Looks to be only thirty or so of us women in this special prison. Maybe it has something to do with what we used to do."

"Could be, but it's probably more on the lines of: We have captured members of the Anarchy March and we can break them if we keep up with the torture," Darla scoffed.

"I used to tell my students that a just human spirit is the hardest thing to break."

"Sounds like you were a great teacher."

"I was," Zee admitted, shaking her head in disappointment.

"What grade did you teach?"

"Ninth grade, the foundation of morality. It was like I went to sleep one day, and I woke up to this. It just snuck up on us, society. In retrospect, I never asked why when they brought back the Pledge of Allegiance. I didn't think twice when history was not in the curriculum anymore and books were slowly disappearing. I mean, we always had cutbacks." Her eyes welled at the thought, and she shook her mangled hair to cover her mounting despair.

"Is that why you're in here, you started teaching the fundamentals, and they didn't like that, right? Didn't fall into their plans?" Darla's face showed anger, pondering her own disagreement with those so-called "necessary budget cuts."

"No, it was simply worse. I asked my class: What is an exchange of opinion? You go to the P.M. with your opinion and after torture, you return with theirs." Zee drummed her hands.

"That's funny."

"They didn't think so. I was in the middle of a lesson plan when they broke in, slammed me against the chalkboard, and told me that I was a traitor to our nation and a terrorist." A teardrop ran down Zee's downtrodden face. "Is there hope, Darla? Please tell me that there is hope."

"That's all we got."

"Oh no! I hear them coming again, this is it! They heard us

talking, it's over, throw in the towel."

"Relax, breathe with me." Darla took a deep breath, held it for a couple of seconds, then exhaled.

Two dark guards walked right up to their cell and unlocked the door.

Zee screamed, "Stay away from us!" She retreated back into a corner, under the palladium of her sheets.

"She's a feisty one," the squat, grotesque guard grunted and grabbed Zee and pinned her down. He pulled out a syringe and injected her rump, she kicked and screamed.

"What kind of human being are you! This isn't right! Help! Ah...!"

The other more diminutive guard pulled out his syringe and stared at Darla's cold eyes.

"If you think you are putting that thing in me, you're in for a fight."

"I'm just trying to do my job, ma'am." The guard walked toward Darla, and she assumed an attack posture.

"I don't want to hurt you, alright? This is a medicine that will help you not get sick," he tried to assure her.

"Stop being a pussy and inject that bitch!" The obese guard ripped the needle out of Zee's buttocks, leaving her on the ground bleeding.

"I can handle this, alright." He took another step closer as Darla pushed herself back against the wall with fists clenched.

"Please, how about if I give you the needle and you can inject yourself?"

Darla stood firm, maintaining defiant eye contact.

He knew she did not believe a word he said, it was all in her embittered stare.

"My number name is 18211919, you can call me Fig. Your name is Darla, right?"

Darla nodded with uncertainty.

"The last thing I want to do is hurt you and I—"

"Give me the fucking needle! I'll show you how it's done!" The guard grabbed the needle from his reluctant partner and rushed in toward Darla.

She kicked the needle out of his hand, and it slid across the cold concrete.

The guard replied with a back slap across her face, "I dare you to do that again, cunt!"

"Hey! This is my prisoner and my responsibility, Milhous!" Fig grabbed the beastly guard's arm yanking it back.

"What did you call me? My number name is 8466, and don't you forget it." Milhous pulled his arm back from Fig's grip. "And don't ever lay your fucking little rat fingers on me again, rookie. I'm your superior, and I outrank you."

Fig backed off and stood next to the door.

"In fact, I wouldn't be in my right mind if I didn't report your behavior to our commanding officer. I'll have you back in the sewers, sloshing shit around before you can say *Fig*."

Fig's face went pale with worry. "No! I'm sorry, please. I need this job. I have bills to pay, 8466," he pleaded.

"That's better 18211919, now get out of this cell and wait for me outside. I want to teach these little girls a lesson." Milhous unzipped his pants.

Fig stood motionless and dumbfounded.

"I said move!"

Fig hesitated then walked out of the cell and stood off to the side. The cell door slammed behind him. He leaned up against the wall and crouched to the floor. He could hear the horrible sounds of clothing being ripped, desperate whimpers, and the gruesome guard grunting and moaning.

Three high-ranking officers rushed through a secured door in an ultra high-tech room. Inside, sitting around a large round table, was the emergency president of the P.M. He stared at a proposed legislation as if it were a paradox. The emergency president conversed with General Stripes and Lieutenant Bachmann, discussing important projects in the works. A man in a white lab coat conducted a presentation.

"Officer Walton, Hill, and Buck, so glad you could join us,"

The emergency president blurted out upon seeing their panting faces.

"Sorry, Mr. President, we had a few pressing matters to—"

"Just sit down, Gabe. I don't want to hear your excuses today."

Officer Walton took a seat, embarrassed that the emergency president scolded him in front of everyone. Hill and Buck followed and took their seats careful not to disturb the meeting.

"Okay, where was I before I was rudely interrupted? Oh yeah, in addition to their superior intelligence, they will also be ten times stronger, attractive, and completely obedient. Furthermore, this new liquid wonder drug will now increase the fertility time and always keep the ovaries ovulating."

"What's an ovary?" the emergency president asked Lieutenant Bachmann.

"I believe it's a part of a woman's brain, Mr. President."

"The first steps have already been taken. Women prisoners in block 13 are receiving their shots as we speak. Soon we will have a superior race lead by our enemy's children. Any questions?"

The whole room nodded in compliance with the Prominent Municipality connivances except for a lone officer at the far end of the table who raised his hand.

"Yes? You don't have to raise your hand."

"I'm not saying that this idea is not ingenious," he stammered. "By all means it's great, but I do see a Hamartia in your diagram," the uncomfortable officer noted.

"Hamartia?"

"Yeah, well, besides the obvious flaw, the one problem I see is how do you propose you get these women pregnant?"

"Well, it's simple really. We have been injecting high levels of testosterone compounds in the turnkey's water supply. With the guards increased libido we can just let nature take its course."

"Oh? ... Oh! A baby conceived by rape, born a bastard with a reconstructed deoxyribonucleic acid to enhance attractiveness and intelligence will lead our future?"

"And don't leave out obedience," the man in the white lab coat reminded him, tapping his pointer against the graphic display.

The emergency president sat puzzled trying to figure out the incoherent conversation, "deo ... deoxbonulcar acid?"

"D.N.A., sir." Bachmann explained.

The emergency president stood up and exclaimed, "I like it! This will secure the dream that our forefathers so proudly laid out."

"Onto other projects. Operation Koch's Ark is at a standstill due to a lack of funds. Do I need to remind everyone of the importance of this exit plan?" General Stripes asked.

"Cut the hospital funding and raise taxes!" The emergency president slammed his fist on the table with all the gusto that presidents before him had done.

"Mr. President, we demolished the last of the public hospitals decades ago." Officer Hill checked his handheld computer. "The only public funding that we maintain is in ... public bathrooms?"

The emergency president gave Officer Hill a look of tremendous disappointment. He slammed his fist on the table again and said, "Well, then cut public bathrooms. Do I have to think of everything?"

The secured door swung open, and a military officer entered the room. He walked up to General Stripes and whispered in his ear.

"Bring him in."

The officer walked back out the door and reentered with Lee, who was limping and covered in bloodied bruises.

General Stripes covered his nose with a handkerchief and leaned as far away from him as possible. "My men said that you have an urgent message for the Prominent Municipality about the fate of our beloved nation."

"Thank you for seeing me," Lee wheezed. "As you can see by my physical appearance, I just escaped a vicious attack from the A.M. They have taken over at least two sections that I know of so far, Section X and S."

"A.M? That doesn't ring a bell." The emergency president's eyes glossed over with uncertainty.

"The Anarchy March, it's a terrorist group, Mr. President,

which operates on the per-periphery of society outside of the Great Apartheid Wall." Officer Walton explained.

"I know of the Anarchy March, but who is this A.M.? How do you know this bit of information, huh? What, are you smarter than me?"

"It's, it ... I just..."

General Stripes spoke up. "No need to Mr. President, I'm handling the situation, personally. It will be taken care of. As I said earlier, a few stragglers will only pose a minor threat."

"I beg to differ. They have with them a new bioweapon that can destroy this section and its regions." Lee limped around the room, energized by having knowledge unknown to them, those that outranked him.

"Impossible! Destroy us, why would anybody want to do that?" The emergency president quelled his temper by pouring himself some water and drinking it with a small white pill.

"I do have information that can stop this threat in exchange for a section of my own."

The general stood up and walked over to Lee, slapping his hand on Lee's shoulder. "So, let me get this straight. After our original deal to bait the A.M. into your previously owned section, Section X — which I don't need to remind you, you've lost control of — you want to sell me information that is rightfully ours only to fix your problem, in exchange for another section of this great land?" he asked massaging Lee's shoulder.

"I have been loyal to the Prominent Municipality for years now, betraying the A.M. and risking my own life, and I feel that I deserve—"

"You have failed!" the general accused, "and under Law 4954923-489982-432224788-Z, this is punishable by death. So, let's make a new deal, shall we? I will let you live and limp out of here on your own two little legs if you kindly share your information that can stop this treason against our proud nation."

Stunned, Lee looked around at all of the unsympathetic faces.

"Right now!" the general wailed with anger, and grabbed Lee by the collar, throwing him to the ground. "We don't make deals with terrorists! Officer Buck, please shoot this man in the head."

"With pleasure." Officer Buck stood up and pulled out his gun.

"Wait, wait! Stop! Okay, all I know is that the leader of the A.M. is a punk kid named Doyle, and his fiancée Darla is imprisoned somewhere."

"Is that all? I have taken her in, personally. I hope for your sake, that's not all you're selling." The general stepped away from Lee and signaled Officer Buck.

He cocked his gun.

Lee pleaded, "No, wait! They have help from a Dream Child!"

The word Dream Child was something that General Stripes knew intimately. When he heard the title, an uncontrollable facial contortion evolved on his composed face. "What did you say?" he growled, pivoting on a heel, now facing Lee.

"A Dream Child."

"That's a Goddamn lie ... Officer Buck!"

Officer Buck pulled the trigger, shooting Lee in the head. The general stomped out of the room.

"What in Tar Heel is a Dream Child?" The emergency president leaned over, asking Officer Hill.

"It's nothing. You know, Mr. President, you look like you had a rough day, maybe you should rest and let us deal with it." Officer Hill called over a military guard. "Take the president to his quarters."

"No, I'll do it!" Officer Walton jumped up and ran to the president's side. "Can I have a word with you, sir? In private."

"Sure, Gabe." The emergency president walked out of the room with Officer Walton escorting him closely. Before they reached the secured door, the emergency president turned around and said, "Good work men, keep up the good work! I know soon we will have this mess cleaned up. And, oh yeah. Can someone clean this bloody mess up here? As you were." The emergency president saluted the men and clicked his heels together, stepping over Lee's body, as he left the room.

"So, what is it, Gabe?"

"Well, first off you can stop calling me Gabe in front of everyone.

They will not respect me if you keep disparaging me by calling me by my first name, the title is Officer Walton. Remember what father's last words were?"

"Clean out this bedpan, it smells of shit?"

"No damn it!"

"I was just kidding, lighten up, Gabe." The emergency president wrapped his arm around Officer Walton. "You have always been a worry wart, don't worry ... as long as there is breath in my lungs, you'll always have a position in my cabinet. What are brothers for?"

The general walked down the hallway in Block 13 with Fig, who despite being shaken up, maintained his composure and sense of duty. Glancing at the general often, he waited for him to initiate the conversation that he had summoned Fig for.

Without breaking stride, he asked Fig, "Did you notice anything different with prisoner 3459320532 since she arrived?"

"No, not really. She keeps quiet and to herself. She's actually a really nice person."

The general stopped and pivoted, now face to face with Fig. "Nice person? Did you know that this nice person is a plague on our society and would rather see you and your family die than to live free?"

"You're right," he faltered. "Sorry, sir."

The general continued walking. "Maybe you should think first before you speak," he cautioned. When they reached the cell door, the general cracked his knuckles and twisted his neck, loosening up his shoulders. "Open this door," he demanded.

Fig unlocked the cell door. Darla looked up, a calm fear vibrated through her body. Zee saw her fear, and it was contagious.

"Well, hello there. What's the matter? Not the person you wanted to see?" The general towered over her. "I want you to tell me a story. A story about a person named Doyle and a new bioweapon."

"Fuck you!"

"Now that is just flat-out rude. Here I am asking you a simple question and you respond like that. Maybe we didn't learn anything from the last time we sat down and talked."

"Leave her alone." Zee stood up.

"Well, what do we have here? A little A.M. co-conspirator?"

"She doesn't know anything, leave her alone."

"But you do. Don't you?" he sneered.

"And I'm ready to die for it." Darla knelt, bowing her head in mock execution.

"I see that, but is she?" The general walked over to Zee and looked into her frightened rabbit eyes. "Are you ready to die for her cause? How about this, you can go free right now if you tell me everything she has told you. Free as an eagle."

Zee looked at Darla and clenched her jaw.

"Anything at all?"

Zee breathed deep, and upon exhaling, she feigned calm, "I'm sorry, but I don't know this person, and I have no relationship with her other than being cell mates."

"Now that's just not true, because Mr. um, what is your number name again?"

"It's 18211919, sir."

"Mr. 18211919 over here says that you two are like Frick and Frack."

Fig saw Darla shoot him an angry look.

"Excuse me sir, I never—"

"18211919, you can wait outside. Now!"

Fig left the two girls in the hands of the tyrant.

The general pulled out his gun and pointed it at a shaken and scared Zee, aiming it at the side of her head and explained, "Now Darla, you actually have a chance to change something. Save an innocent life or let her die. It's your call."

"I'm so sorry, Zee." Tears began to run down Darla's face wiping away the dirt caked upon her cheeks.

Zee breathed in and out again, remembering what Darla taught her, she smiled through her fear. "Don't be, I—"

A puff of smoke streamed from the hole in Zee's head as her body collapsed. Darla whimpered and turned in horror.

"I guess I'm gonna have to do this the old-fashioned way." The general ran up to Darla and beat her mercilessly. Punch after punch landed with painful precision. Fig unlocked the door and stared at Zee sprawled on the floor.

General Stripes continued beating Darla. "What do you want?!" he asked Fig. "Can't you see I'm questioning our prisoner here?"

"Your presence is required immediately at the command center, sir. The emergency president has called for you direct." Fig clicked back on his handheld transceiver.

"Today is your lucky day, whore. When I get back, you better be singing a different song or, so help me God, I will bury you." The general straightened his uniform, wiped away the blood splatter with Zee's sheet, and then exited the cell. "Leave the body in there. I want her to see and smell the outcome when she doesn't talk."

"Sir, yes, sir!" Fig waited until the general disappeared around the corner and then entered the room. Darla leaned up against the wall bleeding from the multiple gashes that had broken open on her face. "I'm not going to hurt you, have some water." Fig unscrewed his water canteen and knelt down as he put it up to Darla's mouth.

She gulped down the water that she had been deprived of. Fig got a good look at Darla's face, swollen from weeks of abuse. Some of the older cuts looked to be infected, oozing with puss.

"We have to get you out of here. I didn't sign up for this." Fig stood up and got on his handheld transceiver. "Come in base, this is 18211919 from block 13. I have two dead prisoners. I need extraction, A.S.A.P., over."

"10-4, standby, over," the responder replied.

Fig's heart raced with the anticipation of the call being placed. It seemed like his whole life was encapsulated in those few moments. He reflected on his partners rage and lust, the general's brutal abuse, and his own blind allegiance. He felt ashamed.

"The proper call to the disposal unit has been made, over," the voice from the handheld transceiver said.

"Okay Darla, I called for a disposer. I'm going to need you to stay absolutely still and lay next to your friend over there."

"I'll try," she stammered out. "My insides hurt." Darla tried to move but it was clear she was in terrible condition as she coughed up blood.

"If you want out, this is how it is going to happen." Fig helped up Darla and laid her next to Zee, whose terrified eyes were frozen open. Darla could hardly bear it.

"And what happens after this?"

"I don't know, maybe it's best not to know."

Darla looked up at Fig with bloodshot, swollen eyes and replied, "Thank you."

"Don't thank me, I knew about this for a long time now and decided to ignore it. I'm just doing what I was supposed to do as a human being."

"I still thank you." Darla grunted in pain as she moved her legs across the frigid floor.

Fig cracked a smile. "You're welcome, it's been years since I smiled. When you live in fear, there isn't any room for happiness."

"I hear footsteps," Darla assumed the position and remained still despite the pain shooting through her body.

A rotund man and a younger, skinnier teenager unlocked the cell door and entered with two rolling stretchers.

"Ah, not again! This is the third time today. Why can't these Povs just fade away?" The teenager stared down at the two bodies with contempt.

"Shut up, you! If they did, we would be out of a job. I ain't going back to the Clone Factory."[1]

"Don't tell me to shut up. This is the second time today that you said that."

---

[1] Livestock was rare and fleeting fast. To keep up with carnivorous demands, cloning animals for mass consumption was needed. These hybrid animals were grown in acre-sized Clone Factories resembling large watermelon patches. They were genetically modified to have no legs, no ears, no eyes, just layers of fat tissue that tasted like a variety of different meats.

"This is the second time, the third time, I'm sick of hearing about how many times things happen."

"Then close both ears if you don't like what I'm saying."

Fig listened and watched the two bickering back and forth with their petty problems. "Come on guys, we have some bodies that need immediate extraction."

"Hey! We don't tell you how to do your job," the rotund man asserted, and jabbed his middle finger in Fig's chest.

"Yeah, we didn't come here to be ridicu ... ridicu ... laughed at," the novice stuttered out.

"Come in, disposal crew 49, come in."

The rotund man unlatched his two-way radio.

"Go for 49."

"We have another call at detainee station 23, over."

"Can you send another disposal crew, we are currently onsite."

"Negative. It is in your jurisdiction, over."

"10-4." The rotund man reddened with irritation as he put back his radio. "Oh, come on! This is the fifth call today about that."

"Hey guys, maybe I can help you out. I get off pretty soon, and I can bring the bodies to the compacters for you."

"You want to help us?"

"I mean, you know, I don't want these dirty Povs stinking up the place," Fig said. "I was thinking of getting into your line of work anyway. It would be good practice for me," he added.

"I don't know? Our job is really difficult, and it requires a high level of intelli — intelli ... You gotta be smart," the teenager stuttered and stammered while he picked his nose and flung a booger onto the wall.

"I think I can manage. Do you have any pointers?"

The teenager pulled out a large plastic jug from underneath the gurney; it was filled with a clear liquid. "If the body doesn't fit in the compacter, then use this acid."

"Yeah, it helps with any stubborn body parts." The rotund man grabbed the jug from the hands of the teenager and walked over to Darla, unscrewing the cap, "Here, let me show you how it's done." He began to tip the jug.

"Wait! Stop!"

Darla flinched as a drop of acid landed on her arm. The burning acid sizzled on her skin, yet Darla remained quiet.

"What's the problem?"

"Um, I just wanted ... maybe to spend some time alone with them, he-he." The two disposers looked at each other and grinned.

"Oh ... I see. Here is another tip then." The rotund man leaned in and whispered, "You have to get them while they are still warm. My partner over here likes 'em when they are cold, but whatever floats your boat." The disposers stashed their equipment, leaving the acid and the gurneys behind as they walked out of the cell. "Don't have too much fun now, you hear!" the rotund man yelled. The disposers disappeared down the hallway.

Without any further hesitation and despite Fig being physically sick by the inhumane environment, he helped Darla up to the gurney. "Alright, keep absolutely still and quiet." Fig rubbed the white sheet in the blood-soaked ground and covered Darla with it. He rolled Darla down the florescent-lit hallway to its end where he was met by a locked door with a mounted camera.

"18211919, shift is over and asking to be relieved from his duty today, sir."

"18211919, what is that with you? Did you need me to call another disposal unit?" a distorted voice boomed out from the overhead speakers.

"Disposer unit 49 has given me the honor of helping them as they have other pressing matters to attend to."

A few seconds of agonizing silence passed as Fig rocked the gurney back and forth, waiting for the door to be buzzed open. He sighed deep as the security door gave way. Fig increased his pace but maintained his calm as best he could as he approached an overhead passageway to his transport.

Overhead motion-sensitive lights turned on at each step of the way. Although the long passageway seemed to grow longer and darker ahead, Fig pressed on despite his mounting fear. When he reached his transport, he picked up Darla and lifted her into the back.

"Whad'ya got there?" said Milhous, appearing out of nowhere, startling the already uneasy Fig.

"The disposal unit asked me to take this body to the compacters for them because—"

"Whoa, whoa, whoa, they asked you?" he pulled the sheet from Darla's swollen face and smacked his lips together, jiggling his body in a quiver of lust. "I better go with you. I don't want you to goof this up."

"I can handle it."

"Do I need to pull rank again? This prisoner was in my block, and I don't want this coming back to haunt me. Now let's go!"

Fig shut the rear door of the transport and walked to the driver's side but was shoved out of the way.

"Better let me drive also."

"This is my transport. I'm driving!" Fig shouted.

"Don't you dare raise your voice to your commanding officer! Now get in the transport before I report this unruly behavior."

Fig walked over to the passenger side and got in as Milhous squeezed into the driver's side. He adjusted the seat to accommodate his obese frame but still seemed to be squished and awkward behind the wheel. "There we go, now we are at a real man's position, not little girl Fig's." Milhous let out a laugh as he started up the transport.

Fig bit his tongue and took the verbal abuse, knowing that relief was only a few miles away.

"What model is this? And what is that smell?"

"It's Volkswagen's new line, and that smell wasn't in here before you came."

"Keep it up 18211919. One day your insolence is going to get you into a lot of trouble," he warned while setting the G.P.S. on the dashboard. The transport headed to the magnetic highway. "Volkswagen's new line? Maybe for a Pov."

Fig ignored him as he stared out of the tinted windows at other transports passing by in a heavy traffic. He saw a little boy, sitting in the backseat of a car, playing with a toy bomb. The P.M.

logo graced its side while his parents quibbled in front. Fig could not help but wonder about the outcome of his dire situation. As the transport reached the compacters, each lane had long lines, each one labeled.

"I don't see Human Waste signs anywhere."

"It's over there, next to the art compacter." Fig pointed to the sign.

Milhous steered over to the correct lane and parked on automated escalating tracks. The tracks moved them to the top of the three-story compacter. The smell of human refuse lingered in the foul tainted air.

Fig got out and walked to the back of the transport opening up the rear door. He whispered to Darla, "It'll be alright, I'll figure out something."

The grotesque Milhous got out and walked over to the compacter and pressed the button. The compacter walls began to move as he walked back over to the transport.

"You get her feet," he ordered.

Fig grabbed Darla by the ankles as the guard grabbed her by the head. They shuffled over to the gaping hole. Fig looked down. The updraft of stench made him gag.

"Okay, on three. Ready?" Milhous began to rock Darla's body back and forth. With every swing, the draft of decomposing flesh wafted into Fig's nostrils.

"One, two—"

Fig dropped Darla's feet and walked off gagging, "I can't do it," he said, the dry heaves had taken over.

"Stop being a pussy and be a man for once in your life! Look, she's dead," Milhous pulled the sheet off of Darla's face to see her staring back at him. "This bitch is still alive!"

Darla kicked him in the head, energized by rage, and jumped to her feet. Milhous recovered and tackled Darla to the ground. Fig watched in horror as the beast wrapped his hands around her neck. "Die you fucking Pov!"

Darla's face began to turn a dark blue. She wheezed, grabbing his thick forearms. She kneed him in the groin, which further infuriated him. Fig noticed that the compacter walls were about to slam shut. He picked up a large bloodstained two-by-four lying next to the compacter. He raised it and with a powerful swoop, cracked Milhous across the back of his skull.

The stunned Milhous stumbled to his feet, asking, "Why, What are you...?"

Fig dropped the two-by-four, realizing what he had done as images of consequences passed through his mind. Darla regained herself and stood up, punching Milhous in the face. He stumbled back arching into the compacter. The compacter's heavy door slammed shut on his huge head, crushing it like a grape. The door re-opened, and Darla tried to lift the rest of the body inside. "Fig! Hurry! Help me get him in there ... Fig!"

Fig shook off his daze and ran over to help. They lifted the large limp body inches at a time and rolled it into the compacter. Darla lunged at the red button and pounded it. She slumped down and sat next to the compacter, sighing in relief as it sealed shut.

Fig took a seat next to her. "God help me, what did I do?"

"The right thing. Now let's get out of here."

They both jumped into the transport and sped off. They remained quiet until they entered into the suburbia of Section A.

"I thought I would never see the day." Darla admired the seemingly utter blissfulness of the town, while the repetitive white picket fences dividing the manicured lawns framing the family homes sickened her. "I can't believe you people live like this while others die beyond these walls."

"Others? What are you talking about?"

"The rest of the sections in this former country. Where the hell have you been living, under a rock?"

"There isn't anyone living in the wasteland. Is there?"

"You people don't even know that we exist? Where do you think I came from?" she asked. "These walls hide more truth than you can even imagine." She watched white fence after white fence pass them by.

Fig tried to calm his racing thoughts to figure things out. "What am I going to tell my wife?" he asked in dismay.

"We'll tell her there's a revolution coming."

"Revolution? What is that?"

"Wow, I got a lot to teach you, Fig, a lot. Let me introduce myself, I am the Anarchy March and boy do I have a story for you."

They drove into a scenic world that had not been seen since the innocence of the fifties.

Testament IX

ON THE CORNER OF SHANGRI-LA AVENUE AND UTOPIA DRIVE

Across the copy and paste landscape of suburbia, they arrived at Fig's house and pulled into his driveway. Darla was stunned speechless by the block of identical homes in a varying array of pale pastel colors. Fig's was no different — it had the stock white picket fence, two-car garage, plastic grass, and large window planters with lush blooms that overhung the wall.

"I need you to stay in the transport. I have to inform my wife that we are going to be harboring a fugitive."

"Good luck with that. If you need anything, I'll be in here." Darla laid down out of sight.

Fig hurried out of the transport and opened up his front door to a worried and frightened wife. He took a few deep breaths.

She put down her ball of yarn and helped him out of his jacket. "Where have you been? You didn't get fired again, did you?"

Fig looked out the front window to see if anyone had seen him come into the house.

"You know, it didn't bother me that you got fired from that computer programming job, and I just chose to ignore it when you got terminated from that pipe repair position, but you can't just keep changing professions!" She stopped complaining and watched him as he paced in front of the window, worriedly glancing out past the curtains.

"My knitting can only pay for so much ... are you, are you even listening to me?"

"Honey, I love you, but you need to be quiet right now and listen to me."

"I almost used the G.R. card to locate you. That would have put us in the red again. I can't support the both of us with my nursing."

"Please tell me that you didn't!"

"Do what?"

"Use the G.R. card! Tell me you didn't use it, Coy!" a fearful Fig shouted.

"No, why? What's going on? Why didn't you use my number name?"

Fig sat down and covered his face with his hands. He peeked through his fingers, deep into her eyes, searching for the right words. "I helped a prisoner escape today."

"You, what?! Jesus, Fig. Oh brother, now you got me cursing. Why did you do that? Oh my God, is the Prominent Municipality coming here?"

"I don't know how long it will take before they can connect the dots, but I had to do it."

Coy stashed away her knitting needles and began to organize the sparkling room. "What did you do? We have a good life. We have friends and family, a new transport," she said fluffing pillows and rearranging coasters.

"It's all a lie, Coy, and you know it. The Prominent Municipality owns everything."

"You are not the man I married. The man I married loves his government and the great things they provide for us."

"For a price!"

"Keep your voice down," Coy cautioned.

"I'm sick of it. I'm sick and tired. All I do is work, and it seems like we never get ahead. All the bills keep adding up, and for what?!" Fig picked up a handful of unpaid bills, shouting, "Oh look! A new tax, what a surprise! Looks like there will be a new side street tax, on top of the highway tax, road tax, street tax, which I still don't know what the difference between a road and street is!" Fig's face flushed with anger, and Coy watched him pace the living room yelling at the bills, shaking them in the air. "Let's see what else. Oh yes, of course, a pet tax. Now every month we are required to pay for an animal park. We don't even own a damn dog! You see what I am saying, Coy? It never stops! I'm living to work and not working to live."

"I don't understand what you are saying. Where is all this coming from?"

He walked to the kitchen. Coy followed. He unlatched a secret panel in a cabinet and pulled out a bottle of whiskey to pour himself a drink. He paused, shrugged, then quaffed down the cheap liquor straight out of the bottle.

"Where did you get that?" Coy asked, following him around the house. "Please don't tell me that you're drinking an illegal substance in this house."

"I'm sorry, Coy. I can't live like this anymore." Fig collapsed on the couch. "After seeing them beat and rape a woman imprisoned only for telling a joke, then to shoot her after not telling them information she never had..."

"What are you talking about? Why would they do that?"

"I don't know. I don't care anymore. All I know is that when I look around, nothing seems right." His dejection multiplied remembering that he accepted a new overwhelming responsibility. "I love you, Coy. I love you so much, but I need to know where you stand and if it's going to be next to me."

Coy knelt next to Fig, she sensed his sincerity and the heartbreak welling inside his chest. "I love you too, but what is our alternative?"

The front door creaked open, Darla walked in. "Hi, sorry, but it was getting kinda cold out there."

"Coy, I want you to meet Darla. She is part of a resistance called the Anarchy March, and she wants to fight for our freedom, real freedom."

Coy went into the kitchen, attempting to not really notice the fugitive who was bringing her husband down with her. "Um, hi. Do you want a cup of tea?" Coy was appalled seeing the woman's beaten face. She had never seen so many gashes and welts and on someone who seemed so frail and harmless.

"Tea? That would be fucking lovely."

"Hey, you can't go in there! The emergency president is engaged in a very important meeting."

The general stopped at the Oval Office doors, straightened out his jacket, turned around, and walked back toward the desk of the secretary with a piercing stare. "Hey? Is that how you address the general of the Prominent Municipality?"

"I'm sorry, sir, but the president gave me strict orders not to be bothered until his official business is finished. I'm just doing my job."

"Your job is to obey, and as your commander, you shall." General Stripes stepped back giving the defiant secretary some space. "I want you to give me a ten count."[1]

"Excuse me? Sir?"

"You heard me."

She slowly cleared her desk, moving her family photos and a framed letter of commendation from her superior to the side. The general's intense stare stabbed through her as she extended her neck and then slammed her head on the desk.

"Ten! Nine! Eight! Seven! Six!" a drop of blood emerged, "Five!" her eyes crossed as she raised her dazed head, the room spun around and around, she grit down, her teeth slipped and she bit her tongue.

"Is this going to take much longer?" the impatient general asked, checking the time on his wristwatch.

"Four! Three! Two! One!"

"Do it again."

"Please, I ... I can't."

---

[1] There were many rules in the Institute of Indoctrination for the youth of Section A; and for every rule broken, there was a specific punishment. The Ten Count was a self-implemented punishment ordered by a superior while being viewed by his or her peers. Apply a forward and forceful motion to a surface harder than your skull. Count down on each impact and avoid unconsciousness or one would have to start over when woken back up.

"Do it again!" his beet red face blurted in anger.

She wiped the blood from her forehead and pushed off the blood-spattered photos, "...Ten!" the violent impact knocked her out, and she collapsed to the floor.

"You're fired," he said leaning over her. He then stormed into the Oval Office.

The emergency president sprang out of his chair, his pants half down, sweating profusely. "I told everyone, no walk-ins today! Doesn't anyone listen to the president anymore?"

"You sent for me, Mr. President? You said you have an urgent message." General Stripes saw a pair of high heels sticking out from under the desk.

"I never made such a call!" The emergency president pulled up his slacks and zipped in his erection.

"I see." The general scratched his chin and took a seat placing his feet close to the high heels. "Mr. President, I see treason afoot. The people are getting unruly and undisciplined. We need to stop this uprising before it gets out of hand."

The president dabbed his face with a handkerchief and stared out the window overlooking the rose garden. "I don't see it, Stripes. All I see is birds chirping and crazy squirrels nutting around."

"I was lied to today. A diversionary tactic from inside Section A."

"A civilian lied to you?" the President asked with shock.

"We have a problem, Mr. President, and I'm going to take it upon myself to solve this problem personally."

"Uh, you are the general of the Prominent Municipality. Don't we have people on staff that can deal with this matter?"

"Mr. President, you forget, earlier in my career I was a field operative, and I'm not afraid to get my hands dirty."

The president admired a chirping bird delivering a nut to the squirrel sitting on an apple blossom branch. "Maybe you are right about the people, you give them an inch and they walk all over you. Do what you have to do, general, to secure and uphold the name of this great nation. Shut down all amusement parks until further notice."

"Yes, Mr. President!"

"Good work, general, and God bless you."

The general nodded, stood up, and marched out of the Oval Office.

The emergency president sat back down, sighed, and pulled his pants back down around his ankles, "Now, where were we? Oh yes, an executive order." He leaned back in his chair in complete bliss.

Darla was enjoying her cup of tea; the delicious flavor of Earl Grey had not graced her mouth in what seemed like an eternity. In fact, everything she did was with extreme sensitivity and care. She did not want to miss a moment of her freedom, at least what was left of it. She sipped from her cup and looked around at the bareness of their house that shouted *conformity*. Only two framed photos hung behind the couch, one of a person and the other what looked like a will. She broke the silence. "I couldn't help but notice that you have pictures on your walls. Isn't art illegal?" Darla stared at the older man in the photo.

"No, those are the only pictures that we are allowed to have. It's just a friendly reminder showing that the emergency president is always looking out for us, the people."

"Friendly reminder, huh?" Darla stood up and walked over to the picture. "So that's the man. Funny, I was expecting somebody with horns and a lizard tail."

Coy jumped out of her chair, losing her composure, and shouted, "He is a good man, and I will not just stand here and listen to you bad mouth our savior. If it wasn't for him and his family, we would all be in the wasteland." Coy ran upstairs to their bedroom.

"Excuse us for a moment," Fig said and then ran after.

"What did I say?" Darla studied the other picture. Shock and shivers ran down her spine as she read the fictitious iniquity in print. She ripped it off the wall and followed the hushed voices to the bedroom.

"What the fuck is this?"

Fig held Coy as she cried in his arms.

"It's the Constitution. What, is there something wrong with the Constitution? The Constitution that we've honored for over two thousand years now?"

"I have read the Constitution and this is not it. Why do you have this hanging next to the E.P.'s picture? Quite frankly, that scares the hell out of me."

"Amendment 66 clearly states the Bill of Rights should always hang six inches from the President's picture. It's always been like that! Since as far as I can remember!" Coy shouted in between sobs, then blew her nose in a knitted napkin.

Darla sneered at the altered Constitution as she began to read out the amendments, "This is absolutely absurd! I was never a big fan of the Constitution, but this is flat-out wrong. The First Amendment is not the right to go to church every Sunday! What is this garbage? The Fourth Amendment is supposed to protect the people from unlawful entry, not condone it!" Darla was amazed by the mockery of the real Constitution. "It all makes sense now, in time it becomes truth," she muttered.

"Are you sure? I mean this is all very farfetched."

"Am I sure? You think I'm just saying this for the fun of it? Are we having fun yet? I'm not going to even dignify that with an answer, Fig."

Their discussion was interrupted by the bird-chirping doorbell.

"What the hell was that?"

"Oh no! I forgot that 3248924 and 2384989 are coming over for dinner tonight."

"Who?" Darla took cover behind the door.

"Our neighbors. Alright, everyone act normal, we don't want to raise any suspicion." Fig pointed at Amendment number 44. He stood up and walked to the front door. Darla glanced over the Amendment that read: Under the Prominent Municipality, We the People shall report any and all suspicious acts that do not follow the Constitution, or the same consequences will be endured by both parties.

Fig tucked his shirt in, swept his hair back, and opened up the door to his neighbors wearing "his" and "hers" knitted sweaters. "Hi, how are you doing you two? Wow! 2384989 did you lose some weight? Those sweaters fit you perfectly. Coy will be pleased."

"Thank you, I'm so glad that you noticed. I'm on a new diet." The neighbor blushed. "No Christmas lawn ornaments this year?"

"Haven't got to it yet, he-he. Where are my manners, do come in. Coy ... I mean 8739293 is just finishing up dinner." Fig reached out to give his neighbor a handshake. "3248924, always a pleasure." He responded by crushing Fig's hand.

"Is this sweater supposed to be this itchy?" 3248924 pulled Fig in close, inches from his face, and through a forced smile said, "I hope it's not organic veggies again, you know I can't stand that fake food." The neighbor walked into the dining room and sat down at the table.

"Oh, where is your Constitution?" 2384989 asked politely.

Coy and Darla came down from the bedroom carrying the Constitution. Darla was dressed in a flowered frock that was a little too large for her. "We were just thinking about maybe hanging it in the bedroom, to keep us warm at night." Coy hung the frame back up. "But if we did that, our guests wouldn't be able to bask in its presence while having dinner."

"Good thinking," 2384989 said, sitting down at the dinner table, staring at Darla's poor makeup job.

A bit of vomit crawled up Darla's throat. She spit on the Constitution's glass frame, and rubbed it down with her sleeve, "Nothing that an old-fashioned spit-shine can't fix."

"Yes, well, uh, I want to introduce to you my, um, uh, my cousin, 3459320532." Fig introduced Darla to his suspicious neighbors.

"I was not aware you had other living relatives in Section A," the man replied.

"Oh, I'm the quiet one. I keep to myself, just trying to survive in this great nation. You know, not ruffle anyone's feathers."

"Ha ha, anyways, hope you're all hungry." Fig grabbed Coy and went into the kitchen.

"I know I am! I haven't eaten for what seems like years." Darla's sarcasm did not go unnoticed.

"Where did you say you were from?"

"I didn't say, and I'd rather not. Hey! Who is up for a game of name that sin?"

Meanwhile in the kitchen, Fig was trying to calm the tense atmosphere. "Do we have something we can nuke really quickly?" he suggested.

"I don't know. I'll find something. You better get back in there. I don't think leaving Darla with them is a good idea. Have you seen her face?" Fig's eyes widened, and he hurried off back to the dinner table.

"So, do you like living in Section A?"

"Whatever do you mean? Where else would one live?" 2384989 was puzzled by her question.

"Ha ha, she's quite a cut-up, isn't she?" Fig suggested, then tried to change the focus. "Did you take your medicine? She got a little work done and those pain killers, well I don't have to tell you." Fig added on the fly, staring at 2384989's perfectly constructed jawline, bobbed nose, and taut complexion.

"Oh, I feel fine." Darla shot a quick glance at the neighbors. "It is just a simple question," Darla probed.

3248924 huffed. "Better to live in here than to die like Povs in the wastelands," he boasted.

"So, you know that there are people living beyond these walls, and it doesn't bother you?"

"I used to be an Apartheid Wall gunner, back in the day. Those disease-racked Povs got what they deserved."

"Hungry women and children is all they are!"

"Young lady, I don't like where this game is going."

"Hey, hey, she's just not feeling so well. Hey, let's see what's on T.V. before we enjoy my wife's lovely cooking." Fig switched on the television panel hoping to defuse the ticking time bomb of an argument. He flipped through the channels littered with news programs and commercials, trying to find something worth watching. "Oh, I almost forgot the execution is on tonight."

Coy walked out of the kitchen as Fig invited the guests into the living room. The channel's broadcast showed an innocent-looking man with glasses sitting in a chair. Tubes were jammed in his arms, and a noose hung around his neck. The announcer walked into view and greeted a happy civilian sitting in the front row. "And this week's lucky winner is 438758439! She will be helping our firing squad this evening. How do you feel?"

"Like a billion bucks!" the contestant shrieked.

The announcer walked over to the prisoner; his demeanor morphed into an ominous state. The lights dimmed and music belted out a deep mesmerizing tone. "6986898699 is sentenced to death for crimes against humanity and the Prominent Municipality. Under law 759843275-B, for water consumption abuse, under law 785743875-R, walking off the sidewalk in a non-walking zone, under 874328724-Y, not picking up your dog waste..."

Darla watched the television in complete awe as the announcer continued with a rap sheet of crimes one might commit walking through a park. Her face turned pale as the ridiculous allegations continued to pile up. She was bewildered by how the people were forced to live.

"And finally, under law 3244893427-K, over-extension of time spent sitting on a bench. Do you have any last words?"

"The voice of God is government," the condemned man stated.

"Commence the execution!"

"How exciting this is." 2384989's crazed eyes glossed over with blood lust.

The tubes sticking in the man's arms began to inject a purple liquid into his veins. The man jerked as the poison ran through his blood stream. An invisible toxic gas filled the room as the man coughed, spewing out blood from his mouth and nostrils. A switch was turned on, and fifty thousand volts of electricity shot through his wilting body. His body quivered then stopped after the electricity was turned off. The floor dropped from under him, the chair crashed down into a fire pit. The flames rose and engulfed his body as it hung from a noose.

"Ready, aim, fire!" The firing squad riddled the body with bullets as the fire licked the charred flesh. It burned for a few moments longer then a large saw swiped across the room, decapitating the burning corpse. The head swung from the noose as the camera zoomed in.

"Oh, I'm sorry, but it looks like contestant 438758439 missed her shot. Better luck next time. Tune in tomorrow for the season finale. It is going to be a killing!"

Darla grabbed the remote and turned off the television.

"Hey! They were going to announce who's on tomorrow's execution. I hope it is 432809324, so we can finally get our credits," 3248924 boasted, grabbing the remote away from Darla and turning the television back on.

"We reported him last month. Boy we sure could use that baksheesh reward."

"What! What! This is..." Darla stammered, at a loss for words.

Fig stood up and escorted Darla to the stairs, "She's not feeling too good after the, um, the enhancements." Fig and Darla disappeared up the stairs and into the bedroom.

"Is she going to be alright? She's not sick, is she?" 2384989's left eyebrow perked, already cashing the reward.

"Oh, no, no, no. It's just her Eve's time of month. Not mixing well with her prescription drugs."

3248924 huffed, "Figures. Woman stuff. Anyways, where's food?"

"Please take your seats, I'll have it ready in just a few..." Coy walked back into the kitchen as the neighbors sat down.

"They are acting really strange, don't you think, dear?"

"Yeah, unfortunately acting strange is not reportable. Not yet! Ha ha!"

Coy brought microwaved dinners out and put them in front of her guests.

"What is this?" 3248924 poked around at his peas.

"I'm sorry, but the pot roast overcooked. I hope you're a Hungry Man!"

"I feel sorry for your husband. Can't even enjoy a home-cooked meal in his own castle."

"Now 3248924, not everyone is blessed with talents in the kitchen."

"Well, thank God you are! Right, honey? Or I would have to upgrade to a newer model. Ha, ha, ha!" he said between mouthfuls of food.

Fig came walking down the stairs. "My wife's cousin will not be joining us. She hasn't been sleeping much." He sat down and they all began to eat.

3248924 stopped chewing on his soggy peas and said, "Your wife's? I thought you said she was your cousin."

"Our cousin, by marriage," Fig said gulping down a forkful of mashed potatoes.

Not another word was spoken between them. The background television audio provided the conversation. The consistent flow of commercial advertisements polluted their conscious.

A cool brisk southern wind blew through the window curtains. The empty bed where Darla had laid was now just an imprint. The open window revealed her escape. She found herself walking around lost in the suburban town. What caught her attention was that every ten feet there was a sign posted about some law or other. It was a constant reminder that freedom was a figment of the Section A citizens' imagination.

She walked around in the dark, no streetlights, only the dull light from the law signs. After seeing a sign about curfew, she tried to stay out of sight, bouncing from shadows to shadows like a lost rat. *I need to get out of here. I can't handle this anymore. I'll take my chances on the outside,* she thought as she noticed the surroundings becoming increasingly bare. The trees and natural green lawns turned into hard pavement. She looked up at a massive warehouse with a bright light coming through the windows, smack in the middle of the suburbanite oasis. *What is this?* Darla wanted a closer look and walked toward the front door. It creaked open and she dashed around the corner of the building as two men came out on a cigarette break.

"You got one for me?"

"No! This pack cost me a lot of credits. Get your own."

"No? So you don't want to share your illegal substance with me," the man said with a smile.

"Just joking, here you go buddy." He gave a cigarette to his co-worker for fear of getting reported.

Darla looked around on the ground for something she could use as a weapon. A few rocks was all she could see. She grabbed the biggest one and feigned a limp around the corner, hiding the rock behind her. "Help me, I've been raped! Help me!"

"Oh my God! Are you okay, ma'am?"

"Who did this, who raped you?"

Darla swung her rock, smashing the first man in the face, knocking him out.

"The System!" Darla leaped onto the other man's back as he tried to flee. She tightened her grip around his neck, choking off the blood flow to his brain. He fell limp, and she jumped off and smiled at her handiwork. She dragged the bodies into some bushes off to the side of the building and entered the mysterious warehouse.

Thousands upon thousands of glass coffins lined the warehouse. They hung suspended in the air like clothing on a garment conveyor. The coffins were filled with tiny tubes and wires that ran from the heads of elderly people encased inside. These tubes stretched out and hooked into a main computer brain that was set in the middle of the warehouse. She walked over to the ten-foot-high super-computer and looked at the hundreds of monitors in amazement. "What is this? Some kind of fake reality?"

The elderly people on the monitors were walking and talking to each other, going on with their useless existence. Darla walked up to one of the glass coffins. A hairless, old naked man, stripped of any identification, stared back at her. She tapped on the glass but received no response.

"Don't touch that!" a voice said from behind, startling her.

"What the hell, Fig, you scared the shit out of me!"

"Good, serves you right. You can't just sneak off in the middle of the night. If you get caught, I get caught and so does Coy."

"What is this place?"

"You've never heard of a Social Security warehouse? Oh yeah, I forgot, outsider. This is where you go after you hit the age of sixty-two. No use for you anymore. If you are too old to work, then you're too old to live. At least in this reality."

She stepped back to take it all in.

"Welcome to The System, a virtual reality world for the living dead. Their social security pays for a hope that one day they will actually ... I really don't know what they are looking for, an age rejuvenator or the fountain of youth. In any case, they're waiting for an answer."

"They are going to be waiting for a fucking long time under this government."

Fig stared at the monitor; a lonely old grandmother was feeding some birds at a park bench. "They say some have been in here so long that they don't even remember what reality is." Fig was delirious in his thoughts of his own loneliness.

"This place freaks me out, let's get out..." Her words trailed off as she lost consciousness and fell to the floor. She went into another seizure.

"Darla! Darla! What are you doing? Oh my God!" Fig tried to comfort her, but he was scared, unaware of her condition. "Tell me what to do!"

Darla foamed at the mouth as she bit down on her tongue, blood gushed and mixed with the foam.

Fig picked her up and carried her running out of the warehouse.

Darla's mind roused to a familiar and soothing voice. "Honey, wake up."

"Huh? Doyle? Where am I?"

"Don't be silly, honey, we are in our beautiful two-story house and it's Sunday. Get dressed. We are going to be late."

"Late for what?"

"Church, of course, buttercup."

"Buttercup? Church? What's going on? Doyle is that really you?"

"The man you married. Now stop playing around, I have some

great news for us. We were invited to the inauguration of the new president."

"The emergency president is gone? We won?"

"Of course we did. The new president is a great and wise man known across the land for his reason and responsibility to the people under the Prominent Municipality."

"What! Please tell me you're joking."

"I really think his son is going to be a better president than he was. After all, he promised us he would."

"No, this can't be happening, and why are you okay with this? What happened to the Anarchy March?"

"The Anarchy what? Are you feeling okay? Do you need me to call a doctor for you, honey?"

"No! No! Don't call anyone. This is not real!"

"Here, take a few of these." Doyle gave Darla two electric blue pills. "This will help you sleep."

"I don't want to sleep! I want my Doyle back!"

"I'll just tell the president that you were feeling a bit under the weather. I'm sure he will understand; after all, he is wise beyond his years. Now that I think about it, he's almost God-like."

"God-like? You stupid fuck! You sold out! What happened to the cause, the liberation ... and us?"

"You're cute when you're sleepy. Wasn't it you that told me if you can't beat them, join them?" Doyle's sadistic smile stretched across his face.

"Ah! No!" Darla woke up screaming, terrorized from the conformist nightmare.

"Whoa! Whoa! Calm down, Darla. It's alright, you're safe now." Fig laid her back on the bed.

"What happened?" Darla's bugged eyes scanned the room.

"I don't know, you just collapsed and started rolling around on the ground inside of the SS warehouse. You're not sick, are you?" Fig asked.

"I just had an epileptic fit."

"It's not contagious, is it?" Coy backed away covering her

mouth.

"No, it's not contagious! Maybe if you people would learn about things rather than just killing us off, you'd understand more about my condition."

"I'm sorry for our ignorance, we're trying."

Darla rubbed her forehead. "I just had the worst nightmare any human being could possibly have. And you know what? I think I'm still living it. I got to get out of here and find Doyle."

"You're fiancé, right? Maybe when you find him, we can go on a double date. Remember when we used to do that, Fig? Oh, the good old days."

"I don't think your wife comprehends what is going to happen when my fiancé arrives with the Anarchy March. This way of life will cease to exist. There will be no leisure time for double dating. A revolution is coming unlike anything you have ever seen."

"Surely there will be time for a double date. Oh! Or maybe we can have a Tupperware party."

"Yeah! Like that's gonna happen, the Anarchy March and the P.M. is going to have a giant Tupperware party, sitting down and talking out their differences." Darla's sarcasm thickened the tension in the room. "There will be bloodshed in epic proportions!"

"That doesn't sound very nice. That's terrible!"

"It's not supposed to be nice! It's war!"

Coy straightened the curtain pleats. "I don't know if I really want this to happen. Fig and I had a good life until you showed up. Maybe if you go away, things can go back to normal."

Darla stood up, turned Coy around, and pressed her against the wall. "Go away? What are you going to do, rat me out, huh? Listen to me, sweetheart. You have no idea what these fucks have been doing to millions of people for almost a century now. I saw my mom's brains fly out at me and cover my face from a bullet, just because she couldn't understand the reality. I've seen children die from starvation as their mother takes the last of their food capsules. It's hell out there, alright. I'm fucking sorry if this little world you live in suits you just fine. But let me ask you something, would you feel different if you were on the other side? Because, sweetheart, you are now!"

"She's right, Coy, we're in this too deep now. In fact, I have to go to work and erase any and all records of me working there before they catch on."

Coy followed Fig to the front door and said, "Jesus, bless your soul. Be careful, won't you? I don't know what I would do without you." They collapsed into each other's arms, shutting out the world crumbling around them.

Darla watched their love soothe the anxiety. "You two give me hope. I know we can change the world when the people unite and show some compassion for one another."

"Well, on that note, I better get going. Don't want to be late for work."

"Yeah, you don't want to get fired, right?" Darla snickered.

"No, I don't want to lose another finger." Fig waved goodbye, the finger count on his hand ended at four.

"Trust me, it's going to get better." Darla cupped his hand.

He grabbed his hat. "I hope so."

Fig went into work as if it were a normal day at the daily grind. He sat down at his computer and began to delete his workplace existence and time in Section A. Hours passed by as he pounded away on the keyboard. He stood up and paced, paranoid there might be records he had forgotten or any lose ends he should tie up. "Oh yeah! How can I forget about the T.M.V.?" Fig ran to the desk.

He noticed that a ceiling security camera was pointed at him instead of down the cellblock hall. Fig tried to relax while he typed, keeping one eye on the camera. He stood up and walked over to the water cooler, and the security camera followed his every movement. He trembled as he drank some water. He sat back down knowing his time would soon be up. "Done, only one last thing to do."

He walked down the hallway to Darla's cell and loaded up Zee on the remaining gurney. She smelled of rotting flesh and the maggots had wasted no time incubating in her body. He took his last walk back down the lonely hallway knowing big brother had a fixed eye. He reached the locked door at the end and talked into the speaker, "This is unit 49; I'm here to extract the last body from cell block 13."

"Unit 49, we did not dispatch your assistance today, over."

"Number name 18211919 called for us yesterday and we were a little overwhelmed. I'm here to pick up the pieces."

"Stand by."

A million bad thoughts ran through his mind: *It's not going to work, The System is too big to fail, who am I to say the —*

"You are clear unit 49; have a blessed night," the voice boomed. Fig sighed with relief as the door buzzed open and the long hallway reached out to freedom. Fig pushed the gurney out to his transport, loading up Zee's body, and headed off to the compacters to get rid of the last bit of evidence. He kept one eye on the rearview camera in his transport. His clothing stuck to his skin drenched with perspiration. *What am I doing? Where am I going?* Thoughts of doubt clouded his mind as he passed a sign reading: The Prominent Municipality is here for you. He looked in the rearview camera to see flashing red and blue lights. P.M.P.D. was pulling him over. An electric pulse was fired from the police officer's vehicle, disabling Fig's transport. As the P.M.P.D. car slowed to a halt, the officer stepped out, his helmet in place wearing thick dark glasses that hid his eyes and most of his face. He walked up to the driver's side.

"How are you doing, officer? Nice night we are having."

The police officer silently stared.

"Um, what seems to be the problem? Was I driving too fast? I'm kinda in a little hurry."

The officer continued to stare at Fig, making him feel increasingly uncomfortable.

"Step out of your transport, now," he demanded.

As Fig got out, the police officer grabbed him and led him to the rear.

"I'm not sure what I did, officer. There's no need for that." Fig was trying his best to stay calm.

"What is this?" The officer pointed at Zee's leg stuck in between the rear door.

"Oh my gosh! Officer, I can explain. I work at cell block 13 and this is a prisoner."

"Shut up! Do you have any idea how many people could have seen this while you drove casually down the road? You have to be more careful, Fig."

"How do you know my real name?"

The officer took off his helmet and glasses. "Long time no see, buddy."

"Is that you, Gamaliel?"

"It's Officer 459049544 to you," he said with a seriousness that ended in laughter. He slapped his friend's arm. "Just kidding. How have you been?"

"You scared the fudge out of me. I'm so glad it's you. Last time we saw each other was, what? Ten years ago, when we worked in that programming job together?"

"Yep, I hated that job. I wanted more people-oriented work, to give back to the community." Gamaliel caressed his baton. "So here I am."

"I'm sorry I didn't keep in contact with you after you moved, life got in the way."

"Maybe another time we can catch up, but for now, I need to ask you about this body. You're not doing anything illegal are you, buddy?"

"Oh no. I'm a correctional officer now, you know, a prison guard."

Gamaliel looked Fig up and down with uncertainty, judging him by his meek facade. "You? Naw, I remember when 62823742 used to put gum in your hair every Friday and we spent all of Saturday cutting it out, missing the stick ball game every time."

"It's true. I swear ... I mean, I don't swear, but if I did, I would. Anyway, I was just taking this dead prisoner to the compacters and—"

A dispatcher's voice boomed out of Gamaliel's two-way radio

and requested an update on the traffic stop. He reached to answer the request, but Fig grabbed his wrist preventing him from answering the status request.

"Remember when we were kids and you stole 1754's pie from her window?"

"1754? Oh, Mrs. Smith." Gamaliel looked around, hoping no one was listening to their forbidden conversation. "Yeah, why?"

"You ran up to me crying, thinking for sure that the Prominent Municipality were coming for you, so I helped you bake another pie to replace it before Mrs. Smith found out."

"Ha, I remember. You were always a good friend to me."

"Come in, Officer 459049544! Are you Code Four? What is your status?"

"I need a return favor, please don't answer that call."

Gamaliel saw the grave look on Fig's face as he picked up his radio. "Officer 459049544, I'm Code Four, pulled over a defective transport, issuing a repair order, over." Gamaliel attached the radio to his belt. "What's going on Fig?"

"I have been contacted by a person from outside the Great Apartheid Wall." Fig looked around cautiously. "She said that a revolution is coming."

"People are living in the wastelands!"

Fig shushed him. "Not so loud. Are you ever just tired of living in constant fear?"

"Sometimes, but I'm working on that in church."

"No! That's not what I'm talking about, that's just part of the problem. Listen to me and hear me out. You need to trust me on this. I really don't have the time to discuss this right now. I need to take this body to the compacter and then I'll explain everything."

"You never lied to me before, Fig, and I do owe you one. How about this, I'll escort you there so you will not have any more problems. Then we can talk about this revolution."

"Thanks, Gamaliel." Fig returned to his transport as Gamaliel pulled ahead of him, leading the way.

Fig took the opportunity to calm down as they drove onto the highway. He called his wife on the videophone to update her.

"Hi!"

"Is everything okay? Where are you?"

"So far, so good. I bumped into Gamaliel, you remember Gamaliel, right? Anyway, he's with the P.M.P.D. now, and he is escorting me to the compacters." Fig could hear Darla shouting something in the background, and Coy trying to shut her up by waving at her.

"Fig, Honey, is it safe for you to be talking to me on this right now?"

Darla jumped into the frame of the videophone, "Fig, get out of the transport, right now!"

"What? Why?"

"You can't trust anyone here, especially a P.M. police officer. Get out!"

"No, you got it all wrong. I'll be home soon. Don't worry. I've known Gammy since childhood; our parents went to church together. Huh? That's weird..."

"What's going on?" Coy asked.

"We just missed the exit to the compacters."

"Get out now!" Darla screamed just as the transmission went dead. Then Gamaliel appeared on the screen, "Just hold on buddy, I know a shortcut."

Fig hesitated; fear set in. "On second thought, maybe I should do this by myself. I don't want to get you involved," he blurted.

Gamaliel had a blank stare, "It's too late for that."

The videophone shut down, and the doors of the transport locked. Fig had no control over the vehicle. He frantically tried all the controls, but nothing.

"No, Gamaliel! Let me out!" Fig punched the windows, barely leaving a mark from his child-like hands. He began to hyperventilate as they exited onto an unknown off-ramp, passing "Do Not Enter" and "Men at Work" signs. A steady incline led to a forested area on top of a hill lit by the pale moonlight that overlooked the Great Apartheid Wall. Fig saw a shadowy figure standing in the dark waiting for them to pull up. The headlights revealed General Stripes standing with his arms behind his back, a snarl curled his lip.

"No!" Fig kicked at the windows but to no avail.

Gamaliel released the door locks and walked over to Fig's transport. He pulled Fig out and threw him on the ground in front of the general.

"Good work, Officer 459049544, or should I say Captain 459049544."

"Thank you, sir." Gamaliel proudly saluted.

"Leave us. We have an interesting topic to discuss." The general waved him off.

Gamaliel walked past Fig, looking down in disgust. "I'm sorry 18211919, what's friendship if you have credits and a new promotion." Gamaliel jumped in his transport and took off.

"What are you doing here?" The general took out his half-smoked Rubusto and lit it up.

"I don't know. I don't know what's happening."

"You don't know? You're a threat to national security and harboring a known terrorist. And you say, I don't know? Let me inform you, if you haven't been paying attention for the last few decades. Your friend there just got a promotion for obeying the laws and the Constitution. His future is bright and promising. You, on the other hand, seem to be on a different path, one of self-destruction filled with poisonous ideas and deluded thoughts."

"I'm confused. Darla said so many things. I don't know what to believe in." Fig trembled.

The general stood proud and looked beyond the Great Apartheid Wall to an old, burned-out town in Section C. "This is where my career started years ago. You see that place over there. That was one of the many towns that I was told to torch while the Povs slept. I didn't ask any questions; I just did what I was told to do. I found out later it was to make room for this Great Apartheid Wall." The general introduced the wall as if he built it himself. "This wall has been our salvation from all threats that oppose our freedom. I trust in our government, unconditionally, and look where I am. The System works for those who want it to work, and most important, those who believe in the Prominent Municipality. It's very simple and it starts with the swaddle at infancy, Fig. Does it not?"

Fig replied, "Yes ... sir..." through chattering teeth.

"You want to be called Fig, and the Prominent Municipality needs you to be 18211919. Do you understand what I'm saying?"

Fig thought to himself and a calm swept over him. He stood up tall, "I do, I think for the first time in my life I understand. You want me to not have an identity, not to think for myself, and to become just another faceless gear in the machine to keep it moving forward for those who built it, namely the Prominent Municipality. For what, though? For material things? Peace of mind? Freedom? I'm sorry, I don't feel any of those."

"Don't apologize. Some people just don't work out and can't be fixed."

"I'm a human being! Not a tool! Look at me!" Fig yelled.

The general stormed up to Fig. "You're nothing! And may God have pity on your soul." The general pulled his gun and pointed it between Fig's eyes. "When will you people learn life is a privilege and has to be earned? I want you to give me a ten count, for seconds you have to live ... Come on, ready? I'll start, ten, nine, eight, seven, six, five." The hammer on the gun cocked back and clicked into position.

Fig closed his eyes and picked up the count. "Four, three, two, one."

A piercing light cut across the sky — thunderous explosions and an enormous glowing mushroom cloud formed in the night sky. The general's eyes widened as sonic blasts knocked him to the ground. He stood back up, awed by the firepower in the distance. While the general stood mesmerized, Fig ran into the nearby bushes.

"It's time, the apocalypse has finally come." The general moved back to his transport and drove to headquarters to deal with the threat head on.

Testament X

RISE ABOVE

Abandoned bulldozers and cranes, mounds of exhumed dirt and discarded trash littered the desolate region. The truck rocked unsteadily over the broken roadway that gave way to a smoother paved road. Doyle and Jack approached the open perimeter gates of Section A. The colossal wall dwarfed them, towering above the horizon. Name's blueprint looked pretty minuscule now.

"Would you look at that." Jack stared at the wall and all of its impregnable glory.

"I'm not impressed. Pull over here."

Jack pulled over to the side of the road a few miles from the security gates. Doyle jumped out of the truck and laid out the blueprints across the hood to go over the last details.

"Alright Jack, we're going to act cool, no sudden movements. In a few hours it will be the Twenty-Fifth. We'll show up, show them the pass card, and hopefully, smooth sailing through those rotating walls."

Jack looked at Doyle with mounting uncertainty. "I'm not trying to be a dick, but I have been fighting by your side for over fifteen years now, and it has never been smooth sailing."

"What's your point?"

"There is two of us and only one pass card. And when we're inside, then what?"

"Why so many questions?" Doyle folded the blueprint.

"Maybe we should go in with a plan this time, that's all."

"We have a plan. It's been the same plan since we joined the Anarchy March."

"You know what I mean, man."

"What do you want me to tell you? I don't have a fucking plan.

Besides, if all else fails, we have this." Doyle pulled out the handheld nuke.

"Sounds like a loud plan to me. But maybe I should do this alone. With the one pass card, it will raise less suspicion. If something goes down, I don't want the leader of the Anarchy March's legacy ending at the front gates."

"What are you rambling on about now?"

"Let me get past the guards and I'll come back and pick you up."

"Are you feeling alright? This is probably the most unselfish thing I've heard from you," Doyle quipped.

"I just have a good feeling about this. I actually feel that we're going to make a difference. Please, let me do it. We're in this together till the end. I give you my word. I won't fuck it up."

Doyle felt some of the burden lift off his shoulders realizing that he was not the only one who carried the world. He patted Jack on the back, "I know you won't, brother."

Jack smiled, swiping up the blueprints and grabbing for the handheld nuke.

Doyle tightened his grip. "No, this is staying with me, just in case. Call it Plan B." He handed Jack the pass card.

Jack nodded and jumped back into the truck, peeling out toward the gates. Doyle stood on the side of the road in a cloud of dust. A sinking sensation struck at him, but he chalked it up to nerves. After a few minutes passed, he took out his binoculars and watched Jack pull up to the security tower. Jack waved the pass card at a sentry. The guard took the pass card and walked into his security tower. Jack looked back toward Doyle and gave him a thumbs up.

"Don't do that, dumb-ass!" Doyle blurted out as his eyes were glued to the binoculars. He could see the guard step out with his gun drawn, then Jack and the guard engaged in a heated conversation. The roar of an approaching caravan behind him diverted his attention. "Shit." Doyle focused in on a very familiar face. "Sunshine?"

She was driving a large bus at high speed along the magnetic roadway, followed closely by a dozen or so transports.

Doyle ran onto the road and yelled, "Get off the road!" The bus screeched to a stop in front of him as he ran to the driver's side. "What the hell are you doing here, Sunshine?"

"They totally said, like, they would rather die and stuff, um, with their Savior than to like die in vain and junk. I wasn't gonna tell them, no."

"What?"

Cutter jumped out of the bus and limped over to him. "The Nukies, they want to fight. And so do the last Anarchy March members we found on the way. Let's finish this."

Doyle looked back at the small army that Sunshine and Cutter had pulled together.

"Well fuck! Get these vehicles off the road, so they're not detected." Doyle picked up his binoculars to see that Jack was being detained at gunpoint. "Shit, they're on to him."

Although the armed guard had a twitchy trigger finger, Jack was able to punch him in the face, diverting the shot into his arm. He jumped back into the truck and headed in reverse as fast as he could. The guard stood up and ran into the tower to trigger the alarm. The piercing siren echoed across the land. And what seemed to come out of nowhere? A barreling battle-ready P.M. convoy from the other side of the gates.

"Fuck, Jack! Why the fuck did I let him go?"

"What's happening?" Sunshine squinted into the distance.

"In about five minutes we're going to be overrun by the P.M." Doyle looked down at his nuke bomb. "No guts, no glory. Cutter, I want you to take Sunshine and all these people, get on the rest of the buses, and get the hell outta here. I'm gonna take this bus and this nuke, and ram it right up their asses." He walked over to the driver's side and Cutter grabbed him.

"I don't think that is a good idea, sir."

"Why not!"

"It can't end here like this. Let me take it," Cutter pleaded.

"No! The last guy I let go fucked everything up. I gotta take care of this myself! After it happens, I want you and the others to get inside those walls." Doyle climbed into the driver's seat but was yanked back once again. "We don't have time for this shit!"

"You have given hope to all of these people, and it's all they got. Let me go, the difference is that I know I'm not coming back. This is my ride and my duty to the Anarchy March, sir."

Doyle looked at all the lost faces that seemed all too familiar. Doyle hugged Cutter, "I hate this democracy shit. You will not be forgotten, I promise."

"I know, sir."

"And stop calling me sir."

Cutter smiled and took the handheld nuke. He slammed the door shut and yelled his war cry.

Jack pulled up in the truck and skidded to a stop in front of Doyle. "I'm sorry man, we were ratted out; they were fucking expecting us." Jack's eyes grew big, surprised by all the new faces. "Where did all these people come from?"

"Shut up! Now is not the time. Let's get out of here!" Doyle gathered everyone. "Take cover inside the buses! Move it! Let's go!" Doyle jumped into one of the buses and led them away from danger.

Sunshine ducked under a seat like everyone else.

Cutter barreled toward the oncoming army, 60, 80, 100 M.P.H., racing to the finish as the army watched the speeding bus approach them. They fired with a relentless attack; .50 caliber slugs passed through the bus's bulky exterior as if it were made of aluminum foil.

He yelled, "FUCK THE WORLD!"

Bullets ripped through Cutter as the bus veered off the road and flipped and tumbled out of control. Sparks flew as the vehicle slid to a stop. Cutter lost his grip on the handheld nuke in the crash. He lay bleeding and mangled; upside down, he reached out the window for the bomb that was mere inches away. Taking one last breath as he groped for the bomb with bloodied and broken fingers, Cutter pushed the armed button and rolled it toward the middle of the road. The P.M. bore down on the wreck. The first transport that passed ran over the nuke, detonating it. The searing light from the bomb's ignition obliterated the approaching army and the ensuing explosion and shockwaves slammed into the fleeing buses, sending them flying. The night sky glowed for what felt like an eternity before turning dead gray, swallowing the moon and the stars.

Doyle woke up in a pool of blood. He looked around in a daze, then he saw her; once a beautiful young girl, twisted pieces of metal had shredded Sunshine's body, she was almost unrecognizable. A blank look of horror burned into her dead eyes.

The loud ringing in Doyle's bleeding ears brought horrific flashbacks. He crawled his way out of the wreckage, the mountain-high mushroom cloud towered over everything. Other survivors crawled from the wreckage, and some began to wander, holding their heads in shock.

"Is there anyone else alive? Jack!" Doyle searched looking for the slightest breath of life.

"Help! I can't feel my legs!" a voice yelled from under a bus. Several survivors ran to his aid. They struggled to lift the bus just enough to pull the Nukie to safety.

Doyle peered around, the beaten Anarchy March lay bleeding and dying. A loud grinding of metal overtook the ringing in Doyle's ears. In the distance, he watched the Great Apartheid Wall begin to rotate. He pressed forward, left foot followed by his right.

Jack crawled up from under some rubble. "We have to regroup! Doyle, where are you going?"

"Jack!" Doyle went over to him, and helped him up. "We are almost there, I'm not stopping now!" Doyle's indomitable attitude inspired everyone to keep going as Doyle hobbled toward the wall.

The rag-tag Anarchy March followed him, their leader. As they formed together, their numbers rose, as did their pride. The thirty or so members of the March inched forward, leaving a bloody trail on the road. They passed the bomb crater. Doyle watched the wall come together, and the opening to Section A was in sight.

"Did you hear that? They made it!" Darla ran to the windows and saw the expanding mushroom cloud just beyond the walls.

The television interrupted to an emergency broadcast over all channels. Martial Law flashed across the screen while the Prominent Municipality flag waved in the background as a voice calmly stated, "Do not be alarmed. We are experiencing minor difficulty. Please remain inside your house until further notice." The message repeated over and over again.

"That's bullshit, Doyle is here. I know it. How do we get to the gates from here?"

"No! Fig said to stay here until he returns. Besides, the television said to stay inside." Coy turned up the volume of the television.

Darla snatched the controller out of Coy's hands and threw it at the T.V., destroying both. "It's garbage for your brain, now let's go!" Darla opened up the door and a reluctant Coy followed.

Families stood outside of their safe havens to gaze at the colossal expanse of fiery clouds rolling upward, stretching out across the sky.

"What is it, Dad?" asked a little boy with a P.M. baseball cap on.

"I think it might be the Second Coming, son. Soon we will be with God." The father wrapped his arm around his son and squeezed him close, he swelled with excitement.

Darla ran down the street with Coy lagging behind.

"It's this way!" Coy changed directions. A forceful hand suddenly pulled Darla back.

"Didn't you hear the broadcast? All civilians are to stay inside," a man said, dressed in military garb.

Darla broke free and rushed toward the open gates.

He tackled her and wrestled her to the ground, slapping on handcuffs. Coy turned around and saw Darla fighting back.

"Stop it! Let her go!" Coy ran to her aid, jumping on the man's back, pounding on him.

While the man fought with the two women, a call came over his handheld radio, "Code Triple Move, Main and Front Street, clear all military personnel. Now! Code Triple Move!"

The man stopped attempting to subdue them. "I'll deal with you two later!" he yelled and ran off.

"What does Code Triple Move mean?" Darla asked, slipping her legs through her arms so the handcuffs were in front.

"I don't know. But he was in a hurry to get away from these streets."

"Let me guess, the wall opening is on Main and Front, right?"

Coy stared at Darla and did not answer her.

"I got to warn Doyle!"

"You wouldn't make it in time; it's too far from here."

"I don't care. They are walking into a trap!" Darla took off running as Coy stood there, contemplating.

"There's just no compromise with that woman," she said and ran after her.

"Sir, the Anarchy March has breached the gates at the guard tower, and they are about to enter Section A!" Lieutenant Bachmann pointed out the obvious.

General Stripes removed his eye device. "I can see that, moron. If they want in so bad, then let them in."

"Sir?"

"I said let them in! Make the call."

"What about the civilians in the area?"

"We will kill two birds with one stone, wiping the Anarchy March from God's green Earth and re-teaching the people the power we possess."

Lieutenant Bachmann hesitated. He stared at the general with a deep sense of fear.

"That is a direct order, Lieutenant Bachmann," the general demanded.

Lieutenant Bachmann jumped in a panic and took his portable radio off his belt. "Code Triple Move, Main and Front Street, clear all military personnel. Now! Code Triple Move!"

The general put his eye device back in. "You can't make an omelet without frying a few eggs. One day I hope for your sake and the nation's, you will understand the responsibility that I have to endure. The hard decisions."

Doyle led the weakened Anarchy March through the wall opening. He took his first step onto Main Street, going forward through the suburban neighborhood. The green irrigation lawns and pristine white picket fences were alien to him. He pulled out a ripped and tattered white flag he had folded away. He held up the war-torn banner with the unmistakable spray-painted logo of the Anarchy March.

"Revolution is here!" Doyle stumbled forward as the rest of the Anarchy March began to yell out oppressed ideas and thoughts.

"Every man, woman, and child are born equal!"

"Taxation is theft!"

"Rules are meant to be broken!"

"Live your life, free your mind!"

"Viva la Revolution!"

The wave of anger attracted the residents as they poured out of their houses to watch the spectacular display of protest that had not been seen in decades. The residents watched in shock as the Anarchy March trekked down Main Street parading their obstinacy. A member of the March fell dead from the exhaustion as others limped and crawled on the road to the C Street House.

Jack took a few steps back and picked up the fallen brother and carried him over his shoulders. Even after death he could still live for the good fight.

A squadron of helicopters flew over Darla's and Coy's head streaking toward the wall opening. Coy caught up with Darla and tried to hold her back, "You're going to get yourself killed. You can't help them!"

"No, I have to!" Darla broke free and took off running, her dedicated spirit intact.

The helicopters began to drop their bombs while Darla watched in dismay as countless weapons of mass destruction rained on top of the Anarchy March. The sounds of protest were drowned by the sound of death; explosion after explosion ripped through the atmosphere. Darla dropped to her knees; tears ran down her exhausted face. The world had officially ended in her eyes and truth had been defeated. Still, she felt the need to be resolute for her fiancé. "I have to see if he is alright."

"Darla, sweetie, he's gone. And the same fate will happen to us if we stay on the streets," Coy claimed.

"No! You're wrong!" Darla was back on her feet and ran toward the smoldering craters.

"Sir, there are no survivors in a two-mile radius. The Anarchy March is dead."

"Good, I have to report this to the president. The people need to be briefed." The general jumped into his helicopter and set out to the C Street House.

Lieutenant Bachmann looked over at the bombed area and the chaotic aftermath. Hundreds of burnt minions riddled the charred craters. Bachmann took a deep breath and exhaled, "Rest in peace."

The general sat back in his seat, a smile was fixed to his face as the helicopter flew through the dark clouds. He looked down upon the charred landscape and the world he had helped create in an iron-fisted fashion, the feeling as if he were God radiated through him.

"Is everything okay, sir?" asked the pilot.

"I don't know. Let me ask you a question. What is your name, your real name?"

"Um ... it's, Herbert, sir."

"Excuse me, I couldn't hear you."

"It's 98438984, sir!"

"Then everything is perfect. I couldn't have made it better myself."

The helicopter landed by the emergency president who was waiting to meet them.

"What are you doing out from your bunker, Mr. President?"

"I didn't understand why I was in there. If we are under attack, shouldn't I be the leader and take command?"

"National security falls under my jurisdiction, Mr. President; your job is to ensure that the people are protected."

"Oh, okay."

"We need you, Mr. President, to make an announcement to the people, to ensure them that they are safe, and most of all, to show the face of the Prominent Municipality."

"I can do that."

"I know you can, Mr. President. Lead the people."

"Lead the people! Aye aye, captain ... ur, general! As you were." The emergency president saluted him and walked off filled with inspiration toward the C Street House.

Darla reached the destruction as the smoke cleared. She could see burned and mutilated bodies. The thought of Doyle dead never crossed her mind. "Doyle! Doyle!" She called for him, tears welled as she searched.

Coy grabbed and shook her. "We have to get out of here!"

Darla hung her head about to give up when she saw someone emerging from cover beyond the other side of the wall. Doyle's smiling face enthralled her heart. She ran into his arms. They embraced and kissed through streaming tears of happiness; theirs was a love that would be for eternity.

"Hey."

"Hay is for horses."

"Well then come here, Horsey." Darla grabbed on to him and pulled him close for another kiss.

"Careful, I'm a little fucked up."

Jack walked in through the opening as the metal walls began to grind shut.

Doyle felt a burning sensation from his pocket. He pulled out the over-heated hologram device that Name had given him. He threw it onto the tracks of the wall, smashing it to tiny little pieces. "Worked like a charm."

The reunited couple kissed and hugged again.

"Alright, alright, break it up. You guys are starting to make me want to puke! Enough of that shit." Jack grabbed Darla's hands wrapped around Doyle's neck and used a bolt cutter to lop off her handcuffs. "I really hate to break up this glorious party but standing here doesn't seem too good for my health." Jack walked off down the street.

Coy stood motionless and stared at the two lovers with an odd look on her face.

"What's her problem?" Doyle asked Darla.

"Oh, I'm sorry, my name is Coy. I just heard so much about you. But your friend is right, we should not be found here."

Darla grabbed Doyle's hand, and they walked back toward Fig and Coy's house.

"Where is the rest of the Anarchy March?"

"I told them to regroup and meet back here at the same time, the same day, next year. We'll be waiting for them at the opening. I promised them things would be different."

They moved fast to the house, keeping a keen watch on every crevice they passed, making sure they remained undetected. Darla and Doyle held each other close, afraid they might separate again. Darla had so much she wanted to say to her lover, but remained quiet, they all remained silent, realizing that caution was of the utmost importance. With breathless anticipation they reached their safe house at sunrise.

Jack strolled in first. "Nice place! Do you have running water?" He no sooner got the words out of his mouth when someone jumped on his back.

"Where is she, you fudging dirt baguette!" Fig clawed at Jack's head. Jack responded by flipping Fig over his shoulder and onto the floor. Jack readied himself with his fists.

"Stop! Get off of him!"

"This little fuck attacked me." Jack clinched his fists tighter.

"That is my husband and you are our guest, so mind your manners!"

Jack repelled her attempt to back him off.

"They're cool, Jack, get off of him," Darla said.

"Don't hurt me." Fig cowered on the floor. "I'm sorry, I thought you were the Prominent Municipality."

"Do I look like the fucking P.M.?"

Jack helped Fig to his feet.

"Doyle, Jack, I want you to meet the … what is your last name?"

"It's um … I can't even remember anymore." Fig's lost eyes came to the realization that his identity and individuality had been stifled for too many years.

"Well, meet Fig and Coy Hope."

"Hope? Huh, I like that." Fig stood an inch taller but fell from his imaginary pedestal when he heard the broken television crackle with an emergency broadcast by the emergency president.

The president shuffled through blank papers and cleared his throat to deliver his maladroit speech. "Hello, fellow citizens. I just wanted to say hi. Um, hello there … Today, our fellow citizens, our way of life, our very freedom came under a flagrant attack by terrorists. As your proud leader and mentor, we want to assure the people that this minor attack from an insignificant terrorist group called the Anarchy March has failed. This group would rather see your way of life, your freedom taken away from you, your children burnt alive than to work in a promising job. They'd rather see chaos and mayhem than church and sections. I promise as your emergency president that this Anarchy March has ended. And as a special treat for you good people, we have caught the leader, and on a two-hour special tonight we will see the execution of this evil-doer. So, rest assured my people and swaddle that little one for me tonight because there are no worries as long as your government is in command. On behalf of the Prominent Municipality, good night and God bless."

Doyle walked up to the television panel and punched it in, finishing off its last bit of life as it sparked dead. "What a load of shit."

"This is great! They think they caught you and the Anarchy March is dead. We're on easy street from now on. Maybe we can sleep for about a month or so. What do you say?"

"I don't think so, Jack, no rest for the weary. We hit them hard, now while they think that the threat is gone, I need to figure out how to get to the pipelines that lead to the C Street House."

Coy glanced at Fig. "Fig, you used to work for the Epidemic Prevention, right? I remember you complaining about working on the pipes all the time. Well, before they cut that program."

"Is this true?" Doyle asked.

"Yeah, for the Water Purification Department, just a glorified plummer. I patched holes, but it was a long time ago. I'm sure that it's different down there now."

"It doesn't matter, if you know just one percent more than I do, then you know best." Doyle's eyes lit up. He took out a few canisters of the Boysenblast. "Come on, Fig."

They all stared at Fig waiting for a response.

"Alright, alright! Just let me get something." Fig disappeared upstairs and returned with a hard hat with a light.

"What, are we going mining?" Jack mocked, laughing at the oversized hat.

"It's dark down there."

"Dark? Try living underground for three years fighting off rats the size of dogs while you slept. Try substituting your piss for water and shit for food. Dark, give me a fucking break."

Doyle took off Fig's hat and put it on Jack's head. "Save it, we'll leave tonight, after the sun goes down, and hopefully, we'll have a better tomorrow."

Doyle and Darla sat a breath away from each other as Darla tended to his wounds. Fig and Coy rested on the couch across from them.

"Oh, that looks nasty. You still haven't bandaged up your finger?"

"Didn't have the time." Doyle held up his hand, saddened that he would not be able to salute his enemies properly.

"This one looks infected, where did you get that holy wonder from?" Darla caressed the branded cross that had been seared into his back.

"I don't know, could have been from the Section X battle or the Evangelist Nukies fire fight. It's all a blur to me."

"Looks like I missed a lot."

"You didn't miss anything." Doyle grimaced as Darla began to stitch him up.

"That's not true, I missed you a lot." Darla batted her eyelashes.

"Well that's a given. I mean, I know I'm a catch and all." Doyle perked up his chest to tease her.

"Oh yes, you're a big boy," Darla remarked with a coquettish smile.

"Oh! Before I forget." Doyle pulled out a microchip and slipped it into Darla's ribs.

"Ouch! What was that?"

"An R.I.T. chip."[1]

"Where did you find that at?"

"I got it from an old naked man. He told me love could not afford to be lost again. I'm assuming it is for you."

They began to whisper sweet nasties to each other through their chorus of giggles.

"Um, excuse me, do you want us to leave you two alone?" Fig inquired; their vulgar conversation made him squeamish.

"Why?" Darla and Doyle asked in harmony.

"It seems like you two are getting a little too *comfortable*, and it's starting to make me feel uncomfortable."

"It's just love, Fig. Don't you talk to Coy that way?"

"In Amendment 69, it says that all sexual desiderata are forbidden unless it's for procreation."

"Fuck that noise! Love between two people is a beautiful thing and should be expressed, especially when its love between two ladies."

Darla slapped Doyle's fresh stitches.

"Ow, what!"

---

[1] The Required Identity Tag was first introduced to newborns in Section A as a way to identify the populace and/or track them at any time. The chip was implanted under the skull, in the soft spot. In time, it would mesh with the forming skull tissue and become virtually irremovable. This was the first known incident of data collection, and the information would be sold to the highest bidder, corporations, law enforcement, investment companies, family members, or friends. Nothing was secret, communal thoughts, shared by all.

"Stop it." Darla smirked, reprimanding him. "Yeah, Fig, come to think about it, I have never seen you even kiss Coy."

"We kiss, when the time is right, and now is not the time."

"It's always the right time for a kiss." Doyle grabbed Darla for a kiss, and with heated passion, they slurped on each other.

Coy and Fig watched the X-rated kiss in shock.

"Yeah, that's right baby." Darla wiped her lips, sloppy from the wet kisses while the Hopes stared back.

"You've never seen a French kiss before?"

"French kiss? You mean freedom kiss, right? We have the same kiss but without the tongue thing."

"No Fig! It's called a fucking French kiss." Doyle stood up and looked around the room. "Where is Jack, he has a better history of the French culture?"

"He's probably in the bedroom sleeping or 'stress releasing.'" Darla laid back on the couch.

"It's almost time, we should get going." Doyle looked out the window. The sky began to fade into a hazy dark blue. He walked upstairs and opened up the bedroom door. Jack, startled, hung up the phone.

"Don't sneak up on me like that, man."

"Who you calling, Jack? Do you know someone in Section A?"

"No, of course not. I was just checking if the phone line is tapped."

Doyle didn't know if he should believe him or not. "It's time. Get your shit together." Doyle walked out and went back downstairs.

"A please would be nice," Jack mumbled as he got off the bed and followed.

Fig led Doyle and Jack through the dark underbelly of the beast as the world above laid in a contented slumber.

"Um, I think it is this way. No, it's this way." Fig fumbled around in the dark of the sewer. "Wait? Did we take a hard left or a far right?

"Are you fucking kidding me? This guy would get lost in a cardboard box. We have been down here for hours! He doesn't know where the fuck we're going."

"It's alright, Fig. Let's stop and think about it for awhile."

Fig used his headlamp to light up the sewer wall, illuminating some etchings. "No, it's this way, I remember now. I used to mark the days I had left from each job, till the transfer. Come on, we are almost there." Fig continued down the dark pathway with renewed confidence. The constant thumping of water dripping echoed through the gloomy, cold tunnels. One last turn and they reached the end of the tunnel. "I'm sorry."

"This is it?" Jack threw his arms down in a fit.

"We must have taken a wrong turn somewhere."

"You think?!" Jack kicked water at Fig. "This is stupid, and I don't want to be down here anymore, it stinks. Just like this idea."

"You know, you're not much help at all. In fact, all you do is ... gosh darn it, complain!"

"Did you say something to me, you fucking little shithead," Jack threatened with clenched fists. "How do we even know this guy is not just fucking with us, until the P.M. shows up?"

"Why would I do that? I didn't ask for this!"

"Yeah, well you got it! So now what are you gonna do about it?" Jack bullied Fig into a corner.

Doyle laughed at them, and they stopped bickering looking back at Doyle. He leaned up against a pipe, grasping another.

"I used to squat in a place like this, dark and smelly, forgotten by society. It was right before I joined the Anarchy March. I had nobody, no family, no friends, nothing of my own. All I could hear was the gunfire from up above, people's death screams. Try sleeping through that."

"You okay, Doyle?" Fig asked wondering if Doyle might be losing it.

"Just thinking about how I never wanted nothing to do with that world up above, and here I am again. It's a full circle, you know?"

"What's next then, man?" Jack asked.

"We systematically search the sewer, day in and day out, as long as it takes. We have to keep our heads up and keep pressing pertinaciously. That's the name of this game."

Fig understood what Doyle was talking about and took his words literally. He arched his head back, "That's it! Fig, you're an idiot!" slapping himself in the head.

"What's going on?"

Fig's headlamp lit up a number 39 spray-painted on a pipe up above. "I forgot that each pipe was labeled from the center of the water pump. Like a spider web it spreads out, all we have to do is get to number 1." Fig pointed out pipe number 38 that led around the corner, "See! We just have thirty-seven more turns and we're there."

"I'm impressed, Fig. See, Jack, good things happen to those who wait." They walked off toward the right direction.

"And bad things happen to those who wait too long." Jack followed, dragging behind.

After many corridors and turns they came upon a cavernous space. The three-story water pump resembled a small building and supplied most of Section A. Hundreds upon hundreds of pipelines ran through the walls in an intricate web-like pattern.

"Let me ask you a question, Fig. Why is the water system set up like this?"

"I didn't make this thing; I just used to patch up the holes."

Doyle dropped down, pulling Fig with him. He covered Fig's mouth and pointed out a person up a flight of stairs working at the main console.

"You two wait here," Doyle whispered, and crawled up to the engaged worker. Doyle screamed in his ear; the man jumped out of his chair.

"You scared the living daylights out of me, boy. Who are you and what are you doing down here?"

"I'm a punk and I am here to fuck it up. The better question is who are you and what are you doing down here?"

"Is this a joke? I'm doing my job!"

"Really? And what might that entail?" Doyle leaned in for an answer.

The man didn't answer. Doyle stepped into him, grinding his

foot down on his.

"I'm just doing as I'm told, alright. I don't know anything. I press these buttons right here when I'm told to."

The crimson phone next to the console rang. Doyle looked at the phone and picked it up.

"We have reports coming from Sector Five about questionable conversations and ideas," the voice said.

"You don't say." Doyle gripped the phone receiver tighter as he looked up at an inspirational poster hanging above the console that read: Ideas are more powerful than guns. We would not let our people have guns, why should we let them have ideas.

"Better give that Sector a double dose," the voice ordered. The line went dead.

"They want you to give Sector Five a double dose. What the fuck are you doing down here?" Doyle demanded, slamming the phone on the receiver.

"I swear, I don't know. I just take orders."

"Well, you better do as you're told." Doyle pulled out his blade. The man shook in fear and did not move. "Now!" he exploded.

The man pushed the buttons in haste as Doyle watched. A red flashing light spun, one of the machines that had multiple hoses started. Two hoses locked into a pipe and injected a strange substance that resembled thick silvery syrup. Doyle looked down on the console as the digital display read: Inserting Lead. Inserting Mercury. Please stand by ...

"You piece of shit! You're making the people brainless!" Doyle wrapped his hands around the man's neck and squeezed. "Is there no soul in you people?!"

"I'm ... ju ... doin ... uh ... my ... job ... please ... I ... don ... wan ... die!"

Doyle released him. "Which one of these pipes goes to the C Street House? I bet you never had to put any of this junk in that pipe, huh?" Doyle pushed the man away.

The worker regained his breath and pointed at a gold pipe. "That one ... the pipes around it, too, I've also never had to put stuff in."

"Should have guessed. Now get the hell out of here, I don't want to see your corrupt fucking face ever again! Mirrors are your enemy now." Doyle kicked the man down the staircase.

He pulled out the three Boysenblast canisters and went to the gold pipe. "Here goes nothing." Doyle twisted and ripped off the cap, but he fell to the ground, dazed by a sharp crushing blow to the back of his head. As he looked up, he saw Jack hovering over him with a pipe wrench and a dead expression.

"Sorry man, I can't let you do that." Jack took the canister from Doyle.

"You? No, Jack." Doyle blinked in and out of consciousness.

"Fuck the world? No, fuck you man! I'm tired of listening to you talk! Fight this and anarchy that! Why can't you just accept that this is the way things are?! You're not going to change the world, Doyle! The Prominent Municipality has shown me a new way, the light to unconditional power."

"You're ... wrong..." Doyle made his way to his feet and pulled out his blade.

Jack replied by pulling out a small gun.

"You shouldn't bring a knife to a gun fight. You should know that of all people."

Doyle took a few steps forward. He could feel blood dripping from the back of his skull.

"Don't make me kill you, brother. I won't hesitate, not even for a split second to splatter your brains on the walls."

"Fig! ... Fig!"

"Don't worry, I already took care of him. He won't be annoying anybody anytime soon."

"You do what you have to do, or should I say, programmed to."

Jack aimed the gun at Doyle's face and pulled the trigger ... Jack pulled the trigger again and again ...

"I keep my friends close but my enemies closer. You think I don't know where you hide your gun?"

Jack's face turned purple with rage. He charged forward, slamming Doyle against the metal wall. "I'll kill you!"

Doyle landed a head-butt to Jack's nose, backing him off. "I don't know what they did to you, but I'm gonna fix it. One fucking stab at a time!" Doyle raised his knife and thrust downward, stabbing Jack in the arm, who had blocked his head and neck from Doyle's attempt to deliver a fatal blow. Jack screamed and pulled out the knife and lunged at Doyle. Doyle grabbed for the blade as it sliced across his hand. He stumbled back, still dizzy from his head wound. He fell to the floor, ghost white.

Jack towered over him. "I'll take good care of Darla for you. See you in Hell!" Jack moved in for the finishing blow, but his head seared in pain, his body convulsed. Blood streamed out from his eyes, ears, and nose. A rapid popping sound and then Jack's head imploded, brain matter, blood and skull shards spewed out. Jack slunk to his knees and then one last contortion, he slumped onto the floor.

Doyle was sprawled out on the ground in shock. He slowly got to his feet. "Hell? If you believe in that sort of shit."

He grabbed the canister away from Jack's lifeless body and pushed it into the pipe, replaced the pipe cap, and the ensuing vacuum sucked the can through the golden pipe. He put the last two canisters in the other pipes that surrounded the gold one. He stumbled off and came across Fig's leg sticking out from behind some debris.

Doyle looked over the sad scene. Fig crumpled in a heap, a pool of blood surrounding him. A large bloodstained rock lay on the ground next to Fig's broken headlamp. Doyle leaned in and felt a faint breath of life.

"Hang in there." Doyle picked him up and carried him out of the water pump station.

In a light sleep, Name opened up his eyes, he thought he heard a noise and stared at the digital clock that had a T-minus count down; three, two, one … the clock flashed then blinked zero in big red numbers. He rolled out of bed and put on his fuzzy slippers. He yawned as he walked outside to his weather machine and flipped the large switch. "Good job, Seeker." Name strolled back into the house as the machine revved up, illuminating a string of multicolored, festive lights. It shot a pulsating beam into the heavens shattering old theologies. A glowing static electric cloud formed over the land. The cloud grew larger, violent lightning struck the earth in anger. Name crawled back under the covers, "Mother Nature, Heaven has no rage like love to hatred turned, Nor Hell a fury like a woman scorned..." Name fell fast asleep like a newborn.

Doyle kicked the front door open, startling Darla and Coy sitting on the couch. He stumbled in and placed Fig on the couch next to Coy.

"Fig! What happened to him?" She ran into the bathroom and returned with medical supplies.

"Jack happened. He turned against us."

"Jack? Oh no, they must have gotten to him."

"His eyes were empty, almost digital," Doyle said as he collapsed on the couch.

"Are you okay, baby?" Darla comforted him, wiping away the blood from his brow.

"I'll live, it's Fig I'm worried about. Help me up." Weary and worn, he managed to stand up with her help.

"Is he going to be alright?" Darla looked down at Fig slumped on the couch, blood flowing.

"It's not as bad as it looks. His vitals seem steady. He's just lost a lot of blood." Coy dressed Fig's head wound in gauze.

"Hey, Horsey. Where are you going? Sit down, you need to rest."

"I know, but I need to see this."

Darla grabbed a blanket as Doyle led her out the front door and then climbed up the side of the house to the rooftop. Darla held her stomach and turned a little pale climbing up after him.

"You okay, baby, still hate heights?"

"No, not exactly. I believe its morning sickness, apparently it lasts all fucking day long." Darla breathed in and out, rubbing her belly.

It took a few moments before her words sunk in. "Are we having a baby?"

Darla smiled, she seemed to glow, and he knew the answer. He wrapped the blanket around both of them. Doyle laid back, staring at the stars, grinning.

"Is it finally over, Horsey?"

"I don't think it will ever be over, but it's the first step to a better future." Doyle caressed Darla's stomach.

"So, what are we supposed to see up here?"

"Fireworks, like the pictures in the books of Independence Day."

"Really? I have never seen fireworks before." Darla cuddled next to Doyle. "Did I tell you that I love you today?"

"No, actually you didn't. You kinda just hit me earlier." Doyle lifted a sleeve, revealing a bruise.

"Baby, love is pain and the more I hit you, it means the more I love you." Darla giggled and kissed him.

Doyle caressed her hand. "I noticed we both lost our rings."

"It's alright, Horsey. We can start anew, just two people in love."

A thunderous storm brewed in the distance, growing, rolling closer. Ominous clouds approached swallowing everything in their path.

"We better get inside; it looks like a nasty storm is coming."

"Let it rain." Doyle covered Darla with the blanket as the raindrops fell. The thunderstorm lit up the skies with brilliant lightning bolts. The storm consumed Section A. In the distance, millions upon millions of small reflective flakes filled the air as the Boysenblast gas leaked from the C Street House and engulfed the military facilities.

"That's odd? Why is the sky shimmering?"

Blinding lightning bolts struck the C Street House, answering Darla's question. The gas ignited an explosion that rocked across Section A. A shockwave hit their house and shook its foundation. Doyle and Darla covered their eyes. A mile-high fireball shot into the air and illuminated the night sky, sending a powerful message of change.

"Hello? Hello! Shit!" General Stripes hung up the phone and

grabbed Lieutenant Bachmann by his lapels. "We have to get the president out right now!"

"What? Why?"

"The Anarchy March made it inside with the bioweapon. We don't have much time!"

They both ran to the general's military transport and tore down the road. The law-abiding driver stopped at a crosswalk while a family hurried across to make curfew.

"Driver! State your name."

"190593055656, sir."

"We are under a national security alert! I order you to not stop until I say to."

"Sorry, sir." The driver continued to wait until the family was safely across the street.

"Did I stutter?" The general wrapped a wire around the driver's neck.

The driver gagged and kicked the gas pedal to the floor mowing down the last few stragglers. The horrified driver gasped as the car rolled over the screaming bodies.

They reached the front gate of the C Street House and were greeted by a guard.

"Sir, what can I do for you, sir?"

The general shot the driver in the head and pushed him out. "Do something with this and open the gate."

They walked into the C Street House and went straight to the emergency president's bedroom. The general and Lieutenant Bachmann barged in, waking him up.

"Mr. President, we have to relocate you to a secure location."

"Huh? Who are you, is that you Stripes?"

"Mr. President, we don't have time, I will explain everything later." The general pulled off the emergency president's blankets, there were two naked young girls.

"Can they come also?"

"No! We have to go, now!"

"How about just one of them? This one right here, I gave her a special name. She's my Southern Belle." He smiled down on the sleepy girl.

The general pulled out his gun and shot both girls. "Let's get going, Mr. President."

Two military guards broke in the door. "Is everything alright in here, sir? We heard gunfire."

"Yes, fine, the president needs to attend to an important midnight meeting. Carry on." The general escorted the president out of the room as Lieutenant Bachmann flanked them.

The two guards resumed their positions outside the bedroom doors.

They jumped into the transport and peeled out through the C Street House gates. The president looked back, watching his mansion as it faded into the darkness.

"Sorry, Mr. President, but we needed to leave. I had an inside informant contact me about an evil plot to kill you."

"Really? Who would want to kill me?"

"It doesn't matter. Project Red, White, and Ruse was a failure. The enemy was able to penetrate the Great Apartheid Walls. Lieutenant Bachmann, the remote detonator, please."

Lieutenant Bachmann handed the general the remote control, and he activated it.

"What did that do?"

"Failure is not an option. We need to regroup."

The military transport traveled down the road in the middle of the night to an undisclosed location. A large, sprawling hidden base surrounded a massive aircraft hangar. The president's attention was drawn to the huge spaceship inside the hanger. Thousands of tiny worker ants toiled on the almost completed ship. The transport parked inside the hanger. A sentry opened the door for the president, and he was greeted by Officers Walton, Hill, and Buck.

"Mr. President, welcome to Koch's Ark. Isn't it grand?" The general basked in all his Prominent Municipality glory.

The president stepped into a murky puddle. "You dragged me out of bed for this, Gabe? What is this monstrosity?"

"Sorry, Mr. President. Right this way. We need to brief you on the mission ahead," Officer Walton said as the other officers led the way through the rows of military tanks and planes being fueled from barrels of gasoline. The bustling airstrip was in chaos; the normally well-ordered soldiers scurried everywhere in disarray.

"Where are we going? Why couldn't this wait until morning?" The President rubbed his drowsy eyes. "Damn it, now I have to run another commercial for a new southern belle candidate. Do you have any idea how long it takes to find a good girl in these parts? Well, do you?"

Officer Hill rushed up to a large metal door and put his eye against a scanner. The red beam swept across his pupil, and the door opened to an elevator shaft.

"Quit your damn pushing! I'm coming, I'm coming." The president tilted his head back to insert a few beads of eye drops. "Does anyone have a caffeine capsule, huh? Why is no one talking to me? I demand someone answer me! I am the emergency president of the Prominent Municipal—"

General Stripes reholstered his stun gun. "Sorry, sir. It is for your own good — plausible deniability. Officer Buck, pick up the president and get him ready for his memory briefing ... and for God sakes, get him some pants."

EPILOGUE

"Oi oi and good morning to all. My name is Doyle and I'm the leader of the Anarchy March broadcasting from inside of Section A. We will be running a broadcast twenty-four hours a day, seven days a week, three hundred and sixty-five days a year until the truth is known to all. Despite what you saw on your television panels, I am very much alive and will not be silenced. I want the people to hear what I have to say and not just to listen. You need to forget everything you have learned or have been taught by the Prominent Municipality and to open up your minds to other possibilities.

"I have traveled across this once great land, seeing sites that no one should see. The horrors of war, poverty, greed, hate, and religion; when will it end? As an optimistic man, I would like to say soon, but I live in reality and the future looks bleak. There is hope though, and it lies within you. One person can change it all. It just takes one person to stand up and fight for what is right. Don't walk away from your problems. It doesn't matter if you take a step to the left or to the right, but if we move away from each other, divided we fall, divided we fail. I want to be known as the person who throws a rock in a lake to create ripples, rather than through a glass house. We the People should not be living under anything but the sun. Not law, not government, and especially not under a fictitious God. I want to unite us and bring freedom back. I'm not one to give a great speech. I'm just one man that speaks what's on his mind and for what's in the back of the minds of others. So, if you feel the same as I do and you want to act, I'll ask you to join me for the good fight. Just as evolution formed and shaped us into human beings, I believe We the People can evolve into more conscious beings, realizing every person, old, young, is born equal.

"Until then, I see a change on the horizon, when that sun rises over the fear-mongering wall, realigning on December 25, a revolution will be coming! So please, help me. Pick up that first rock and throw it. Let's say fuck you to the oppression because The System just does not work! Let's see what kind of ripples we can start in this lake. Keep your chins up, for tomorrow the air is always fresher when you face the world head on. I leave you with this quote by the late Emma Goldman, 'The most violent element in society is ignorance' ... Oi oi and good morning to all. My name is Doyle and I'm the leader of the Anarchy March broadcasting from inside of Section A..."

RUSS LIPPITT is the author of *Lion's Share* and *The Showdown*. He was born in 1977 and raised in Hawaii. He attended college in San Francisco and now lives in Los Angeles with his wife.

CPSIA information can be obtained
at www.ICGtesting.com
Printed in the USA
FSHW012148271120
76282FS